D0938944

THE Lending Library

Center Point
Large Print

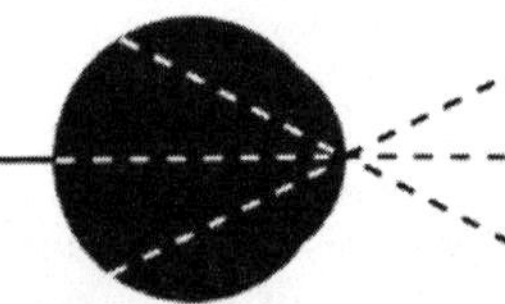

This Large Print Book carries the
Seal of Approval of N.A.V.H.

THE Lending Library

ALIZA FOGELSON

CENTER POINT LARGE PRINT
THORNDIKE, MAINE

This Center Point Large Print edition
is published in the year 2021 by arrangement with
Amazon Publishing.

Originally published in the United States by
Amazon Publishing, 2020.

The text of this Large Print edition is unabridged.
In other aspects, this book may vary
from the original edition.
Printed in the United States of America
on permanent paper.
Set in 16-point Times New Roman type.

ISBN: 978-1-64358-998-5

The Library of Congress has cataloged this record
under Library of Congress Control Number: 2021936919

For my parents, who have encouraged my love of books and my dream of being a writer every step of the way

One

November 2007

I was sniffing glue again.

"Ahem." Kendra delicately cleared her throat as she rounded the stack and caught me in my favorite spot at the Chatsworth Library, the squishy chair in the key-shaped nook. I was now holding the book innocently in my hands, like a normal library-goer. Which I was. Except for my overwhelmingly passionate desire to read books and reread them, hold them, surround myself with them, and yes . . . sometimes even smell them. It wasn't just the heady scent of glue in the spine. It was also the scent of the pages—timeworn or slicked with new ink—and the old cloth cases, how the linen had aged. The smell of imagination and escape.

I wouldn't have been surprised if Kendra had some secret book-adoring practices of her own. At least, I hoped she did. After all, Kendra was the librarian at Chatsworth Elementary School, where I started teaching art last fall.

"I'm going to check this out. You ready, Dodie?" Kendra gestured toward the novel I was holding, *A Charmed Life*.

"Yep." With one last longing glance at all the

treasures lining the shelves, I followed her to the circulation desk.

Both our phones made the shloomping sound of a new text message. I dug my phone out of my "I Brake for Books" tote, and Kendra and I both gasped as we read our friend Sullivan's text:

> ALL CLEAR! Heading out to Addis Ababa tomorrow. Olive's in 20?

"She's really going!" Kendra said.

"This is so exciting!" I clapped my hands. Kendra raised an eyebrow. But how could I not be excited? A baby! Sullivan's baby!

On our way, I typed back.

> Hurry! Have to pack etc . . . plus they just took the cc chip cookies out of the oven!

Twenty minutes later Kendra and I burst through the doors of the café. Sullivan was shaking her head as we sat down. "We missed it?" I cried, my grin fading quickly. "I risked my life and limb for a cookie, and they're gone?"

"Hey!" Kendra objected. "I wasn't driving that fast."

"That's because I made you slow down."

"Wasn't the idea to get here quickly?" Kendra said, smiling in spite of herself.

"Well, you didn't exactly succeed," Sullivan

pointed out. "But did you really think I wouldn't have saved you a reward for your efforts?" She handed both of us a wax paper sack. I could feel the warm cookie steaming up the insides. My mouth watered.

"Thank you."

"You're the best!"

"I even waited to eat mine," Sullivan said proudly. I could tell by the tiny streak of chocolate in the corner of her mouth that she hadn't *completely* waited . . . but who could blame her? Olive's straight-out-of-the-oven chocolate chip cookies were legendary—more warm dough than actual cookie, which was just how I (and, apparently, most of the other residents of Chatsworth) liked it. After having caught me licking the beaters all through childhood, my mother always joked that it was no coincidence my nickname, Do, was pronounced the same way.

None of us spoke as we savored the cookies. We got lost in the Madagascar vanilla mixed with heady cinnamon and neon-yellow eggs fresh from the farm blended with deep, almost smoky-tasting chocolate chips. I was drunk on pastry. As I sucked the last bit of melted chocolate off my finger, the world slowly seeped back into focus.

"Okay, tell us everything," Kendra said as soon as we finished.

"The passport and clearances from the US

Embassy finally came through, so I can go back to Ethiopia and bring him here!"

"Congratulations! That's amazing!" I wiped away a tear. They both looked at me strangely. "It's just so great."

Sullivan was my best friend from art school and the reason I now lived in Chatsworth. A little more than two years earlier, she had decided she wanted to be a mother and had started the adoption process. After tons of paperwork and sleepless nights, she had met her son six months ago. The wait since then had been excruciating. Now she could finally bring him home.

"What time is your flight?"

"Ten p.m."

"Okay, I'll be by tomorrow morning with a few things." I had actually devoted a corner of my coat closet to presents for the new baby for the last six months—onesies, blankets, books. The pile was starting to get a little overwhelming.

"Are you ready to be a mother?" Kendra asked.

"I am *so* ready. Um . . . speaking of mothers, what is mine doing here?" Sullivan asked, looking over our shoulders as Mackie O'Reilly made her way over.

"Surprise! I had a feeling I might find you girls here. I'm taking you shopping, Sullivan." Mackie's sparkling venetian-blue eyes and heart-shaped face hinted at the youthful beauty she had maintained through the years.

Sullivan got up and flashed us a grin. "Sorry, ladies; Gramma calls."

"Of course," Kendra said, hugging Sullivan goodbye. "Safe travels!"

"I'm so happy for you. Can't wait to meet him."

"Thanks, Do," she said. "I'll keep you guys posted."

"Want to split a scone?" I asked Kendra when they were gone.

"Sure. Pumpkin caramel?"

"Why not?"

On the other side of the café, a young mother was strapping her daughter into a stroller. The little girl had a tiny pink bow in her hair, a ruffled dress, and a grin from ear to ear. The mother plopped a kiss on her forehead. Her husband handed her a coffee.

"Wouldn't you like to be that lady right now? Or Sullivan?" I said dreamily. How could anyone not adore babies? With their lovely-smelling skin and their little heads covered with baby-bird fuzz, those dimples denting chubby cheeks, their hiccupy laughs. I had never felt in any rush to get married; I really wanted to be with the right person when that happened. (A good thing, too, since my dating life in Chatsworth had pretty much been nonexistent.) The urge for a baby of my own was like a thirst, though. At thirty-two, I still had time. But I had always envisioned myself married, with at least one child by now, instead of going on a year and a half without a date. And even that one had sucked.

Because our family was small and I hadn't had much chance to be around babies growing up, I started babysitting as soon as I was old enough. In fact, I had spent so much time taking care of little ones that by the time I graduated from high school, the money I'd saved up almost covered my first semester of art school. The year after I graduated from college, I worked as an au pair for a family in a suburb of Paris with their adorable Zen-like baby and their three-year-old, who looked like someone out of *Madeline* and acted as sassy as Matilda. But that was more than five years ago, and none of my friends and neither of my sisters had kids yet, so I was at a serious baby-cuddling deficit.

Kendra shook her head vehemently, waking me out of my daydream. "Nope. Uh-uh."

"You mean not right now," I clarified.

"I don't *ever* want to have kids."

"You just feel that way because you haven't met the right person yet."

"That's where you're wrong. That's one of the main reasons I don't want to have a baby. Once I find that right person, I want to be able to be selfish. I want to stay in bed every weekend until noon." She grinned wickedly. "When we finally do get out of bed, I want to be able to let my Sunday—or whatever day—take me where it will, without having to repeat the same routine over and over again. And when our currently nonexistent but future fabulously rich friends invite us to spend an impromptu weekend on their yacht in the south of where-the-hell-ever, I want to be able to pack my passport and a bathing suit and go."

Okay, well, she did have a point or two there. Even I could see that.

She wasn't done. "I mean, all these people who assume I need a child to feel complete . . . doesn't that say something about their marriages? Shouldn't it be enough to be madly in love with your husband or wife? I get my fix of kids at work anyway. Not that I won't be the most amazing aunt to Sullivan's kid . . . and yours, in the future."

I was silent. I could have tried explaining all the reasons children were essential and amazing, but unlike Kendra's arguments, mine weren't purely logical. Her point of view made sense. My desire was more than a feeling—I was certain that one of my purposes on earth was to be a mother. Not that I was going to let Kendra—or anyone else—know the depths of how badly I wanted that. I thought what Sullivan was doing—adopting on her own—was incredibly brave.

Kendra changed the subject. "So how's school been for you?"

"There's this one student I worry about . . . ," I began.

Kendra rolled her eyes playfully. "Here comes

Savior Dodie again. Always trying to help others, regardless of the cost to her wallet, reputation, or sanity."

I put my hands on my hips in mock anger. We both laughed.

"Elmira Pelle needs my help," I insisted.

Kendra knew me so well, even though I had only been in Chatsworth a few months. She and Sullivan had grown up there together, and we had become friends by proxy.

I owed a lot to Sullivan and couldn't wait to offer my babysitting skills when she was ready for them. If it hadn't been for her, I might still have been in New York trying to make it as an artist and failing instead of falling more and more in love with this town and the people in it. I also might have found art school a lot lonelier if not for her. There had been this weird sense of competition between a lot of the students, and Sullivan wasn't having any of that. Her work happened to be some of the most captivating of anyone's: these gorgeous photo-realistic paintings that captured the subject's personality and mood so vividly you felt like you knew them.

I had gone up to her one day after our studio class. "Could I ask you a question?"

"Sure. Nice work, by the way." She gestured to my canvas.

"Thanks," I said, though my cheerful portrait

seemed juvenile beside hers. "How do you listen so well with your eyes?"

Sullivan laughed, then—realizing I was serious—cocked her head at me. I fidgeted under the directness of her gaze.

"You are . . . quirky," she said after a moment.

It may not have been the first time I'd been called that. But no one had actually called me out in such a straightforward way. "I don't know if I would describe myself as quirky."

"How many pairs of shoes do you have that aren't brown or black?"

I started counting in my head. I was still tallying when she interrupted. "How many times have you brought homemade baked goods to parties? And have you been to Disney World more than three times as an adult . . . by choice?"

I grinned at her.

"Yep, okay, that's what I thought," she said.

"So now that we've established I'm quirky, are you going to share your secret with me?"

"There's no secret. Whenever I can, I do a lot of talking with the subjects before we start. I guess I just look at what's really there instead of what I want to see or what the subject wants me to see."

"Oh," I said, glancing back at the sketch in front of me. I had drawn the model as though she had starry eyes. It was kind of my signature. But now it felt like I was imposing something on her instead of capturing her.

Sullivan seemed to sense my disappointment in myself because she quickly said, "This is beautiful. I love the suggestion of light in her eyes."

"Thanks." I smiled, still unconvinced. Sullivan had made me look at things in a new way; it hadn't occurred to me that I could see if the models would be willing to talk to me and that what they said could inform my portraits.

"Listen, there's a group of us who get drinks every Friday night at the Shaggy Dog Pub around seven. Will you come this week?"

"I'd love to."

We ended up staying out till midnight that night and many others. Finally, I was getting to know other students who were passionate about art—who fiercely debated about how to fix the issue of art programs being cut in public schools or whether performance art was pretentious or who the greatest Renaissance painter was.

After that Sullivan and I always set up our easels next to each other. Sometimes when class ended, we stayed to keep drawing or painting. I could still remember the intense resiny smell of the studio and the squish of the brush into a fresh dollop of paint. In those years, painting always felt like potential.

By senior year, the faculty members had started to commission Sullivan to paint family portraits and to recommend her to their friends. She mounted a few small shows with other artists and sold all her paintings.

"You're going to make a go of this!" I said to her the day after one show over celebratory croissants.

"Do, there's something I need to tell you."

"You got a solo show in Chelsea, didn't you?" A little flair of jealousy disappeared into my happiness for her.

"No. I'm moving back home."

"Wait, what?"

She was making it in New York. That was so rare.

"I miss small-town life. I've had enough of the ninety-nine-cent slice for dinner and mysterious, deafening neighbor noises and seeing rats on the subway and feeling like one myself every time I have to go somewhere at rush hour."

"Okay, that's fair." I couldn't deny that I felt the same way, more and more often. "But you're doing so well. Don't you want to give it a few more months here?"

Sullivan was silent. Then she said, "There's this house I've always loved. It's a little Colonial with an amazing yard bordered by a creek, and I used to pass it on my way to school every day. It's for sale, and I know I'll kick myself if I don't go for it. It's exactly how I'd want to use the money I've earned here from my gallery shows."

For the love of a house . . . I understood. I

scanned the real estate pages every week even though I wasn't in the market.

"What will you do there? Will you still paint and keep representation here for your work?"

"Yes and no. I'd like to make a go of it as a portrait painter in Chatsworth. My elementary school art teacher has been doing that for years as a side career, but she's decided to give it up, which leaves an opening for me since she was pretty much the only game in town."

It sounded so much smaller . . . but wonderful. "I'm going to miss you a ton, but I'm happy for you. It's obvious it's what you want."

"Thanks, Do." Sullivan hugged me. "And who knows? Maybe when you get sick of this place, I can convince you to move to Chatsworth too."

Like pretty much everyone, I'd had my ups and downs with New York. But I couldn't imagine actually leaving. I would definitely have to visit Sullivan and see the town's charm for myself, though.

It took another year and a half before I did. By then, Sullivan's business was hugely successful—she was turning down commissions from all over the region—and Elizabeth, her on-again, off-again girlfriend from New York, had decamped to Chatsworth and moved in with her.

I arrived on a fresh spring morning in a rental car. The two-hour drive up had felt liberating after the tight crush of taxi traffic in the city, and there was so much lush green even surrounding the parkway I could tell it was going to be a perfect weekend.

The town of Chatsworth sat about twelve minutes from the nearest exit, past two towns with friendly-looking little neighborhoods. I slowed down as I approached the center of Chatsworth, where there was a big rotary with a gazebo flanked by trees at its center. A couple and their kids were playing a game of tag around it. On the east side of the rotary, a little street lined with shops unfurled about six blocks. I tooled down the street, continued past the elementary school where I would end up working, and found the neighborhood where Sullivan lived.

Over the next couple days, Sullivan showed me around town and introduced me to the Chatsworth Library. The feeling I had when I walked in the doors—seeing the floor-to-ceiling windows casting light over the treasures that waited on the worn-wood bookcases dotting the room . . . the reading nook that would become my favorite spot . . . the schoolhouse charm of the building . . . and the reading group deep in conversation—probably cinched it for me.

In New York, my dreams of becoming an artist had just been crushed when my first gallery show was savaged by the press. I'd had my heart broken by my boyfriend, Daniel. As a star fashion designer, he had introduced me to life in the fast lane, but it had felt like a beautiful dress that never quite fit. Now I was in this place that was green and slower—in exactly the right way—and full of friendly people. I felt like I was losing something when I left Chatsworth, some part of myself that had been squished down for a long time. I went back to my life in the city, but I kept visiting and imagining what it might be like to live there. When Sullivan told me three years later that the elementary school art teacher was moving back home to California to help her elderly mother—right as I was finishing my art education degree—I saw it as fate. I intuitively knew that watching kids discover their own talent and creating things would be much more satisfying to me than a good art review would have been.

Two months into my first year of teaching, I knew teachers were not supposed to favor one kid over another. And I would never in a million years let on to anyone that I had a favorite. But was it any secret that sometimes there was a student that a teacher wanted to look out for? Maybe one that needed a little more care? Because they had selfish jerkface parents who didn't encourage their talents, who made their kid feel like an inconvenience, who continually forgot to pick their kid up from school so that their kid was left waiting, feeling miserable and abandoned, with whatever teacher happened to be nearby until one of the parents got his or her act together, left his or her manicure/trainer appointment, and got his or her selfish jerkface to the school to take home his or her excellent, smart, sweet kid? Hypothetically speaking.

"Thanks, Elmira," I said as my student passed me some books. "How's Ms. Granger's class?" Elmira Pelle had taken to helping me put supplies away sometimes after our art class. I liked having lots of art and picture books around for the kids to inspire them.

"Awesome." Elmira grinned. "We're reading *Anne of Green Gables*."

"Really? Isn't that a middle school book?" Elmira was in the fourth grade.

"Yeah. Well, *I'm* reading *Anne of Green Gables*," she admitted.

"That's fantastic. You have a lot to be proud of, you know that?"

"My mom thinks my grades should be better."

I tried to breathe slowly through my nose. Elmira got all As. Maybe a few A minuses. But no Bs. *Cool it, Dodie,* I thought.

"Does she ever help you with your homework?" I asked, keeping judgment out of my tone.

"No, I never ask. She's got her hands full with my baby brother, Teddie. She said I'm old enough to take care of myself."

Um . . . what? "Did she and your dad enjoy the fall choir concert?"

Elmira had been fabulous. Before her solo, she had looked like she was going to keel over with stage fright, but when she got to the mic, her clear, high voice rang out, and all our jaws dropped.

"They didn't make it," she murmured.

I hadn't seen the Pelles, but it seemed inconceivable that they had missed it. Elmira had one of the only solos.

"I'm sorry," I murmured back.

Her brow knit. "It was weird. They said they were going to come, and they got a babysitter for my brother, but I looked for them and they weren't there. My dad didn't have a chance to work out last week, and that was his only night to do it. And my mom had to get her nails done while the babysitter was watching Teddie."

Breathe, Dodie, breathe, I thought. But it was too late . . . I felt like an anemone at the bottom of the ocean. I could see the light of reason up above, and I couldn't do any of the cruel and unusual things I was envisioning inflicting on Elmira's parents. I tried to imagine being a calm, serene, yet colorful anemone. It didn't work. I was still pissed off.

The truth was Elmira's situation struck a little too close to home. Her artistic talent and love of books were not the only things that reminded me of myself. My father had run out on my mom and my sisters and me when I was four. But I had ended up with two loving parents throughout most of my childhood, thank heaven. My amazing mother had always been there for us, even before my stepfather came along. I wished I could spare Elmira the pain I'd felt each time my biological father, now known as Not Dad, had missed the important occasions in my life—birthdays, my bat mitzvah, graduations . . .

I handed her a stack of books. "You were fabulous. You're not only a good artist but also a good singer. And a good shelver."

As she turned to place more books on the shelves, I thought I noticed her quickly sniffing one, and the hint of a smile returned to her face.

Anoop startled me when he rang the doorbell the next afternoon soon after I got home from school. He was such a nice postman, and he never seemed to mind coming up the stairs to bring me my mail instead of putting it in my mailbox like he did for everyone else.

My students had been wild all day, and thinking about Elmira was getting under my skin. I hoped Anoop wasn't going to cap things off by delivering me bad news like a jury duty summons. I was annoyed, but I slapped a smile on my face anyway. "Hi, Anoop."

"Hi, Ms. Fairisle." He held a postcard out to me, shifting his weight back and forth. I guessed new folks in town were quite a curiosity.

For the hundredth time, I said, "Please, no need to call me Ms. Fairisle. Call me Dodie."

Anoop just touched his ocean-colored Winslow Homer cap and said, "Good day, Ms. Fairisle."

"Thanks for the mail."

It was exactly the opposite of what I had feared—and what I'd been hoping for: a postcard from my younger sister, Coco! She always drew these amazing little sketches on the front. In this one, she was staring at her arm as if waiting for something.

> Greetings from northern Sudan! Today Mark and I put the final brick into the schoolhouse. It was super hot, so when we were done, we took a delightful swim. Before we got in, they warned us about guinea worm. Ever heard of it? Let's just say I tried to keep my mouth closed so I didn't swallow any water during my swim. If I did, a year from now, a 3-foot-long worm might emerge through my skin. I'm already on the lookout. Bisous! Coco

Mark had come into a ton of money when his aunt Rose passed away, and he and Coco decided to spend the year after their wedding traveling to developing countries to do humanitarian work. Mark had trained as an engineer, so he knew how to build houses and schools. Coco used her skills as a nurse to treat patients and educate the townspeople about basic medical care.

I missed her so much. She and our older sister, Maddie, were two of my best friends in the world. Chatsworth was a couple hours away from New York City, where Maddie still lived. Both of us were a little less than three hours from the Ulster County town where my mom and my stepfather, who had been Dad since I was eight, lived. Our family managed to see each other every few months; sometimes—in a string of holidays or birthdays—it was as much as once a month. In between, we all burned up the phone lines talking several times a week. Now, it was catch-as-catch-can with Coco's scant access to technology. I anticipated her postcards like each one was a missive from heaven.

In just three weeks, she would be in Khartoum, where the phones were more plentiful, and we would finally be able to have a real chat.

That night, I snuggled down under my covers, taking a deep breath of the crisp, sweet air pouring in through the window, happy to return to the embrace of my pillow-top mattress. Delightfully happy. *Almost* perfectly happy. Except that I had a queen bed, which was pretty roomy for one person.

A very small part of me was willing to admit

that the blaring background and constant pulse of New York had become like soothing white noise at bedtime during the years I had lived there. I loved Chatsworth. Loved, loved, loved. Like a croissant loves chocolate. Still, I couldn't help but admit that sometimes the refreshing quiet of Chatsworth could already be a little too . . . quiet. And if I had been the type of person to get lonely, it was possible that I might have felt a teeny, tiny bit of loneliness now. Which was why it was such a good thing that I *wasn't* the kind of person who got lonely.

Just in case, I thought of the least lonely place I could: the Chatsworth Library. Within its walls were longtime friends whose kindnesses and adventures had inspired me and entertained me as far back as I could remember. *Sense and Sensibility*'s Marianne Dashwood would not have sulked in her soup about being boyfriend-less. Miss Nelson wouldn't have gone missing again due to an ice cream hangover from her single lady pity party. Neither would Viola Swamp. And fair Rosalind from *As You Like It* would have dressed up like a man and found her fellow and . . . well, anyway . . . the library. That's where I would go tomorrow, I resolved, and I finally fell asleep thinking about settling down in my favorite reading nook surrounded by books and the shafts of light streaming through the windows.

Two

I poked at my ringing phone to answer it without running off the road. Managing to open it and hit speakerphone, I heard Kendra's voice from far away. "Where are you?"

"Driving to the library," I shouted.

"For a change," Kendra joked. "Dodie, you do realize that speakerphone amplifies your voice, right?"

"I know," I said a little more quietly. "And yes, I've practically melted my library card in the past two months from overuse. Need anything?"

"Nah, I think that new five-hundred-page biography of Abigail Adams that I just got there with you on *Wednesday* should tide me over for a bit." Kendra laughed.

"Cool. I'm in the lot now, so I'll call you later."

I could have chatted with her all the way up to the door of the library, but I wanted to enjoy this moment, the feeling of possibility before walking inside, knowing that endless choices awaited me.

When I lived in Manhattan, I often visited the flower market. I would go first thing in the morning, tea in hand; walk to the very center, where all the heady smells pooled; and then meander from row to row. Sometimes I bought gerbera daisies in just the right shade of red orange, or yellow French tulips with pink veins as I'd planned. Other times, I ended up taking home something unexpected—a branch of cherry blossoms or pussy willows. Either way, whatever I brought home was always perfect. The library was like this too—you could get exactly what you were looking for or surprise yourself. And at the library, you didn't even have to pay!

Instead of a brick schoolhouse building like many New England libraries, the Chatsworth one was housed in a sturdy, cream-colored clapboard rectangle with two small additions on either side for the audiovisuals room and the computer lab. The shingles seemed like a little wink on such a big building, especially since the shutters on each window had been painted a subtle but unmistakable pale green. People often approached the building in hushed tones and left it talking excitedly. *It is definitely hushed today,* I thought. In fact, no one was leaving the building. No one was going up to it either. Except me.

The interior of the library was in utter darkness. My heart sank as I saw the sign in the window: CLOSED INDEFINITELY FOR RENOVATIONS.

I stood there for several minutes. The door to the addition opened. The assistant librarian and my friend Geraldine's bottom appeared, then the rest of her. She was tugging a trash bag.

I rushed up to her as she hitched it into the dumpster. She lifted the surgical mask off her face and said, without a touch of surprise, "Hi, Dodie. Bummer, eh?"

"What happened?" I spluttered.

"Asbestos abatement." Geraldine squinched up her face.

"How much needs to be abated?"

"No idea, but it sounds like a lot. The McClenahan kid went exploring on his own and must have stepped through the floor, which was actually the ceiling, because it started raining asbestos during story circle yesterday."

"No one knew it was there? How is that possible?"

Geraldine shrugged. "Maybe they knew but didn't do anything about it. Anyway, they have to now."

"Why?" I asked plaintively, though of course I knew the answer. I didn't want to be inside an asbestos-infested building any more than the next person.

"Because Officer Frederick was in the story circle at the time with his niece."

"I see."

"Yeah, the inspector said the electricity and pipes are outdated, so they'll probably do a big overhaul while they're at it. I wouldn't be surprised if it took them until next Christmas, judging by how long it took them to renovate the Derbyshire Library," Geraldine mused.

I tried to breathe very slowly through my nose. "The Derbyshire Library?"

I had been there once after running an errand nearby. It smelled so aseptic—like a new car. The books hadn't had time to settle in and exude their historic perfume. It had felt like a place doing an impression of a library instead of actually being one.

"You okay, Dodie?" Geraldine asked. "You look really pale all of a sudden."

"I'll be fine."

She patted my shoulder. "Derbyshire Library is only forty-five minutes away from here." Her voice cracked as she said it. "All of our books will be transferred to other locations within the Connecticut system."

Forty-five minutes! My breathing grew more rapid again. Forty-five minutes was long enough for someone to give birth to a child! When Mom had Coco, she barely made it from the entrance to the hospital to her room before Coco came and the doctor had to . . . not important! The point was that forty-five minutes was a long time for me and an eternity for parents of most children between the ages of zero and five. Or, in the case of my hyperactive student Jonah Brownlee's mother, zero and eight.

"Yeah, good thing," I murmured. "Okay, I'm going to go now."

"See you," Geraldine said, replacing her mask before heading back inside.

As I made my way back to my car, feeling nauseated, two other cars pulled into the parking lot. Lula Cabrera and her kids piled out of one. "Hi, Dodie. We're here for story circle. Are you sitting in?" Lula asked.

"Um . . . no. There's no story circle today or for a while, it looks like," I hedged.

"What do you mean?" Her son was peeking out from behind her leg, listening to our conversation.

"The library is closed indefinitely for renovations," I announced.

A frown creased Lula's face. Her daughter tapped her on the arm. "Closed, Mama?" Her lower lip trembled. "But you said . . ."

"I know, sweets, but there's nothing Mama can do," she replied helplessly, patting the two children. "Let's go get some ice cream."

"Sorry to be the bearer of bad news."

"Not your fault. But they were really looking forward to this," she replied just loudly enough for me to hear. "Their father has been at the new mall's construction site constantly for the last three months, and the library is the only thing keeping all of us sane."

"Good luck," I offered, feeling lame and strangely guilty. Not that the library closing was my fault or had anything to do with me. I just wished I could do something to help Lula and her kids.

And what was I going to do now that the library was closed? Well, first of all, I would go to Wendell Wye's Bookshop to remind myself that there were other places to get something to read.

I was sitting on the ground in the bookstore, looking at an illustrated history of Paris. Elmira Pelle passed by, trailing after her mother, with a stack of books in her arms. I was about to get their attention when I overheard her say, "Mom, can I have one of these?"

"No, Elmira. I bought you a new book two weeks ago. If you can't show any self-restraint and you're going to read them that quickly, you're going to have to check them out of the library."

I goggled at her words. First of all, was she really reprimanding her daughter for reading too quickly? Second of all, did she have any idea of the burning urgency of reading for a book-loving child, how two weeks was a complete eternity without a new book to dive into?

They didn't know yet that the library was closed. I had a feeling her mother wouldn't be up for driving her to Derbyshire. So what was Elmira going to do now?

I bought a nice, juicy historical novel to cheer myself up.

"Here you go, Miss Fairisle." Wendell handed me my book.

"Please, call me Dodie," I replied distractedly, mesmerized by the hair of the man walking out the door in front of me. It was dark with a swirly cowlick. Even seeing his shoulders from the back made me weak in the knees. Who *was* that? And where could I get one?

By the time I had paid and gotten outside, he was driving away. I sighed as I watched him brake at the exit, then proceed out into the street.

It wouldn't have mattered anyway. I was still recovering from having my heart crushed by my last boyfriend.

A few days later, Elmira was sitting on the bench outside the gym reading *From the Mixed-Up Files of Mrs. Basil E. Frankweiler*—again. Now, I have probably read that book more times than there are visitors on a Saturday afternoon in the Metropolitan Museum of Art, where the action takes place. But in the months since my arrival, I had hardly seen Elmira reading anything else.

"Hello there, Elmira. Reading Mrs. Frankweiler again?"

"Yup," she said, sticking a bookmark between the worn pages.

"I love that book. But don't you ever want to read something different?"

"Sure, but I've read all the books in the school library, and the big library is closed, and it's difficult for my mom to find time to take us to the one in the next town or to the bookstore with her schedule being what it is." *Everything in the second part of that sentence sounded parroted,* I thought, frowning.

"Listen, what if I lent you some books?" I offered. "You could tell me a bit about what kind you like—besides Basil, of course—and then you can borrow them from me."

Elmira looked intrigued. "You have books like this, for people my age?" she asked, ever practical.

"Yes," I lied. "A few dozen."

"Okay," she agreed, even though she was eyeing me strangely, as most girls would a thirty-two-year-old who'd confessed to having a collection of chapter books at home.

"Great! I have to go. See you later," I said because now I wanted to be sure that I had time to get back to the bookstore before it closed.

A week after I first lent Elmira the dozen new chapter books I'd bought, she knocked on the door of my classroom.

"Hi, Elmira," I said, stepping down from the ladder I was using to hang the kindergarteners' sock puppet self-portrait gallery. "What's up?"

"Thanks for the loaner, Ms. Fairisle." Elmira

lifted all twelve books out of her backpack and placed them on the edge of my desk.

"Not a fan?" I asked.

"No, I loved them!" she enthused. "I read them all."

"Already?"

"Yeah." She looked sheepish. "Now I have to buy some new batteries for my parents' flash-light so they don't find out I was reading past bedtime."

I winked at her. I would have to get more books.

Remembering Elmira's talent for art, an idea hit me. "As it happens, I could use a helping hand on this project I'm working on, and you're exactly the person I need."

"Really?" she breathed, as though I'd just asked her to join a trip to Narnia.

"Really. Here's the thing. I'd like to gather some books that people don't want anymore so I can lend them to others. I think we need a flyer asking people to donate. Could you help me design it?"

Elmira's ponytail was swinging as she nodded. "I'll do it!"

The next afternoon, she handed me a drawing. Over the edge of a book that someone was reading, all that was visible were two eyes and the top of the person's hair, similar to the little old ladies you'd see behind the steering wheel in

Florida. It was funny and silly and . . . absolutely perfect!

"I *love* it!" I cried, giving her a big hug. Elmira looked surprised.

"Thanks," she said shyly.

"Do you need a ride home?"

"Sure, that would be great. My parents got tied up . . ." She looked down at her shoes.

After dropping her off, I rolled down the window to get my fix of fall air. I could smell burning leaves somewhere. It should have felt more like winter by now. But I loved the slow change of the season, the way the leaves smoldered red for weeks and weeks before sailing dazedly off the branches toward earth. Breathing deeply, I felt my heart lift even higher as I arrived home.

Back in July, my Chatsworth house had the same happy effect on me when my mother and I first visited it. Mom had come to town to help me choose a place to live. Partly because of how amazing she is. Partly because she and Dad were going to loan me a little money for a small down payment, knowing it would take me some time to find my financial footing. But mostly because she feared that when it came to the really big decisions—like which adorable house I would want to buy—I might be a little . . . indecisive. She and Dad had had to listen to me talk for hours about whether I would want Greek Revival style or Queen Anne, or a Victorian or a Federal home. Even before I had known whether those existed in Chatsworth or if any of them would be in my limited price range.

Sullivan had started scouting for-sale houses when she was driving around town. "There's one you have to see. It's got kind of a weird mushing together of different styles, which some people wouldn't go for, but I think it's super cute." When my mom and I pulled up to the house that day, my face flushed. I was certain, right away, that it was meant to be my home. I couldn't describe the architectural style. Turns out, neither could the broker, Bonnie. As we stood in front, she shuffled through the papers attached to her clipboard. "Um, it says Arts and Crafts on one page, Tudor on the other, and Cotswold Cottage on this other description."

Mom later told me my eyes lit up. Three times. Especially at the mention of "Cotswold Cottage." How very fairy-tale-ish!

I loved the fact that it had three different identities all linked by a certain quirky but solid charm. The main foundation was a sensible brick rectangle, but sticking out from what would have been the second-floor level, above the front door, was a projection of sand-colored stucco facing. A single peaked gable bisected the roof rising behind it. Forest-green half timbers striped downward from the peak above the mullioned window. The whole roof was covered in thin, almost pumpernickel-dark shingles. On the left side of the house, there was a tall brick chimney; on the right side, an adorable little room jutted out from the front, also in sand-colored stucco, with dark-green frames on the three floor-to-ceiling windows. A sunroom!

When Bonnie gave us the tour, I saw that the sunroom was smaller than it had looked from the outside—the house itself wasn't all that large—but it would be a lovely place to put a comfy chair so I could read and look out the window with a cup of tea.

As she took us through the rest of the rooms, it felt like a house that had been well loved, lived in, and—most of all—that wanted to be well loved and lived in again.

"And this is the final treat," Bonnie announced, gesturing through the kitchen toward the back of the house. I was busy imagining where all my pots and pans would go, the dinner parties I would throw there, and chatting with my guests in the adjacent living room, which was open to the kitchen. Bonnie opened a glass door at the back of the house that had been covered by a gauzy curtain. "This is the *full* sunroom."

I turned to my mother and whispered, "I want to live here."

She nodded, giving me only a *Shh, we don't*

want to seem overeager look. Instead of being surprised by how sure I was, she recognized that this house was perfect for me too. I smiled at my mom reassuringly. She was probably worried we'd have a repeat of New York, when the broker I was working with to find an apartment to rent claimed that he'd never received my check—after cashing it.

Her return smile didn't quite reach her eyes. She might also have been a little worried about my transition from the big city to a small town. In New York there had been plenty of glamorous parties with my worldly boyfriend Daniel, cultural events featuring artists and literati, and restaurants serving burrata over arugula with Dalmatian fig jam (for example). But New York also meant giving up a lot. As much of an optimist as I was, I could best describe my experience of the New York dating scene as meeting different versions of the same immature, superficial man over and over. I knew there were others, but I hadn't found them. And I missed being able to take long green walks. Central Park was great, but it wasn't a tree-lined neighborhood. I didn't have a yard in New York. I couldn't get a dog. On the salary I'd probably be earning there for the foreseeable future, I couldn't have more than four walls. I had found myself wishing for an escape from the city, not only for a weekend here or there to somewhere I felt less anonymous but to somewhere I could put down roots and belong.

Now, thanks to Sullivan and my parents, I had the perfect house of my own—a blend of city and country, stately and humble and homey and artsy and overall cozy and welcoming.

As I put the key in the door, I felt just how charmed my life was. Now if only I could keep making it better for Elmira . . . and Lula and her kids . . . and all the other people of Chatsworth who had a big, fat, book-shaped hole in their lives without a nearby library to go to.

Three

The flyer was a smashing success. I set up three big wicker baskets in my art room so that the kids and parents could stop by anytime to dump in their donations. The baskets filled up more quickly than I could have imagined.

"Your flyer is a classic," I complimented Elmira on the sidewalk a few days later. "We're swimming in books!"

I set up a community lending library in my classroom, but it didn't last very long. Patrons stopped by and disrupted my classes, and it started taking over all the shelves that were meant for art supplies. When Gibbon's *Decline and Fall of the Roman Empire* fell off a desk and crushed my student Abel's rather miraculous drinking-straw suspension bridge, I knew it was time to reconsider the location.

"Tell me everything," Kendra insisted when I called a debriefing over coffee in the teachers' lounge, and I happily obliged, right down to Abel's stoic response when he heard about the demise of his construction.

"So I've been trying to figure out where else it could go. I was hoping some part of the school library could be used for the lending library, but

I know you only have room in there for a small selection of children's books as it is."

"What about the public library at Derbyshire?" Kendra asked.

"I thought about it, but we need something here. And I really want the place to have a different vibe. I don't want anyone who comes in to feel like they have to be quiet or obey a ton of rules. I see it as more of a social place," I revealed. "More intimate feeling. Plus, Derbyshire Library is so far away."

Kendra nodded. "You're thinking of installing it in your home for now, aren't you?"

I secretly had been. "Part of me realizes it's a crazy idea. I mean, my house isn't that big. But it's big enough, especially for one person. I could use the sunroom in the back of the house for the time being. Move out some of the furniture and try to fit as many books in as I can. There won't be room for tons of people to linger, but that's okay. Hopefully they'll be encouraged to come and find a book, have a cup of tea together somewhere afterward, invite each other over for book clubs, that sort of thing." Actually, I hoped all those things could be squeezed into the back sunroom somehow, but first things first . . .

"It sounds great. You could throw some cheap curtains over the windows that look into your living room to give you some privacy," Kendra suggested. "And you can lock the door between the sunroom and the rest of the house, right? That way, if you need someone else to tend the library when you're out of town or just want to keep people from getting too curious, you'll be all set. I'd love to help you."

"Thanks, Kendra."

Kendra thought my plan could work. And she was the school librarian! I could do this. I just knew it.

On Sunday I joyfully made lists of all the books I wanted to track down for my sunroom library. I hoped that some targeted advertising would bring them in, but I had started socking away a little money for special must-haves anyway.

I also paged through many of the volumes on my own shelves, and a stream-of-consciousness book search began. *A Tale of Two Cities* made me think of the eighteenth-century French Revolution, which made me think of the French Revolution in the novel *Les Misérables*, which came out when impressionism was starting in France.

Soon I was on the floor of my living room surrounded by art books—on Monet and Sisley, and then the Nabis, who followed the impressionists and included some of my favorite painters, like the incredible colorist Bonnard. The open pages cast the room in a glow of apricot and periwinkle, quince yellow green and pomegranate red. As I was tracing the peach-like cheeks of a mother watching over her sleeping baby in a Berthe Morisot painting, the phone rang.

"Hi, honey. What are you doing?" Mom asked.

"Just getting some inspiration for the lending library."

"That classroom must be really full by now," she said.

"Well, yes, I've recently decided to put the library in the back sunroom at the house."

"In your home? Do you really think that's a good idea? I mean, you've only just moved somewhere with more than four walls. Don't you want to keep them to yourself for a little while?"

"No, not really. I mean, I have a whole house now. With multiple rooms. I like reading in the sunroom, but I'm happy to share it with others. And I think this is something the town really needs."

"The town needs it, huh?"

"In my opinion, yes," I said as decisively as I could.

"And you don't think it's taking on too much when you're just starting to get settled in at the school and in the town?"

"No, I can handle it," I snapped.

She was silent for a second, then conceded. "Okay, well, you know best."

I didn't want to leave things this way. My mom

was only trying to help. Sort of. "So what were some of my favorite books when I was growing up? I have a bunch down already, but I could use your help in filling out my list."

"*Mouse Paint* . . ." That had been the first one I'd written down!

"*The Very Hungry Caterpillar*." Ooh, yes, I'd loved that one.

"*Strega Nona*." And that one.

"*The Cat in the Hat*, obviously. *Where the Wild Things Are*. Oh, and your number one favorite was *Jellybeans for Breakfast*."

That definitely made sense. Except today it would probably be more like *Ice Cream for Breakfast (and Sometimes Lunch and Dinner)*.

"Then when you were older, you loved *Miss Nelson Is Missing! Madeline*, of course. And eventually, *Mrs. Piggle-Wiggle*. The Anne of Green Gables series. And so many Judy Blume books."

Mrs. Piggle-Wiggle! The funny British lady who always found the perfect way to get kids to do the right thing. Like Mary Poppins crossed with Mrs. Doubtfire. I sighed with contentment.

"Do you still have my copies of all of them there?" I asked.

"I think so. I've seen some of them around. Let me check and get back to you. So . . . what else is new?" Mom asked. I knew she was wondering whether there were any developments on the man front. Her voice sounded so hopeful, so why did I feel myself bristling again?

"Nothing," I sighed.

"What about giving it another go with that nice Daniel? Nice *and* famous, to boot! I've always imagined you showing up in the tabloids at a fabulous party on someone's yacht."

The smile fell off my face. "Is that your dream for my life?" I said dryly.

"Of course not, Do. You can do anything in the world you want. Books and art have always been your first loves. And I know how much you like teaching. However, in addition to knowing your life would be brainy, I also envisioned moments of glamour." My mom was a voracious reader too—she practically ate books—but she had a soft spot for celebrity gossip. Daniel had made her a beautiful blue tweed suit one Hanukkah and sent flowers on her birthday, so she was a huge fan.

"Well, if that is the case—which I doubt—it won't be with Daniel. He broke my heart, remember?"

"I'm sure it was all a misunderstanding," my stepdad chimed in, having picked up another phone in the house. They used this impromptu, low-tech conference call feature often so that neither would miss a word.

"Hi, Dad," I said. "And yes, it was. I thought he would stand by me no matter what, and instead he made me feel like an idiot right after I was publicly humiliated."

"I'm sorry, Do. I didn't mean to push," my mom said. "It's only that we really want you to be happy."

"Forget Daniel because I could never be happy with him."

"Okay, okay. We're off to dinner. Love you," Dad said.

"And Dodie, it's really great that you're starting a little library," my mom said. "You've loved books so much since you were a baby. I think it's a wonderful idea."

"Thanks, Mom."

I couldn't help but feel unsettled after we talked. They meant well, but sometimes they still treated me like a little girl. The one who had quit horseback riding lessons after two stinky weeks and gymnastics after three when I hurdled into the vault instead of over it.

I gathered all the books into my arms, replacing them on the shelves. All except the book with the Berthe Morisot picture. The woman in the painting looked exhausted, her eyes half-closed. Not only with fatigue, I imagined, but also with joy. She was gingerly pulling down the lacy canopy hung over the crib to keep out the drafts. *Lucky baby,* I thought. *Lucky mother.*

It was going to be pretty challenging to become a mother at the rate I was going. I hadn't felt like trusting anyone thanks to what had happened with Daniel.

After art school, I had worked in a gallery during the day and painted most nights and on weekends. As a reward for gofering for crazy bosses at a fashion glossy, my friend James got to attend tons of glamorous events in the evenings, and he brought me along on the rare occasions when he could pull me away from my paintbrushes and canvases.

At one of these shindigs, I was standing next to a rakishly handsome man at the buffet table. James was flirting with a male model nearby whose cheeks were so sunken he looked like he'd swallowed a vacuum cleaner. I was doing my own impression of a vacuum, hoovering these really delicious little morel mushroom and Idiazabal tarts with sprigs of tarragon and some microgreens with a hint of spiciness to them that was probably from . . . anyway, the man next to me was being interviewed, so I knew he was someone important, but of course I didn't recognize him. I overheard him saying, "Well, I figured Daniel G had a little bit more of a stylish ring to it than Daniel Gargamel."

His eyes smiled before his mouth. Of course I knew who Daniel G was. He had debuted his first couture collection when he was twenty-three and in the ten years since continued to prove how precocious and rare his taste was.

Our eyes connected. “Excuse me,” he said to his interviewer. “I have somewhere to be.”

I turned quickly away from him and stuffed another hors d’oeuvre in my mouth, half-afraid and half-hoping he was coming toward me. A moment later, a deep cinnamony cologne enveloped me, and I felt a tap on my shoulder. “Hello?” he said.

“Yes,” I croaked. The crinkly lines around his eyes suggested he could eat girls like me for breakfast—and probably did.

“I noticed you were interested in my interview.” It was not a question. Such staggering confidence was more intoxicating than the three glasses of cheap Pinot I’d had on an empty stomach. Empty before all the tarts, that is.

“I . . . um . . . I was just reflecting that you have it even worse than I do,” I blurted.

He raised one dark eyebrow in amusement. “Really? And how is that?” Daniel G probably wasn’t used to being told that he was less fortunate than anyone else.

“You see, my name is Dodie Fairisle.” I managed a smile, willing him to understand.

He looked at me in anticipation. Shoot. I was sort of hoping he would pick up on my meaning.

“Uh . . . your last name is Gargamel . . . ?” I backed away. My pajamas beckoned. And a brown paper bag for my head.

He laughed—a practiced, throaty bark that was

neither warm nor cool. "I'm giving you a hard time. I knew what you meant."

I exhaled. "Okaygoodnicetomeetyoubye!"

As I turned to flee, he slipped his hand around my wrist and gently tugged me back to face him. "Wait a second. You are charming. Let me take you to dinner," he ordered.

I reflected for a moment. Most of his face was expressionless, but there was an eager gleam in his eye.

"All right," I agreed. Why bother living in New York if not to take a few chances?

In the early days, dating Daniel G meant I had to get used to half-clad models swanning around his apartment, crashing on his couch, borrowing clothes from the showroom, and cozying up to him in restaurants or clubs whenever I went to the bathroom.

However, after Daniel and I had been out on a few dates, the models disappeared. I wasn't sure how he was sending a signal that he wasn't interested in playing the field anymore, but everyone in New York besides me seemed to have gotten the message. Daniel seemed to revel in having an aspiring artist on his arm at events, and the press ate it up.

As brilliant and funny and charming as he was, something wasn't quite right. I began to notice that when I told him a story, he'd always swing the conversation back around to something that had happened to him. If I mentioned an exciting event or big deadline I had coming up, he never asked how it had gone afterward. If I said I'd had a bad day, I rarely got so far as to tell him why before I was commiserating over one of his problems with a supplier or another designer or an account. And he never remembered to find out whether the next day was better. The reality was Daniel G was very interested in me but not as interested as he was in Daniel G.

"He's a narcissist," Coco claimed. That word always sounded so lovely that it was hard to believe it meant such an unpleasant thing. Ultimately, when I needed him most, he hadn't been there for me. And to add insult to injury after our painful breakup, he'd asked me not to speak to the press.

I pushed those thoughts away. For now, my hands would be full setting up the new lending library. First I had to figure out how the Hatshepsut to do that.

I decided to focus on what was most important: the experience of the library. I had to set aside what other people did in their libraries and forget about what I didn't know. Instead, I would try to think as someone who had been an attentive (okay, compulsive) patron of libraries for my whole life. I wanted to make it a place where I would feel comfortable and happy so that other people would too.

The front entrance of my house faced west, and the back sunroom sat on the east-facing side. Light streaming from the southern window crossed the whole space all the way to the window on the north side. It could get warm in there with the full sun; I would need to set up some shelves in a way that created shade without risking damage to the books by putting them in the path of blazing heat. Some transparent curtains maybe—heavy enough to block the glare but thin enough for sunshine to suffuse the room. The door connected to the house was at the southwest corner three steps up into my kitchen and living room. I sat down on the stairs with a little sketch pad and drew out my vision. I knew I'd have to get in there with an actual tape measure at some point, but tape measures are scary. Like mayonnaise or Rodents of Unusual Size. So for now, I drew.

I knew from all my library visits that the shelves were usually about six feet tall, and I could fit five of them in the center of the room with comfortable aisle space between them, maybe six if I squeezed them in. Then I could have low bookcases lining each wall below the windows except the solid west wall attached to the house and the left half of the north wall, which was also solid and windowless. The circulation desk would go in the middle of the west wall, and I hoped I could snug in a round table on the other side of it, in the northwest corner, for a few readers to sit at. In the south corner of the opposite wall were the french doors leading to the outside, and they were fortunately wide enough that I was sure I could fit the shelves and other furniture through. Well, pretty sure.

I set my sketch pad down and wiped my brow. Beads of sweat came off on my fingers. I was breathing heavily, the blood pounding through my veins. The way the library needed to look was clear to me now, so close that I could practically smell the books.

On Monday afternoon, a few of my closest friends met me at school to ferry some books back to my place. My massive furniture order materialized right as we got home. Actually, the delivery truck was there waiting for us. Oops.

"How long have you guys been here?" I asked, concerned.

"About twenty minutes," the head guy, whose name tag read DANA, said.

"I'm so sorry."

"Nah, that's okay. It's not every day we get to deliver the contents of a library!" Dana gestured at the bookcases lined up in the back of the truck. My palms started sweating.

"Are you going to have self-help books? Like *The Secret*? Or *How to Win Friends and Influence*

People?" a teen-looking delivery guy asked as he headed up the ramp.

"Sure," I said, biting my lip. "We're going to have a little bit of everything, hopefully."

The guys unloaded the shelves, and fortunately—with a little grunting and rotating and probably some swearing that I pretended not to hear—everything ended up inside the sunroom exactly where I'd drawn it. I thanked the delivery guys and tipped them generously, telling them to come back in the New Year after we opened.

When they left, we ordered pizza, and Kendra mixed up a bunch of Bellinis to keep us buzzing along. So some thrillers might get mixed in with the romance section . . . no big deal.

"You look really happy," Kendra said, handing me another Bellini after we'd shelved the last of the books.

"I am."

She clinked glasses with me. "Me too."

The other girls gathered around, wanting to get in on the toast. "Yeah, this place is going to be fantastic," Geraldine said.

"Thanks. That means a lot to me coming from the two coolest librarians I know."

Everyone burst out laughing.

"What?" I asked.

"I've never seen anyone smile so big!" Kendra giggled.

"Just wait until the opening!"

Four

December 2007

The lending library was my new crush. I thought about it when I was at school and when I was driving home. I basked in its presence. I kept imagining ways to make it happy or, rather, to make its visitors happy. I couldn't wait to tell my older sister, Maddie, about it. But first, I was looking forward to a dose of vicarious dating.

Maddie made a bigger effort to meet new people than anyone I knew. She seemed to have some kind of male magnet that I wasn't blessed with, so her efforts were always rewarded with attention. Unfortunately, her own attention span lasted about as long as a fruit fly's.

She answered on the second ring. "Hey, princesspants."

I grinned. "Hi, hot stuff."

"What are you doing right now? I hear something going into the oven."

"Are you a dog? What's with the supersonic hearing?" I asked. "I'm making Yorkshire pudding."

"What the hell is Yorkshire pudding?"

"It's kind of like a popover—"

"Love those," Maddie interrupted.

"—usually baked in the drippings of roast beef."

"Ew, roast beast! But you don't eat roast beast."

"I know."

"Um, Dodie, doesn't that mean you're making popovers?"

"Okay, yes, fine," I harrumphed. "But I was reading Dickens, and he doesn't call them that. He calls them Yorkshire puddings." I wasn't about to tell her that he also described them as blisterous. They really weren't. Okay, well, maybe in shape they were, but as anyone who had ever eaten one knew, they were basically the perfect kind of bread. All crisp brown crust, just the tiniest hint of eggyness inside. When they came out of the oven, I would either butter them or use some Macon Farms cherry preserves or the last dregs of my Fauchon peach-vanilla jam. Or the almond cream Maddie had gotten me on sale at Dean & Deluca. Snapping back to it, I asked, "Where are you?"

"I'm at the gym working off my popovers of a different kind."

"What are you doing?"

"On the treadmill."

"Wow, you sound great," I marveled.

"Thanks, Do. But don't be impressed. I started three minutes ago, so I'm only going one and a half miles an hour at this point."

"How's your Dionysus?"

"Gorge. I sat and stared at his marvelous, endless eyes and dark, full lashes for two hours last night," she said dreamily. "It distracted me from the blather coming out of his mouth."

I snickered. "That's a little creepy of you, though. I mean, is it obvious to him you just think he's pretty? Wasn't he weirded out by all that staring?"

"Nope. He kept saying, 'My eyelashes *are* beautiful, no? Keep looking at me; I think that makes them grow.' "

I rolled my eyes and laughed. "I can see why you wanted to tune him out then."

"Yeah. That's why he's Mr. Right Now. Enough about him. Mom told me you're starting a library?"

"I'm really excited about it. You know that little corner in our attic with the squishy chair where I always used to read? I set up a corner like that in the library here. And I've been cutting up the art from old calendars and turning them into bookmarks so I can write a little note telling people why I chose that book for them. Remember the back sunroom? That's where I put it. It's such a great, sunny space, and the trees all around make it feel homey and cozy too."

"It sounds awesome. I can't wait to see it when I'm there. Listen, I'd better kick it up a notch. Blasting up to three miles an hour! Enjoy the dickens out of those popovers." She laughed.

I rolled my eyes again. “Thanks. Enjoy the workout.”

“If you say so. And hey, I’ll see you next weekend.”

“I know! Excited to celebrate your birthday!”

“It’s really coming along, isn’t it?” I said to Geraldine.

The smell of books was already filling the air. They neatly lined the shelves except for the decorated bins I’d put out with picture books for the kids to rifle through, one low corner bookcase that had a squishy chair shoved in next to it, and a stack of random books on top of it meant to entice people who didn’t know what they were looking for. I would keep refreshing it with totally unrelated books—some delicious beach reads by Sophie Kinsella or Hester Browne or Zane, some Nicholas Sparks tearjerkers, some award-winning new literary fiction, some scandalous memoirs. The rest of the books in the library were divided into fiction, narrative nonfiction, and illustrated books arranged in alphabetical order. People could find their way to the books they loved, and the hunt would be fun.

“Definitely getting there. But it still needs something,” Geraldine said, her hand on her hip, her head cocked as she scrutinized one side of the room.

“Well, I want to leave the bulletin board blank

for now so the kids can fill it up with requests and drawings and stuff." The thought made me smile. A wooden credenza I'd gotten at an auction and moved around my house aimlessly for the past three months had finally found its true home beneath the bulletin board. On top of it, I'd placed a little basket labeled COMMENT CARDS with a stack of them to write on and slip into the envelope, inviting COMMENTS, THOUGHTS, BOOK WISH LISTS for the bulletin board. A handful of pencils sat in a colorful Italian tomato can. There were also a pad of construction paper and two boxes of crayons.

"No, that's not it." Geraldine was shaking her head. She was trying not to smile or to glance at the door into my house, which, I now realized, Kendra had disappeared through a while ago.

A moment later, she returned, gingerly carrying something in her arms.

Oh no. Was that . . . had she . . . ?

"This is what's missing!" Kendra announced, as though she was continuing the conversation Geraldine and I were having.

Even seeing the wood frame on the back of the canvas made the corners of my mouth pull down. Then Kendra turned the canvas around. I clenched my fists hard.

"Yes!" Geraldine clapped. "It's perfect!"

There, staring me in the face, was one of my paintings—two mermaid sisters holding hands, one with red-gold hair, one with honey-gold hair, their tresses trailing, their eyes starry as though lit from within. I sat down heavily in a child-size chair, feeling it creak under me. My knees were shaking; I crossed my arms over them so Geraldine and Kendra wouldn't notice.

But of course they did. Kendra had seen my artwork previously—by accident when we went up to my attic to pull down a box of books and she remarked upon the row after row of canvases turned away to face the rafters—and I had shared the story of my spectacular failure as an artist with her.

Through the many long hours of gallery work in New York—cataloging, stuffing envelopes, entering mailing addresses—I had nursed my ambition as a painter, sacrificing lots of beer-soaked nights with friends to save up for new paints, brushes, and canvases and devoting a corner of my tiny apartment to my easel and a growing body of work.

One day, the owner of the gallery where I was interning finally let me show him some of my paintings. "Stick to data entry," he advised me. I faked a stomachache, went home, and cried for the entire weekend until Daniel returned from a model-scouting trip in Morocco.

"What's wrong?" he asked when he called from the back of a cab. It was early in our relationship, and—considering how nice his apartment was—it hadn't made sense for us to stay at mine before. So Daniel had never even seen my artwork.

"My boss hated my paintings," I confessed.

"What? That's crazy. Let me see what he saw," he insisted. "I'll give you my honest opinion."

"Okay." I sniffed. Thirty minutes and one rapid cleaning spell later, I buzzed him up.

"Seriously, Dodie, you've got something here," he said when he looked at my paintings. He pulled a half dozen of them out of the careful layers of canvases I'd made along the floor around the easel. "They're different from anything I've seen before, and I've seen a *lot* of art."

"Really?" I asked.

"Yeah." He looked thoughtful and said, "Listen, let me talk to a couple friends and see if I can get your stuff viewed by someone else."

I guessed Daniel loved a good challenge because within a month he got me booked for a group show at a small but well-respected gallery in Chelsea.

To make a long and painful story short, Daniel and my family and friends loved my work. The *Times* called it "mawkish and sentimental," and *New York* magazine put it in the Highbrow Despicable column on the Approval Matrix with the line "incomprehensibly childish art from a supposed adult." It should have given me some satisfaction to be featured in such a legendary spot—"Even the 'Despicable' ones are cool,"

Sullivan had insisted—but it didn't. The other reviews were pretty similar. Some of them talked about how all the subjects' eyes shone with a glee that can't exist in a world where puppies are run over, or they snarked that the artist seemed imprisoned in a strange, warped optimism.

Maddie dropped the f-bomb fourteen times in a row trying to convince me that the blasé New York press should take its head out of its glutei maximi (my words, not hers) and stop writing reviews from their postcocaine binge crashes.

Daniel had a friend send me an emergency supply of vacuum-packed cheeses from Paris.

I locked myself in my apartment for yet another tear-filled weekend, packed away my paints and paintings, drowned my sorrows in *tomme vieille* and *comté fruité*, and admitted to myself that I didn't have the talent or the thick skin to be an artist. What people said deeply hurt me. It felt like an attack not only on my work but also on my way of looking at the world. Secretly, a small part of me had hoped Not Dad might be inspired by my success—or, as it turned out, failure—to get in touch with me all those years after abandoning our family. But of course, he never contacted me about the show or the savage reviews.

"What should I do now?" I asked Daniel. A part of me wanted him to say, "Take some time and then start painting again. Screw them."

Instead, his response was: "I was afraid this might happen."

"What? The bad reviews? Why?" I assumed he meant that some mean critics can torpedo new people for the fun of it.

But no. "I want you to be happy, Do. But maybe it's better to accept that your painting isn't good enough rather than spend years trying to make it happen?"

My jaw dropped. Not good enough? That's what he thought? And he had allowed me to expose my work to the world anyway? I wanted to say, "I thought you believed in me." But there was no point. Daniel's meaning was clear, and my heart was broken. I could never be with him again after that.

I had enrolled in teacher education classes a week later figuring I could use my passion for art to help little ones learn it. I loved what I did now. I didn't love seeing a reminder of my failure clasped between Kendra's hands. And I certainly didn't love the idea of all the library patrons being forced to look at my painting or—Geppetto forbid—thinking that I was showing it off.

Kendra and Geraldine had obviously followed the range of emotions on my face. Geraldine patted me on the shoulder. Kendra sat down in the other child-size chair, holding the painting on her lap and resting her knees against mine. The mermaids stared at me. I put my hand over their eyes.

"Dodie, this will warm up the whole room. No one has to know you painted it. Tell them you got it at an auction."

"No, thanks," I said in a small voice.

Kendra was not about to be deterred. She walked over to the wall behind the circulation desk, holding up the painting at the right height. "It's nautical, so it feels like New England. It's happy-making . . . Do, it's really perfect. You have to admit that."

"I don't admit that. It's mawkish and sentimental," I murmured.

"You don't really believe that," Kendra said, trying to meet my eyes. "Do you?"

"It's not for me to judge," I hedged.

"Good! Let the patrons decide!" Geraldine urged.

"That's not what I meant!"

"It may not be what you meant, but it's what you said," Kendra argued. "Listen, Do. We don't have to do this if you don't want to. But first of all, your back will be to it almost all of the time." She sat at the circulation desk to demonstrate. "And"—her eyes narrowed like she was going in for the kill—"I heard Elmira say the other day at school that mermaids are her favorite mythical creature. I'm sure she'd feel even more welcome here with this painting up."

I sighed. Making Elmira happy was more important than my own insecurities. Besides, I planned to find a great piece of art—by someone else—to replace my crappy one as soon as possible.

On Friday night, I had a little grand opening party for the library. I would have loved for my family to be there, but Maddie and my parents graciously declined the drive in, which turned out to be a good thing because there wasn't actually room. As it was, people had to take turns coming in. But no one seemed to mind. I hung some paper lanterns from the trees behind the house so that people could congregate out there and mingle. There was only one thing that could take away from my joy that night: the thought of Elmira with her face pressed up to the window of her room, dreaming of being at the library with us. Suddenly my duck-and-smoked-Gouda canapé seemed cold indeed.

I'd plan a little celebration for her, I resolved—maybe some cupcakes in the lending library one day after school. Right now, I had to pay attention to the guests who were there to celebrate—friends I already had and future friends I was sure to make over the stacks—and their excitement wiped away any doubts I might have had. I could see it already: this little library was going to do so much good for the people of Chatsworth.

Thinking about it made my cheeks glow like the windows of my beloved book-filled retreat, a shelter against lonely nights or difficult days for anyone who wanted to come inside.

"Happy thirty-fifth birthday, Maddie!" I said the next night in New York.

"Thanks, Do!" She looked happy. At least, her eyebrows looked happy. I couldn't see the rest of her face because of the gigantic shellfish tower in front of her. What I could see were periwinkles. And crab legs. Part of a lobster. Some miniature shrimp. And some other whirly-twirly shells I didn't recognize. "Take any creatures you want from that side." Her voice drifted over the ice.

"Oh, that's okay. I'm good with my langoustines for now," I replied, prying a morsel out of the shell and placing it on my tongue. Chef Delain Fremais was such a genius with seafood. These langoustines had a touch of olive oil, some Maldon sea salt, cracked black pepper, a little citrus . . . and something else I couldn't put my finger on . . . a little mystery touch that made all the difference between the magic he worked in his kitchen and the edible but not always inspired results from mine. Then there were the sumptuous surroundings capped with the giant painting of a whale that hovered above us. And the impeccable service. Not to mention the impact that this meal would have on my bank account.

“We’ll go halvesies,” Maddie had said to reassure me on the phone a month earlier when I told her I was coming to New York to celebrate with her and asked if she had any place in mind for dinner. “It’s a milestone birthday, and I feel like doing it up big-time . . . and I’ve always wanted to have a meal at Les Crustacés. You in?”

I had sighed. Whether it was one meal or two meals at Les Crustacés . . . I would be so far in the hole it hardly mattered. There was no way I could let Maddie buy her own birthday meal. She had just lost her job . . . again. She started each one in a burst of enthusiasm that carried her through the first few weeks. Unfortunately, Maddie didn’t care much for fussy little details like getting to work within two hours of everyone else or responding to emails within . . . ever. Her new employers usually lost their enthusiasm pretty quickly.

So, having taken the plunge into the expensive-meal ocean, I was determined to enjoy myself. I didn’t have to worry about whether Maddie would.

“Hey, you,” I said as her whole face reemerged. The tower was shrinking. Her side plate was rapidly filling up with empty shells.

“Ahoy there! Okay, so now I can tell you the main reason for the big celebration,” she announced.

"Your illustrious birth?" I said sweetly, giving her a goofy grin.

"Shut up," she returned, "and listen to your older sister's wisdom. I'm celebrating my liberation." Maddie smiled.

"From your latest disastrous job? Liberation, huh? Is that what the kids are calling it these days?"

She ignored me. "I'm ready to embrace being footloose and fancy-free!"

I clinked glasses with her, but something gnawed at me.

"Sure, right . . . um, what do you mean? How is that different from your usual footlooseness and fancy-freedom?"

"Well, just that, you know, now that I'm thirty-five and still single, my chances of having kids are shrinking based on every medical study ever, and especially since Grandma tried to have kids at age thirty-five, and she couldn't. She had Mom and Uncle Charlie, then no dice."

A chill ran down my spine. That didn't prove anything, though.

"And Mom couldn't have kids after thirty-five either."

"What are you talking about?"

"Don't point that thing at me," Maddie said. I lowered the langoustine claw, my hand shaking.

"What are you talking about?" I repeated.

"That was part of the reason Not Dad made a

run for it when we were young. Mom wanted more kids. But after a year of trying, Not Dad didn't."

"Really?" I said faintly. The sounds in the room came roaring at me like a wave, then subsided, then roared toward me again. I focused on Maddie.

"Yeah." She looked at me levelly. "I guess it makes sense since he's our real father, but he didn't even want us, apparently." The corners of her mouth pulled down. That snapped me out of my shock. I couldn't let Maddie be unhappy on her birthday even if this conversation was making me feel seasick.

"So where does the celebration part come in?" I forced myself to say.

Maddie shrugged her shoulders as if to shake off the negativity and perked up. "Well, the beauty of it is now that I'm thirty-five, I don't need to worry about it anymore. The decision has been made for me."

"That's ridiculous." I laughed. It sounded strangely hoarse. "That doesn't necessarily mean anything for us . . . um, for you."

Maddie leaned in as if to tell me a secret. "And here's the best part. I've discovered I don't really care! I almost feel relieved. And I mean, you still have time, but obviously it's a good thing that you don't have a kid yet either."

"Obviously? Why is that?"

Maddie was watching my face, and she plastered on a smile when she noticed my expression. "Never mind, let's just enjoy the mollusks," she said, waving her hand in a gesture of conciliation.

"No, I want to know what's obvious about it," I insisted.

"You've got lots going on," she continued, "between settling into Chatsworth, and your new library, and hopefully some dating. Do you really want to have a kid alone?"

I was silent for a long moment. "What makes you think I'll still be alone?"

"I'm sure you won't be. But what if you are?"

"Mom did it alone for years."

"Yeah. And it sucked. Besides, you loved painting more than anything, but you gave it up after a few crappy reviews. How do you know you'll be like Mom instead of Not Dad? You love babies, but what about when it gets really hard and there's no out? How do you know you won't want to cut and run?"

"I would never, ever do that."

"You don't know that."

"Yes, I do," I said louder.

"No, you don't," Maddie replied.

"Do you know me at all?"

"Yeah. I do. And I know myself. Let's face it. Coco may be our little sister, but she is the only one of us who has her act together enough right now to have a kid. I'm too selfish, and you live in a fantasy world where everything comes easily. You probably think magical elves will zip down from the North Pole and take care of your child if you can't."

"Give it a rest, Maddie! You've just lost, what, your twenty-third job this year? If any one of us is going to turn out to be a deadbeat like Not Dad, it's *you!*" I yelled.

Maddie's eyes opened wide. So did the eyes of every other person in the restaurant. I felt a tap on my shoulder. I looked up.

"Excuse me, Mademoiselle," the maître d' said smoothly. "May I speak with you a moment about your dessert?" I had arranged for a special croquembouche for Maddie—one of those crazy towers of pastry puffs stuck together with delicious hard caramel.

My face was on fire. "I'm sorry, sir," I whispered, staring at my napkin. "My sister and I were having a friendly debate. It's her birthday."

"That's right. She didn't mean anything by it," Maddie chimed in.

"*Oui*. I understand, and that's fine." His face was impassive. "May we invite you into the bar area to take your dessert? There's a lovely little table by the window."

Maddie was leaning across the table to hear the conversation. We both glanced at the bar area.

How embarrassing. We'd have to pass by all the patrons on the way there and back. A double walk of shame thanks to my outburst. Maddie was apparently thinking the same thing.

She shook her head. "May we take it to go?"

Maddie didn't know what was in store, so fortunately she wouldn't share my current vision of a sadly disassembled pyramid. Which, when disassembled, would look like a bunch of gloopy, oozing cream puffs, I reckoned. At least it would taste delicious.

"But of course, Mademoiselle. It would be my pleasure."

As if he was already expecting our decision, I was handed the bill, my credit card was whisked away and back, an LC-monogrammed doggie bag appeared under our noses, and we made our way awkwardly toward the door.

When we got outside, Maddie tromped toward the subway so quickly I had to run to catch up with her.

"Can you believe that guy? Not even letting us eat our entrées or stay at our table for the special dessert I ordered . . . it's not like we're some kind of hooligans," I babbled.

Maddie whirled around. "Dodie, shut it. I really don't want to hear anything more from you tonight."

"But, but you told the maître d' I didn't mean anything by it—"

"That was not for *your* benefit. That was because I wanted some goddamn chocolate tart with the gold leaf and the coulis on the plate, not on Styrofoam," she roared, peppering the sentence with other unrepeatable curse words.

"Okay, well, I'm sorry, but you know you sort of just dropped a big, fat bomb on me about babies and the reason Not Dad left us, and then you insulted me and . . ."

She put a hand up to stop me. "You do not get to make excuses. You know how to behave in a restaurant. And babies aren't everything." Maddie dared me with her gaze.

I wasn't about to rise to that bait. "Listen, Maddie, I don't want to fight with you on your birthday. Let me buy us a bottle of Veuve, and we can go back and enjoy dessert at your place. It's a croquembouche!" I announced, forcing a smile. "Let's not let this ruin our night."

Maddie grabbed the bag out of my hand and threw it into the nearest trash can. "Too late. You already ruined my birthday."

I lay awake that night while she breathed evenly. It was a good thing she'd run out of steam so that my remorseful tears didn't keep her up. Maddie had really needed something good after her firing. She had been trying to look on the bright side. Maybe she'd been a little harsh and a little callous with a family bombshell she knew would affect me. Still, it was her night. And I'd ruined it with my baby-fever-fueled outburst and my defensiveness.

I couldn't believe I'd compared her to Not Dad. Our biological father had left my mother when Maddie was seven, I was four, and Coco was two. Maddie had a handful of memories of him. Mostly of him yelling at Mom or coming to get clean laundry before his next "business trip." There were only a few scattered memories left in my mind, a hazy picture of his face. Coco didn't remember him at all. We never heard from him after he walked out. For years, Mom had told us that he was living high on the hog in a villa in the south of France. She later admitted she'd lied to spare us from the truth: he had lived around the corner from us throughout our entire childhoods with a new wife and two kids younger than Coco.

It was wrong of me to say Maddie could turn out like him. She was probably just putting on a brave, uncaring face, secretly freaked out about the age thing. And besides, it wasn't that he hadn't wanted kids. It was that he hadn't wanted us.

And I couldn't deny that there was some truth to what Maddie had said about me. Maybe I did sometimes have my head in the clouds. Maybe I was thirty-two and starting over again. But Chatsworth was where I wanted to be. I knew it in my bones. I would make the lending library work. And I would become a mother too—soon—before it was too late.

I called my mom right when I got home. “Mom, Maddie said you and Grandma couldn’t have children after thirty-five. Is that true?”

Mom was silent for an ominously long time. “Yes, but Dodie, everyone’s different. That doesn’t mean anything for you. Just think about the Kaminsky girls. Jana struggled for years with infertility, but Eleanor got pregnant at forty on her honeymoon.”

The words *struggled for years with infertility* didn’t help matters.

“Why didn’t you tell me this?” I asked.

“Because I didn’t want you to stress about something you can’t control. You’re single right now, and so what could you actually do?”

“I don’t know,” I replied. “But at least I have to find out what I *can* do.”

I spent the rest of the weekend researching. Apparently there were some tests that gave you a sense of whether you were likely to have a baby-factory-in-waiting in there or reproductive tumbleweeds. I set up an appointment to see Dr. Len, my ob/gyn, for the second time in the six months I’d been in Chatsworth—this was an emergency.

“Let’s do the testing,” I said to Dr. Len as soon as he’d walked me through the basics.

“Your insurance probably won’t cover it since you’re so young and have no history of infertility.”

“I understand, but it’s worth it to me.”

“Then we’ll need you to come back during your next cycle and draw some blood on day three. I can look at your ovaries today and get a sense of where you are if you want to proceed.”

“Yes, please.”

“I’ll be back shortly.”

An aide came and prepped the ultrasound probe. It never occurred to me that I might be using one except if I were pregnant.

Dr. Len came back a few minutes later. The testing was a little uncomfortable, but mostly I was just so nervous about what he would find.

He was silent while looking at the screen, then said, “Why don’t you get dressed, and we’ll go over what I saw?”

The aide led me to his office. I figured that if it was categorically good news, the doctor would have come right out with it.

“Your ovaries are on the small side,” Dr. Len began, “and I only saw a few egg follicles in each one—three on one side, two on the other.”

My stomach began to churn even harder like a salmon swimming upstream.

"So what does that mean? How many are you supposed to see?"

"We would like to see more follicles in someone of your age. Now, it's possible that IVF would spur more or that this is just an off, low-producing cycle for you, but we'd rather see somewhere more in the neighborhood of twenty follicles and upward."

"So this is bad, right?" Tears began to threaten.

"Listen, from the current research, age seems to be a much better predictor of reproductive success than this testing. Chances are, all will be fine for you. And it only takes one egg. I do think it's a good idea to have the blood work done so that we'll have a little more information."

"Okay." But I wasn't sure I would. What was the point? I mean, I was already looking at probably reduced fertility at age thirty-two. By age thirty-five, it seemed pretty darn likely that I would be in the same spot as my mother and grandmother—minus the children.

"You know Sullivan's back from Ethiopia with the baby, right?" Kendra said as she organized the library cards in the circulation desk drawer one night after school.

"Mm-hmm," I replied, doodling the number thirty-five all over the paper in front of me. That number had all-new sinister connotations to it ever since my conversation with Maddie. "We've been texting."

"I don't know what's up with you," Kendra said, probably surprised by my lack of enthusiasm, "but do you want to talk about it?"

"No, I think it's just the weather," I fibbed.

"But you always talk about how much you love the winter . . . how 'the whole world becomes like a doily with doves nesting near the holly berries,' " Kendra pointed out, smiling.

"Yes, I did say that, didn't I?" I replied.

Kendra gave up. "Okay, well, you know I'm here if you want to talk about it."

"Nope. Tell me about your day."

"Oh, it was good. I mean, other than when Benton gave me a twenty-minute exhortation on the magic of math to mold young minds and suggested we get more math books for the library. The library!" Kendra was shaking her head. "What kid's going to want to check those out?"

Benton might have been a third-grade teacher, but he took his duties with the seriousness of a college professor. Come to think of it, he dressed like one too. He definitely had more corduroy jackets and sweater vests and styles of glasses than anyone else I had ever met. And I had spent time in Brooklyn.

"Sounds like true pleasure reading."

It was a running joke with me and Kendra that

encounters with Benton in the teachers' lounge were akin to being locked in a room with a genius parrot. Sometimes we wished we could throw a blanket over his head to silence his monologues. He seemed to have a sort of homing device for Kendra. Almost as soon as we sat down to lunch, he would appear with a story, formula, theorem . . . although to be fair he sometimes came out with a fascinating detail. Like the fact that my house was its own special architectural style after all—Garden Court style, inspired by a section of West Philadelphia architecture that a man named Clarence Siegel had invented.

"How's your mom doing?" I asked. Kendra had lived with her mother in Chatsworth for the past seven years, since Kendra's father died of pancreatic cancer, but her mom had moved down to Florida a few months before I'd gotten to town.

"Great. She's adjusting really well. She loves the weather, and there's plenty of shopping to make up for the fact that she's not in driving range of New York anymore."

"You're visiting her over Christmas, right?"

"Yep, for a few days. Then she's going on a cruise with her new girlfriends down there!"

"Sounds awesome." I tried to perk up my voice.

Kendra wasn't fooled. "You going to be all right?" She slung her arm around my shoulder.

"Yeah, I'll be fine. Thanks."

"Well, if you want to talk about it, you know I'm here," she repeated.

"Thanks, K. I know." I stopped doodling and went to open a box of donated books. It was a comfort to think about who would discover them on the shelves or piled on top of the bookcase of randomness.

Five

I was temporarily brought out of my sulk by the arrival of an important addition to life in Chatsworth. A very, very small one who ignited a lot of big crushes. A few weeks after their return from Africa, Sullivan was ready to introduce us to her adopted son.

About two years earlier, Sullivan had decided she wanted to be a single mother. She'd had a longtime lover named Elizabeth before I came to town, but they had such a big blowup that Elizabeth moved back to the city. When Sullivan had first started the adoption process, Elizabeth disagreed with her choice. Not the adoption in general but the Ethiopia part specifically. Elizabeth accused Sullivan of being selfish for adopting an African child and said that people already saw her as different because she was a lesbian and that now she was going to make it even worse by choosing a child with a different skin color than hers. Kendra had told me Sullivan's response had been unrepeatable . . . but I think I got the gist.

Twenty-seven months, a ton of paperwork, and two trips to Ethiopia later, Sullivan was the delighted new mother of an eight-month-old baby named Terabithia. Terabithia! Like *Bridge to Terabithia*!

His big debut happened at Sullivan's parents' house. Sullivan's father, Jeff, and her mother, Mackie, were so excited about the new member of their family that they insisted on throwing a welcome party and inviting about fifty people.

On the day of the party, I was practically bursting. This was not only because I was about to meet Terabithia. Or because I knew Mackie and Jeff would be storybook grandparents who would serve you freshly baked cookies for breakfast and string up fairy lanterns in the backyard on your birthday. It was also because I couldn't wait to see the look on Sullivan's face when she opened the second part of my present. The first part was a blanket made of the softest cotton dyed the bright reds and blues of Childe Hassam's paintings of flags on Fifth Avenue.

I almost missed the big reveal of the second part of my present. I was playing "This Little Piggy" with Terabithia's toes, and his giggles were making his stomach shudder like the top of a popcorn container in the microwave.

Mackie realized I wasn't sitting in the gift circle when Sullivan opened the blanket. "Dodie," she called me over.

Yeees! I thought. I wrapped Terabithia right up and plopped into a chair with him nestled in my arm. He didn't seem to be disturbed at how abruptly our game had ended. He was making cooing noises into my elbow.

No one could see what was underneath the paper, but Sullivan laughed. "Pee-pee Teepees!" she cried. "Exactly what I needed."

Now, that may not seem like the most essential present, but really. A little blue cone that looks like you could eat Hawaiian ices out of it meant to protect parents' faces from a wayward stream during diaper changing? What could be more perfect?

Terabithia stirred from his little nap a few minutes later. It was time for me to hand him back to his mother. I wanted to keep holding him. He was so lovable. So near. I held him up to my eye level. "You are a sweet one. Here's your mama."

Sullivan took him in her arms. He was looking over her shoulder, and his eyes were sad, as if he didn't want to say goodbye to me either. My heart ached. Poor little guy. So much change in his life in such a short time. Now he had Sullivan, Mackie, and Jeff. But still, being a single mother wouldn't be easy for Sullivan. I thought about my mom and how tough the first years were before my stepdad, Walter, came along. I thought about the perpetual bags under her eyes as she worried about money and childcare and getting us to school and rushing to and from her job and keeping all the balls in the air. The buried memory of two-year-old Coco's lost look resurfaced, and I recognized a little of it in Terabithia's expression now.

"He really likes you, Auntie Dodie," Sullivan observed as I said my goodbyes. "He's been fearful around new people so far."

"It's no wonder—he needs some time to get adjusted," I said. "It's a huge change for such a little guy."

"True. Thanks for coming." She kissed me on the cheek. "And for the Pee-pee Teepees. I love those Pee-pee Teepees." And then for good measure, "Who wouldn't love those Pee-pee Teepees?" She grinned. I grinned back. As much fun to say as to use!

"Good luck with that cutie. And if there's anything we can do, let us know." I gestured to include Kendra.

"Awesome!" she enthused. "I'm sure I'm going to need a lot of help."

"You're really not going to be home for the holidays?" Mom asked plaintively for the fourteenth time. Christmas Eve was days away, so she was finally coming to terms with reality.

"Maddie will be an only child," Dad added for good measure. Neither of them knew that things were off with me and Maddie. We'd spoken a few times since her birthday, and I had given her a half-hearted apology. I was still embarrassed about how selfish I'd been, thinking only of myself when she was probably pretty sad to have actually reached the no-baby milestone. Yet somehow I couldn't bring the subject back up again. I would rather pretend it didn't exist. That wasn't why I wasn't going home, of course.

"I know, but since it's my first holiday season here, I should stick around and keep the library running. It's only been a couple weeks, and it's a time of year when people might feel really lonely and need a good book."

It made me sad to think of being away from my family at the holidays for the first time, but I'd started the library, and I couldn't abandon it at such a critical moment. Not to mention I continued to be as obsessed with the library as a teenage girl with her brand-new star-quarterback boyfriend. I practically sleepwalked into the lending library more than once and awoke to find myself cuddled up in a chair with a book as my pillow.

"Okay, honey," Mom conceded after a long pause. "We're going to miss you. Bundle up and stay warm."

I was feeling a little bit down when Anoop rang the bell.

"Here, these are for you." I passed him the plate of cookies I'd baked.

In return, he gave me a handful of holiday cards and something from Coco! Her latest postcard had a drawing of Mark on the front. His face was purple as an eggplant, and he was wearing a sheepish grin. He looked a little like Violet Beauregard in *Charlie and the Chocolate Factory*.

> Dear Do,
> Mark accidentally ate the flower that's meant to dye the royal chieftain's robes, instead of the one that's supposed to go on salads. Don't be alarmed, though—it looks much worse than it is. Rokiki said this particular flower can dissolve your appendix, but that's a good thing, right? I mean, I'm sort of attached to the idea of mine, but not having one means it won't ever explode. Plus Mark said our appendix is an evolutionary vestige. Apparently, our toes are obsolete too, but I'm not about to give those up. Hope all is well in Chatsworth and that you aren't breaking all the small-town boys' hearts. Got to go reason with the chieftain. It's a good thing he likes Tabasco sauce; I brought plenty. xxxC

The ring of the phone startled me out of my sleep. "Hello?" I grunted.

"Do!"

"Co!" I sat bolt upright. "It's really you! I just got your postcard."

"I'm here . . . I'm there . . . I'm everywhere! You couldn't get away from me if you tried!"

"If only that were true . . ."

"Oh, don't get sentimental on me," Coco said, but her voice quavered. "Each tear will cost me thirty dollars in phone charges, and I'm standing in a phone booth that smells like the toilet a toilet uses."

I laughed and wiped my eyes. "Tell me everything."

"It's been amazing. We've helped vaccinate three whole towns for polio. The other day, a patient who'd had a chronic infection for the past year finally got a clean bill of health. It's amazing to see what we can do here—with the leftover antibiotics that most people would throw away as soon as they start feeling better. And Mark, he's been building like you wouldn't believe. He's tireless. He's . . . Dodie, I swear every day he does something that makes me think, *That's why I married him*."

I swallowed hard. "That is so fantastic, Coco."

"How are you? How's Chatsworth? Are you bored? Lonely?"

I laughed. Coco was always gentle but direct. "No, I'm really happy here. I opened a lending library in my classroom—"

"Yes, I got your postcard. That's so perfect. First teaching, and now this."

"Well, that's not even the craziest part. It's gotten bigger, so I moved it into my house."

"Whaaat?"

"In the back sunroom downstairs, so it'll be pretty separate. And I am so excited!"

"I can't wait to come visit you."

"So when do you think that will be?" I gave in to my selfishness.

"I don't know yet. We still feel like we have so much to do. I mean, obviously if that were the measure, we could be here forever. But I think we want to head to at least one more country before we come home."

"You two are doing so much good. I'm sure it's hard a lot of the time."

"We enjoy it and seeing people's lives get better, so it doesn't feel like a sacrifice. Except, you know, whenever we have to go to the bathroom. Or try to get clean. And sometimes meals. But most of the time, it still feels like a huge adventure and an opportunity to do something for other people."

"It is, Coco. And even though you're my baby sister, I want you to know how much I admire you." I said it to her all the time. I was way past the point of worrying I'd overinflate her ego. Coco wasn't like that.

"Thanks, Do. Listen, I gotta run. Take care of

yourself, and good luck with the library. I'll talk to you really soon."

"Coco, I . . ." I wanted to tell her about Maddie so badly. About the ticking clock. But it wouldn't be fair. I couldn't keep her on the phone to talk about my problems. "Speak to you soon," I said, knowing I had a much sooner "soon" in mind than she did. "Love you and Mark."

"We love you too. Bisous."

I laid my head back on my pillow and heaved a deep sigh. I missed her already. "One more country" could of course mean months. Years even. I gulped. Wishing for her to come home was definitely selfish, and yet I couldn't help it.

The next day was the *first-ever story circle at the library!* After the kickoff party, I posted the library's regular hours: it would be open from 4:00 p.m.–7:00 p.m. on weekdays and 10:00 a.m.–3:00 p.m. on Saturdays. The first Saturday of each month would be story circle day; one for the kids at 10:30 a.m. and one for the adults at 2:00 p.m.

By ten thirty that morning, there were eight kids in the circle with their parents. At least, some of them were in the circle sitting on their parents' laps. A little boy named Guillaume was currently rummaging through my book bag, and two other kids were pulling every book off the shelf in front of them and chuckling with glee.

"Who wants to hear some books about snow?" I asked. The two kids stopped throwing books on the ground and wandered back over to see what was in my hands. Guillaume's mother extracted him and put him next to her knees.

First I read them *Oh!* A hush fell over them as they looked at the soft colors and listened to the quiet rhymes about the animals in the snow.

"And this one's called *The Snowy Day*." I thoroughly enjoyed the looks on their faces as I read it to them.

"Did anyone know this book before?" I asked, closing it.

"No!" yelled Guillaume. "But I wannit."

"We have it at home," said Lula's daughter, Margarita.

I couldn't read the expression on Jefferson Hendrow's face, but I was curious about what he was thinking. "Would you like to take a closer look?" I handed him the book. He flipped to the page with the little boy, Peter, and his mother.

"This looks like me and my mama."

I realized he'd never seen a book before with anyone in it that looked like him.

I smiled at him through a pang of sadness. Jefferson went to Eagle Ridge, not Chatsworth. Kendra hadn't wanted to wait to go through all the budgetary red tape before buying more diverse books for the Chatsworth Elementary School Library, so she had bought *The Snowy*

Day and a bunch of others herself right after she became the librarian. Eagle Ridge's library was even smaller than Chatsworth's, but couldn't they make room for books that reflected all the kids?

I'll have to change that, I thought.

"I'll show you some other really good ones on the shelves too."

Later that afternoon, the grown-ups' story circle attendees mingled in the small space between the shelves and the table in the corner. A few people helped me pull over some of the child's chairs in addition to the ones I'd taken from around my kitchen table and carried into the sunroom.

"What a lovely idea. A story group for old fogeys like me!" a woman named Roberta joked.

I gasped, horrified.

"I'm teasing," she laughed.

Kendra was cracking up. So was Geraldine, who had already come several times to the lending library, getting her fix while the Chatsworth Library where she had worked was undergoing much more extensive renovations. Very little progress had happened so far from her account of the situation.

"Oh, of course," I flubbed. "Well, help yourself to more of the milk punch and chocolate-raspberry jam squares." I gestured to where Kendra and I had set them up along the top of the bookcases under the kids' bulletin board.

“Dodie, want to start us off?” Roberta suggested.

“Sure. First of all, has anyone else been to one of these besides me? One for adults, I mean?”

The other fourteen women who had squeezed into the tight space shook their heads.

“Okay, well, some story circles have a writing period, and then people take turns reading what they’ve written. We could do that, or we could tell stories off the tops of our head. I mean, top of our heads. Tops of our heads. Whatever!”

The three other younger women besides Kendra and me were quiet, deferring to the older ladies in the group. “Let’s just start telling stories,” Roberta said.

“Why don’t you go first?” Kendra encouraged.

“Okay.” She paused, collecting her thoughts. “I first met my husband, Ray, when we were working together at a notions shop. For those of you who were born after 1960, a notions shop is where you sell buttons and ribbons and bits and bobs of that sort. Ray never said a word to me for the first three months we were working there. He was scared to death of girls. Well, okay, he was scared to death of me.

“I had quite a lot of beaux in those days. They couldn’t wait until I was done working to see me, so sometimes they came into the shop pretending to need something for their mothers. I flirted with them something awful. I never noticed Ray reacting any way or another to the boys. He was steady, steady. At the end of the day, he never left until the place was in shipshape shape.

"Three months into my time there, I fell ill with an awful cold. The kind that shakes your bones with aches, and you can hardly bear to lift up your head. But I went in to work anyway. I was real proud of having a job.

"It was one of the busiest days of the year—near Christmastime, when everyone was gussying up their old dresses and suits. Even if I'd been well, I could barely have kept up at the register. At the end of the night, I counted the money. I counted it again. Something was very wrong. Fifty dollars was missing. If it had been in the till like it was supposed to be, it would have been a banner day. A record sales day, even. But at the time, losing fifty dollars' worth of merchandise was a catastrophe.

"I couldn't for the life of me figure out what happened. Had customers left without paying? Had they underpaid? Had someone gotten their hands in the till when I wasn't paying attention? My head was a fog. I sank down on the stool behind the counter and tried to think what to do. Ray came up and, real soft-like, said, 'Is something the matter?'

"I figured things couldn't get worse at that point, so I told him.

" 'That's real bad,' Ray said, but in a kind way.

'Let's think on what to do tonight. We don't have to tell Mr. Bell anything until the morning when we give him the count anyway.'

"That was the first time Ray had spoken to me, and I felt so reassured. Not reassured enough that I wasn't up all night wringing my hands (and blowing my nose) anyway, but enough that I could talk myself into walking through that door the next morning instead of calling in sick to postpone my firing.

"When I showed up, I stared right at the floor. Ray was straightening some baskets of buttons stuck on cards that didn't need any more straightening, and when Mr. Bell came through the door from the back room, his face lit up like the sun. 'Good job, Roberta!' he said. 'I've already told Ray I'm taking you two to lunch.'

"There was a great little diner with a soda fountain in the middle of town back then. We went there, and I ate a tuna melt with cheddar cheese and drank a black cow milkshake. I will never forget how great that day was as long as I live. And Ray smiled at me over his chicken and rice plate and soda pop, and then I knew that even though we'd hardly spoken a hundred words to one another in three months, he'd made things right. I admitted to myself that he'd been part of the reason that I came to the shop even though I was sick as a dog. I also knew, from our record-breaking night of sales and our months of quiet, steady work together before then, that we made a good team.

“Ray was a gentleman through and through, and even though I asked him dozens of times over the next few weeks—we had become inseparable after that day—he refused to say how he’d gotten the fifty dollars. I told him that he had given me the best Christmas present I could have wanted. He replied that he hoped I would change my mind about that, and then he held out his mother’s ring and asked me to marry him.

“The first night we were married, he said, ‘Okay, my beloved wife, here’s what happened. I noticed Mr. Slocum and Mr. Barnes both bought scads of notions for their wives but hadn’t remembered either of them paying. So I went to their homes and said, real polite-like, that it seemed there had been a misunderstanding and that they might not have realized there are no running accounts at the store. That’s all I needed to say; each of them paid me straightaway, cash in hand, and that’s how the money came to be back in the drawer and the count all square by the time Mr. Bell got in.’ ”

Roberta paused to look at us, her expression dreamy. “I tell you, ladies, I just about married him again right on the spot.”

Afterward, Kendra and I agreed that it had been a pretty fantastic story circle. Our expressions might have been a teeny bit dreamy too. “Can you imagine falling in love with someone you've known for three months all of a sudden like that? Especially not having talked to them before?" Kendra asked.

"Well, I suppose it could happen," I mused.

"I think I'll know when I find my fish. I'm not much of one for the slow-building romance," Kendra said. "Lightning strikes, or the storm is over."

"Yes, it's always been pretty black and white for me too," I agreed.

Even so, Roberta's story sure was romantic. I *loved* story circle. I wanted to go to one every single day! Or better yet, two—just as I had today.

"You went to the Christmas Craft Market *again?*" Kendra marveled when I called her on my way home. "You are Jewish, right?" I could practically hear her shaking her head in disbelief through my newfangled hands-free setup.

"Yeah, so what? I like the mulled wine and the speculoos cookies! And the trees and the garlands and the ornaments . . ." I was actually shopping for decorations for the library. I had some Hanukkah stuff of my own to put in there, but since most of the population of Chatsworth was Christian, I wanted to make it nice and homey for the visitors who would come in around Christmas. Anyone who was at the library a lot in late December might need a bit of holiday cheer, I figured. I would have to borrow some Kwanzaa stuff too. I didn't think anyone in Chatsworth celebrated the winter solstice, but I would have been happy to put up some of those decorations, too, if I learned otherwise when I asked around.

"I got to go, Kendra. I'm meeting Sullivan and Terabithia now."

"Ooh, have fun! Tell them hi for me."

"Will do. Bye!"

When I got to our meeting place, the playground at Little Duck Park, Terabithia was already in one of the swings, and Sullivan was pushing him. Seeing me, she slowed him down to a stop.

"Hi, Sullivan. I'm so excited to see you guys!"

"Hey," she said, looking down at Terabithia. He was eyeing me as if he vaguely remembered me. He looked a teeny bit scared. Then he gave me a gummy smile.

"Hey, Terabithia." I patted him on the 'fro. It had gotten bigger. I was amazed at how happy that made me—that and the fact that he was wearing overalls with the cuffs turned up at the bottom and a pea-green shirt under a matching wool cardigan. He patted me back on the arm, sending my heart jetéing for joy.

"Can I push him?" I asked Sullivan.

She nodded and stepped aside, shading her eyes with her hand. I started out slow, then pushed a little harder when he let out a pleased hoot. After a while, the pleased hoots were replaced by grunting noises.

"That means no," Sullivan explained, catching the swing to stop the motion quickly and to steady Terabithia. She lifted him out of the seat. His little face was puckered like he'd eaten a lemon. "He loves it but then starts to get kind of seasick."

"Oh." That hadn't occurred to me.

"I'm going to put him in his stroller, and we'll push him around until he recovers," Sullivan said, a tiny smile around the edge of her lips.

"So tell me, what's he like?" I asked while we were circling the pond. The water looked green from far away, but when we approached, it was clear. Long reeds grew from the bottom, swaying gracefully like mermaid's hair. A few ducks circled lazily, their feathers glistening as they plunked their heads under the surface looking for fish. Water streamed off their backs as they brushed them with their bills.

"What's he like?" she echoed.

"Yeah, what are his favorite foods? What's his favorite book? Stuff like that."

"Well, he really likes mashed sweet potatoes. And pear-and-apple baby food. He's still pretty small, so I haven't introduced him to too many things yet."

"Sure."

"For books, he makes me read *The Bumblebee's Bed* over and over. And parts of *Where the Wild Things Are*. He's got a good growl going at this point. It's pretty funny." We grinned at each other. Terabithia was making a sort of humming noise under his breath; the cool air by the water and the sight of the ducks seemed to have rejuvenated him.

Sullivan made a visor again with her hand.

"You okay?" I asked. It was bright out, but she was wincing.

"My eyes have been sensitive today."

"I'm sorry."

"No big deal." She shrugged. "I keep losing pairs of sunglasses."

I got in front of the stroller and walked backward, covering up my face to play peekaboo with Terabithia. He kept laughing a wicked little old man laugh, as though he was seeing it for the first time.

"You have a way with kids," Sullivan noted. "I mean, I've heard you talk a ton about them and your teaching and babysitting and au pairing, but it's really cool to see it in action."

"Thanks, Sullivan. That's nice to hear."

"You'll be well prepared to be a mom when your turn comes."

"If it comes" popped out of my mouth.

She put her hand on my arm. "It will. First of all, we're young."

My frown deepened as I thought of Maddie's news.

"Second of all, if it doesn't happen for you naturally, you can always do what I did."

"It's incredibly brave, what you did."

"Well, I knew what I wanted. So I went for it. I'm determined to be the best mother I can be to Terabithia. And you know me: I'm a pretty stubborn person."

We both laughed.

"I hope I've done the right thing for him and not just myself," she said quietly.

"I'm sure you will do everything you can for him."

Sullivan knelt in front of Terabithia's stroller, her serious tone lightening to playful. "What do you think, Boo? Are you happy to be here?"

Terabithia waved his arms up and down wildly in reply.

Dr. Len had agreed to squeeze me in on December 23 to go over my blood work results.

"Your hormone levels indicate that getting pregnant could potentially be challenging for you. The one that's supposed to be low is on the higher side for someone your age, and we'd like to see a higher number for the other one for someone your age."

"Is there something to do to reverse them?"

"No, I'm afraid not. But I do want to caution

you not to take these numbers as any kind of determinative diagnosis. There's no telling what will happen. And usually, as I said, success rates correlate with age rather than strictly with these numbers. You're a healthy young woman, and you may not have any problems at all."

"What about my family's issues?" I protested.

He shrugged again. "Not any clear indicator that you'd have that problem. Could be coincidence. Or not. There's not much you can do but see what happens when you're ready to try. Or freeze your eggs."

My head snapped up. "Freeze my eggs? Should I think about doing that?"

"That's up to you. The younger you do it, the healthier the eggs are likely to be. You're still quite young yet, as far as that goes. But it is an option that might be worthwhile to consider if you're not ready to try conceiving in the next couple years and if you're worried about potential genetic obstacles to conception."

In other words, he wasn't going to reassure me that Maddie's news was definitely a silly fiction.

"H-how much would that cost?"

"We charge eight thousand dollars for one cycle."

I felt my paper nightgown flap open dangerously as I steadied myself on the examining chair. Freezing my eggs was definitely *not* an option I could consider. I didn't have $8,000. I had a mortgage. A new library. And a lovely but not very plush salary as an art teacher. “I’ll think about it,” I managed to force out, producing a festively beribboned zucchini chocolate chip loaf for Dr. Len and his wife from my roomy purse.

After that, I barely went out over the holiday. I called Sullivan once to check in on Terabithia; she told me he was doing great and that they were staying at Mackie’s sister’s house till after the New Year. “When you’re ready for a night out—or a daytime escape or even a little time to run errands—let me know. You have a wide-open babysitting IOU,” I told her.

I spent all day in the library mostly moving books around (and sometimes sniffing them). Kendra and Geraldine took turns dropping by to keep me company—as it happened, not that many other people came in after all—and tried to enlist me in fun activities. I begged off, claiming sometimes that I had stuff to do for the library, other times that it was too cold to venture out. But when I wasn’t distracting myself in the library, I would find myself sitting on my couch, watching sappy movies, or—even worse—spending hours looking up the causes of infertility on the web, trying to figure out how important a role genetics played.

I had my mom’s hair, which generally co-operated unless there was even the tiniest hint of dampness in the air, in which case it puffed up like a soufflé. And all my life, every one of our relatives had remarked upon the fact that I had my grandmother's eyes. Did I have their ovaries too? Did Coco? And was it really already too late for Maddie?

It was as if a kitchen timer had been set and I could hear its ticking. *Stop with the pity party,* I ordered myself.

Sometimes when a song got stuck in your head, the only way to get it out was to play it over and over until it ran its course. I decided to embrace my obsession in order to get rid of it. After closing up the library one night, I drove to Robshaw's Hardware and Art Supplies.

"Hi, Dodie," Mr. Robshaw greeted me. "I wasn't expecting to see you here now. Not home for the holidays?"

I had been a frequent visitor during the fall. The school's budget was never close to enough to support my sometimes rather ambitious kiddie art projects, so I supplemented my stock with regular trips to my friendly local craft store.

"Nope. Actually, I need a calendar," I said.

"Right over here. Postholiday sale." He led me to the aisle. I picked out a five-year one. I wouldn't even need two years' worth for the purpose I had in mind. The thought depressed me. I grabbed some paint pens from the bins next to the cash register. Motivating colors like red and orange and gold.

When I got up to the cash register, Mr. Robshaw waved me through. "On the house," he said quietly so that the people in line behind me wouldn't hear. At one point in the past few months, he had tried to explain to me that he was keeping track in his mind, like an unofficial rewards card, and giving me free stuff when I'd earned it.

As his generosity began to increase in velocity, it eventually started to occur to me that if I added up my purchases versus the freebies, the stuff he gifted me would far outweigh what I had bought. When I had tried to suggest that to him, he waved me off and threw another handful of Mrs. Grossman's stickers on top of my pile of goodies.

"Thanks, Mr. Robshaw," I said, waving my bag at him.

At home, I spread out the calendar and some sheets of paper on my kitchen table. I pulled down the blinds and shut off my ringer. And then slowly and arduously I called upon my very rusty math skills to make some calculations.

Okay, I thought, *it is now December 30, 2007. I turn thirty-five on February 17, 2010. So I have more than two years to fall madly in love, get married, and get pregnant. That's not so bad.*

I was about to highlight February 17, 2010, on my calendar. Then I could put it under the bed and forget about it for a long time.

But wait. My mother and grandma both had their children by the time they were thirty-five. When they tried after that, they couldn't get pregnant anymore. So maybe they had to get pregnant before they were thirty-five. Maybe if they'd tried any time after they had actually gotten pregnant, it wouldn't have worked because they were too old.

All these hypotheticals were making my brain hurt, but this was serious business. I wanted a child. Better to be safe than sorry. So I counted backward nine months from my thirty-fifth birthday. Then I remembered seeing a program about baby otters on the Discovery Channel, and it had said how pregnancies were actually more like ten months long (for humans, not for otters, although it was actually really surprising how long the otter gestation period could be because of delayed implantation of the egg and . . . well, that wasn't important). To be safe, I counted ten months back from my birthday, which put me at May 17, 2009. That was a year and a half away. Which suddenly sounded a whole lot shorter than before.

I gulped down a glass of water, trying not to panic. What was I going to do?

I was going to do exactly what I had intended. I was going to mark the day of importance, then put this calendar away and not think about it or take it out again for as long as possible. I would know it was there, but I wasn't going to fixate on it. Definitely not. I was going to think about other things. Like all the library visitors that we'd have after the holiday! And all the fun wintry activities coming up! Where I might meet a wonderful man who would want to conceive with me in the next seventeen months.

I was panicking. But in one way, the calendar exercise had been clarifying. I could blame the mess on my ovaries, my DNA, my Y chromosome or whatever the one is that makes you a lady, but I couldn't blame the messenger anymore. Besides, it was the holidays. Granted, I had a feeling the only candles my sister lit during Hanukkah were scented with red quince and meant to be an aphrodisiac for her latest conquest . . . but I hoped she missed me and could forgive me too.

"Hey, Mad," I said when she picked up the phone.

"Hey, Do," she replied. "What's up?"

"Listen, I'm sorry things have been weird between us. You were right. It doesn't help to obsess. It's not fair to blame you for what happened with Not Dad or for my own freak-outs about what you told me. I'm here, and I care, and I know you're probably sad about what this milestone might mean. I want to talk about *you* and how you're feeling about it."

"Thank frickin' hell you've come to your

senses," Maddie said. "Listen, I thought a lot about the circumstances, and I realized it really did come as somewhat of a relief. I don't feel pressure anymore. But thanks for asking. So what else is up? Any sex?"

Well, then, I guessed we were going to put the past right behind us.

"Only in my mind," I replied desultorily.

"Ooh . . . color me intrigued. Tell me about him."

"There's not much to tell."

"Well, make something up. I'm so bored waiting for this damn glacial take-out place to deliver my food that I could eat my shoe."

I smiled at the non sequitur and filled her in on that one brief, shining hair sighting at the bookstore.

"It's really odd, Mad, because I have this feeling he and I are meant to meet."

"That is really odd, Do. But then again, you subscribe to baby magazines, and you have no baby, so I guess there are stranger things."

"I do not," I huffed, nosing my copy of *Happy Child* magazine underneath the sofa with my toe as if she were watching. It was free at the supermarket, and I was curious!

"Whatevs. Listen, maybe it is a sign. Maybe you two are meant for a future of dorkiness."

"Very funny. So what about you? Have I missed anything exciting on your end recently?"

"I've taken a vow of celibacy while I focus on my career," she said solemnly.

"Any good leads?"

"Not yet, but I took a part-time job at Ciao Bella Gelato."

"Yum! Is that something you're interested in pursuing, like from a marketing point of view?"

"No, I just like the free ice cream. I'm hoping that if I eat enough of it, I'll get so sick of it that I won't end up spending twenty dollars a week there for the rest of my life."

"Ha. Makes sense."

Her door buzzer sounded in the background. "Gotta go—Chicken Till You Sicken is here."

"What . . . ?" She was already gone. I hung up with a big grin on my face. Maddie was back! After a few more peeks at the calendar, I peevishly shoved it into the box and under my bed. Then, only then, was I finally feeling ready to start the New Year.

Six

January 2008

As people trickled back into town, the library started to fill up with visitors each afternoon. Elmira came in the day she returned from her family vacation.

"How was it?" I asked her.

"It was okay. My parents left us with babysitters most of the time. But I got to hang out with my brother, and he's turning into a cool little guy now that he's talking more. Plus I finished three books. *The Penderwicks* was awesome! I can't wait for the next one to come out in April."

"I'll place an order for the collection," I promised as she handed me back the books.

"What are you reading?"

I held up Edith Wharton's *The Glimpses of the Moon*, which I reread every few years. It's a favorite with its Venetian palazzos and cooling dips in Lake Como and Parisian sojourns and the splendid struggle of Nick and Susy between love or money.

Elmira wrapped her scarf around her head. "That looks fancy. Guess what? I nagged my mom until she let me walk here. I think she was relieved she doesn't have to take me. Now that she said okay, I can come whenever I want."

"Oh, good. You're essential to the success of this library," I told her. "A founding member, pretty much."

She flushed to her roots with one of the biggest smiles I'd ever seen from her.

The Mediterranean temperatures were definitely only in my imagination. It was full-on winter in Chatsworth, and after several mornings glazed with frost, the first real snow of the year fell on January 8. I was babysitting Terabithia when the blizzard started; Sullivan had finally taken me up on my offer for an evening out to meet some friends for dinner.

"I've got to be honest. I could really use a night off," Sullivan had said when she and Terabithia dropped by the library earlier that week. "Mom and Dad have been great, but I don't want them to have to pick up all the slack. I want him to get used to other people too. With adoptions, most of the experts recommend the parent and child bond for the first few months before introducing a lot of new people, so I couldn't imagine leaving him with someone besides family or my closest friends. He seems to feel comfortable with you, Auntie Dodie."

I loved that name! "Well, I'm honored. Can I call him Boo now too?"

"Sure."

"Here you go, Boo," I said, placing a piece of construction paper and some crayons in front of him. He soon had a crayon in his mouth.

"Yech," Sullivan said to him to get him to understand that crayons aren't for eating. Boo smiled, a swipe of cranberry color on his teeth. "Thanks, Dodie. I really appreciate it." She turned her attention to Boo's masterpiece in the making.

Indira Varma was wandering the stacks, fretting. I approached her.

"Is everything okay?"

Indira leaned toward me. "I don't know what to do. The other girls in Amisha's class are always bullying her. She's a good girl, and I hear her crying sometimes at night."

"That sucks," I said, my anger flaring. "I mean, I'm sorry to hear it. I have a book for her. Be right back."

I went and pulled *Blubber* off the shelf. I didn't know what to write on the back of one of my homemade bookmarks. Sometimes, I would write why I chose the book for that reader, hoping to nudge them into considering the lessons they might find inside. I thought about putting, "One good friend is worth dozens of silly people," but that sounded patronizing. Instead, on the back of the bookmark, cut from Van Gogh's *Poppies and Butterflies* painting, I wrote, "Cindy Crawford, Bill Clinton, and Jessica Simpson were all bullied as children." I figured that covered a few bases, depending on her interests. It wasn't going to solve the problem, obviously. But if a book could make her feel even a little bit less alone . . .

I handed it to her mom, who read the note and smiled. "Really? All of them? Thank you."

"I can tell you from experience that things change so quickly, and hopefully she'll find her group and it will all get better soon. But it does take years for some people. I know 'Hang in there' doesn't really cut it when you're going through something like that. For her or for you." I tried to imagine how hard that would be, to be a mom and see your child in pain. Sullivan had told me she was worried about Terabithia being bullied when he was older because of being a minority and because he had a gay single mom and no dad. That was on top of her worry about him having a tough time with the fact that he had been adopted.

"Books seem to be the main thing Amisha connects to these days," Indira said.

"We have plenty more of them. I'll think of some for next time."

"We're heading out, Do," Sullivan said. "See you tomorrow night."

"Yep. See you!"

After Sullivan left for her dinner, Terabithia and I were playing with his obsession, a miniature version of that arcade game with the groundhogs that you bopped on the head when they popped up. At ten months old, he could pull up on almost anything, and he was pretty steady on his feet as long as he had something to balance against, but he got so excited when he was holding the mallet that he would tip over and crack up laughing when he landed on his bum. We took turns bopping away. He would grunt to cheer me on.

The phone rang. “Hello?”

“Dodie, is everything okay?” Sullivan sounded worried.

“Yeah, we’re having a great time. We’re playing the groundhog game!”

“Still? Since I left three hours ago?”

That couldn’t be right. I looked at the clock. Oh. Eight p.m. How did that happen?

“Anyway, I’ve been trying to get through but haven’t been able to get a signal. My car’s stuck in the snow. I tried calling Mom and Dad to pick me up, but their cells aren’t working, and I worry about them driving farther across town to get me in this crappy weather anyway. I left a message telling them to meet me back there so they can help you with Terabithia if you need it. I’ve got a ride, but it’s snowing so hard we might need to wait until it lets up a bit.”

Snow? I looked out the window. Good grief! It was a blizzard out there. Drifts had already formed on the lawn. "It doesn't look like it's going to let up anytime soon," I observed.

"No, it doesn't. I'll try to get there as quickly as I can. Could you give Terabithia his bottle and put him to bed?"

"Of course. Don't worry, and don't rush. I'll see you soon."

Okay. Put Terabithia to bed. I could do this. Sullivan had given me instructions, and I'd succeeded tons of times while babysitting. Of course, that had been years ago. But Sullivan trusted me. Let's see . . . where would I start? Um, by removing Terabithia's mouth from the middle groundhog's head.

"Time for bottle and bed, Boo." I lifted him gently.

"Waaaa!" he wailed, squirming to get down.

Uh-oh. Sullivan had said he usually went down really easily when he was tired, but maybe Terabithia was a night owl like me. What had she said to do if he wasn't ready? She'd said to rub his back, and he'd quiet down, take his bottle, and fall asleep soon after.

At first, as he drank, his eyelids got heavy. Yes! He was going to fall asleep easily. Then, as if his milk were laced with coffee, his eyes shot open, and he started twisting on my lap, trying to grab my hair, knock the empty bottle out of my hand onto the ground, and turn over onto his belly. He let out a squall as I tried to keep him from diving off my lap. When I carried him up the stairs, I rubbed and rubbed his back like he was a genie's lamp, but I sure didn't get my wish. Terabithia's wails were getting louder and louder. Poor kid. He was probably confused by the absence of Sullivan. And overtired since it was now past his bedtime.

Hopefully, the familiar surroundings of his room would quiet him down.

They didn't. My pajama-putting-on abilities came right back to me as if I had babysitting muscle memory. Which was helpful since it was hard to think straight at that decibel level.

Then it hit me: the diaper! It was soaking wet. Clearly, I was out of practice.

Thanks to my patented Dodie Fairisle speed diaper-changing technique, Terabithia was dressed and dry less than a minute later. But still wailing.

I tried singing to him, told him stories, and read him three books, the same ones Sullivan or Mackie read him every night. I gave him his blankie, which he threw out of his crib. I tried to get him to lie down. I put a cold compress on his head the way Mom used to do for me when I wasn't feeling well, but he threw that at me too. He was like a different person. One I didn't know how to reach. It was an awful feeling. I kept checking my watch. It was already eight forty-five. *The roads must be really bad,* I thought, *for it to take everyone almost an hour just to go a mile or two.*

I brought Terabithia's face right up next to mine, gently looking into his eyes and willing him to calm down. That sometimes had worked with some of the babies I'd taken care of before. Terabithia's big brown eyes were full of more than tears. They were full of fear. A shock of recognition rolled through me. Poor sweetie. He was probably afraid Sullivan was never coming back. It had only been a few months since his big transition, after all. He had no reason yet to be sure that the people around him would stay.

Don't get carried away, Dodie. Terabithia has not been abandoned. It was healthy for his mother to get out, to have a little time away.

At 8:53 (and 41 seconds), the garage door groaned open. It was one of the sweetest sounds I'd ever heard. Help was on the way. Terabithia's cheeks were flushed, and his forehead was hot. I wasn't sure if it was a fever or if he'd just gotten himself worked up.

The three O'Reillys materialized together—apparently Mackie and Jeff had pulled up next to Sullivan's ride, and they'd made the rest of the trip together. When they opened the door to the nursery, Terabithia began to bawl as if with relief to find he hadn't been abandoned after all.

"Shh . . . shh . . . there, there, now," Sullivan soothed, picking Terabithia up.

"You all right?" Jeff asked, patting me on the back. I nodded but couldn't look him in the eye. I had done a terrible job. I had failed. Terabithia would never become president now.

Terabithia gradually proceeded from sobs to snuffles, and soon he was asleep on Sullivan's shoulder. She laid him gently down, and Mackie, Jeff, and I tiptoed out of the room.

"I'm going to put the kettle on," Mackie said when we got downstairs.

"The little bug can be quite a screamer, huh?" Jeff was so nice, trying to reassure me.

"Yeah," I said morosely. "I tried everything—singing, bouncing, walking him around . . . nothing seemed to work."

"That happens. He's not used to going to sleep without any of us. And sometimes, the worst nights are the ones on which he has the most fun. He doesn't want to miss any of the action and kicks up quite a fuss."

I was starting to feel a little better. Especially when Mackie put a cup of tea into my hands—some of the Surabaya I'd given her from Mariage Frères, my favorite tea shop in Paris. "So the drive was difficult?"

"It was. We began to consider whether it might not be best just to sleep at the hair salon, sitting up, in one of those chairs with the big helmet dryers," Jeff joked. I appreciated the effort. Despite the tea, I couldn't help replaying

Terabithia's squinched-up, unhappy little face, over and over in my mind. *What if I damaged him irreparably?* I fretted. *What if he never wants to be around me again?*

"I should go," I said when I finished my tea.

"That's ridiculous. You can't go out again tonight," Mackie tutted. "Sullivan will probably stay in there with Terabithia for a while. You can sleep in the guest room without any fear of disturbing him."

Mackie laid out some pajamas in the guest room. I didn't think the pink crocheted collar was my best look, but I wasn't about to argue.

"Good night," Mackie said as she began to close the door behind her and Jeff. She studied my face for a moment. "Don't worry, Dodie. He won't even remember being upset in the morning. It happens all the time. He'll be fine."

Mackie was right. I hadn't needed to be up half the night fretting that they would never let me babysit again. Or that Terabithia himself would break his silence to pronounce as his first words, "Dodie is inept; please don't let her near me!" When I woke up and padded downstairs in the morning, Terabithia was sitting in his chair with some form of baby food all over his face, his eyes shining almost mischievously. His face lit up even more when he saw me.

"Did you look outside?" Jeff asked.

"Not yet." I peeked through a slat of the blind.

Wow! It was gorgeous. The whole yard looked like the bun part of a big steamed vegetable bun. Thinking about food gave me an idea. "Mind if I make something?" I asked, already on my way to the kitchen. I grabbed four bowls from the cabinet. After throwing my coat, scarf, and hat on and pulling boots over my pajama pants, I ventured out onto the back porch with the bowls in hand. After pushing aside the top layer of snow, I scooped a heap of the fresh stuff underneath into each of the bowls. A few minutes later, Sullivan appeared, having succeeded in getting Terabithia dressed for the cold. The drifts were practically up to her waist. Terabithia squirmed in her arms, gesturing wildly at the snow. She knelt down so that he could touch it. When he patted it, a look of pure shock came across his face so extreme it was as if he'd never seen snow before.

Which, it dawned on me, he probably hadn't. He was a baby. Right.

Terabithia had apparently decided he didn't care for the snow. He was pointing back inside. I followed them, balancing the full bowls. I rushed to the fridge and pulled out a carton of milk and some Hershey's chocolate syrup, poured a little of each into all the bowls, and mixed everything up well. Snow cream, a Fairisle family tradition! Terabithia's happy slurps confirmed that he was instantly converted.

• • •

When I finally got home, I put on *Gossip Girl* and forced myself to pay attention to the stack of bills that were almost due.

I always treated bill paying like ripping off a Band-Aid, opening all of them at once and spreading them out in front of me.

Oh. Holy. Halifax. $2,562 on my credit card. $406 on utilities and phone bill. Plus I owed $1,839 for my mortgage. That came to $5,807. That was . . . a lot. That was . . . definitely more than I was expecting. And more than I made in almost two months. What had I bought? I scrolled through the charges.

Almost a hundred each on cans of paint and on toilet paper (it goes fast with all those visitors tromping in and out!). There was a small bathroom next to the kitchen right on the other side of the sunroom door. I'd had to pay to have someone install an extra door to create a teeny bathroom annex that my library patrons could get to without being tempted to continue farther into my house. It was unlikely that anyone would take the liberty, but it seemed worth my peace of mind to be sure that no wayward kid would nick some cooling cookies off my kitchen counter or make themselves comfortable watching a scandalous program on TV in my living room while their mothers or fathers were chatting away obliviously between the stacks.

I'd also spent a few hundred on curtains, another $500 on rugs to warm up the place. There was a scary amount for shipping some books and a table from Brimfield Flea Market, and even though the bookshelves had been $50 each, sixteen of those added up to $900.

I breathed in through my nose and out through my mouth very slowly.

It's only this first bill. It won't ever be this bad again, I reminded myself. There were always up-front expenses in these kinds of ventures. One-time investment costs, if you will. I was obviously never going to need to buy sixteen bookcases again. And I still had a little money socked away from when I was a teacher's assistant during my master's program and living off cheap Thai food in New York. My heartbeat began to slow down. The thought of spending a hundred dollars a month on toilet paper was still shocking, but as long as I kept the other expenses under control, I should be fine with a little extra spending.

As it turned out, I didn't really need to be at an official story circle to get to hear all about the interesting lives and problems of the people in Chatsworth. The library seemed to bring them out all on its own.

"I think you should just call her," I advised the woman standing on the other side of the circulation desk later that week. She hadn't told me her name yet, but she had already shared the story of how she and her mother had become estranged. It was really sad, but it was also clearly a misunderstanding. "Here, read this little Maya Angelou book called *Mother*. It's so powerful. And I'm sure your mother misses you. You've probably both changed since that fight three years ago. Would you give her another chance?"

Her eyes glistened. "Yes, I would. Thank you, Dodie!" She was about to leave, then did a 180. "Almost forgot the book. Can I get a stamp?"

Who needs bar codes? After my own heart, my visitors were partial to checking their books out the old-fashioned way—complete with that cool mechanism that let you move the letters and numbers of the stamp each day to reflect the date.

"Dodie?" the woman said.

I wasn't looking at the stamper. I wasn't looking at the book. I was looking out the window at a man looking in. Even though he was wearing a yellow hard hat and his hand was making a little visor to shield out the glare of sunset on the window, our eyes met long enough for me to realize . . . I had seen him before.

"Um, Dodie?" the woman tried again.

"Sorry," I said, unable to remove my gaze from the window.

"Hey!" the woman protested as I stamped her hand instead of the book.

"Sorry," I apologized again.

"It's okay," she said graciously, as if remembering my advice.

Was he coming in? He seemed to be scrutinizing the number of people inside the library. *It is definitely on the crowded side,* I thought in consternation. People lined up at the desk were actually standing sideways so that other visitors could get around them to the stacks. Not the perfect setting for a conversation. To top it all off, Jonah Brownlee took the opportunity at that exact moment to let out a bloodcurdling scream. Of course. By the time his mother determined that someone had accidentally shelved Edward Gorey's *The Gashlycrumb Tinies* in the bins of books for young readers, I turned back to the window to see the hard hat retreating.

He was leaving. I lurched forward, startling the next person in line at the circulation desk. "Would you excuse me a moment?" I practically begged.

I wanted to run after him. But what would I say? I was too nervous. Plus, I had a library to run. I rushed to the bathroom instead, splashed cold water on my face, and took deep whiffs of my Diptyque Baies candle until I finally felt like I could be a proper librarian for the next hour and twenty-nine minutes before I could close up the library for the night.

• • •

The following day at the same time, 5:21 p.m., my eyes were fixed on the window. Then the door. Back to the window.

"What the heck is going on with you?" Kendra demanded. True to her word, she had taken to helping out a lot at the library, and she seemed to like it as much as I did.

"What are you talking about?" I asked innocently.

"I'm talking about your incredibly twitchy behavior today. Did you get hit by lightning yesterday or something?"

That wrapped a grin right around my face. "Something like that," I laughed.

"You met someone? He came here? Tell me everything!" She perched on the edge of the desk as if there weren't dozens of people around.

I lowered my voice and described him and his hat and his eyes. "He didn't come in. It was crowded, and Jonah Brownlee kept screaming, 'I don't want to get thrown out of a sleigh! I don't want to be smothered underneath a rug! What if I fall down the stairs?' "

Kendra stifled a snicker. "He'll come back, obviously. The guy, not Jonah Brownlee. Although probably him too once he calms down a bit."

"Would it be too much if I proposed when he comes back?" I joked.

"Um, yeah. But maybe you should do it anyway. Or at least flirt with him for a start."

"No, I can't. I can't." I sat back down, my knees weak at the thought of trying to have a conversation with him.

"Yes. You. Can."

"No, I can't."

"Do you want me to tell him that your pipes haven't been serviced since you moved to Chatsworth and if he doesn't bring his hard hat and tools and get in there soon, they'll probably burst?"

My head was on the desk. I wanted to laugh, but all the air had rushed out of my lungs. What if he never came back?

When Kendra finished giggling at her own joke, she rubbed my back and glanced at the clock. "There's always tomorrow," she pointed out. Except there wasn't, really, because she was womanning the library by herself the next night. I was taking Geraldine out to dinner for her birthday.

Geraldine and I ate a huge meal at Hibachi-Ho-Yes, where we'd met in the early days after my move to Chatsworth. On that all-important night, we bonded after we had both confessed to pretending it was our birthday so that they'd sing us the clapping song and bring us extra pineapple. It had seemed fitting to celebrate her real birthday there.

"So how are you doing with the library being closed?" I asked, dipping a monster shrimp into the ginger sauce.

"It sucks. I like working at Wendell Wye's; he's a nice man, passionate about what he does, and of course I love bookstores. But it's not the same."

"I know."

"Having the lending library to go to makes it better, though," she added, leaning away from the flames and covering her eyebrows protectively as the chef lit up a stack of onions.

I grinned at her. "I really appreciate all your help."

"Sure thing."

"Do you think the Chatsworth Library will be up and running anytime soon?"

She shook her head. "It sounds like a mess. In January I actually started an online course to get my master's in library science. I'll do that until the fall, when I can hopefully start going to classes if I get accepted to one of the programs I'm applying for now."

"You don't waste any time!" I said, impressed.

"Nope. I figured, if Chatsworth reopens soon, I'll keep up with the online course instead. I'm pretty flexible about it as long as I can keep moving forward."

"I know you have lots of 'real' librarian friends, but if you ever need a recommendation for your application, you know I'm here and will be embarrassingly but hopefully effectively gushy on your behalf."

Geraldine laughed. "Thank you. I will keep that in mind."

After our feast, I flipped open my phone. A message from Kendra. My very full stomach attempted a graceful dive. It felt more like a belly flop.

HE CAME IN SWEET JESUS HE IS DREAMY, her text from three hours ago reported. CALL WHEN YOU CAN.

She whistled as she answered the phone.

"What? Is he that gorgeous? What time did he come? Did you talk to him?"

"Okay, slow down there." Kendra laughed. "Yes, five twenty-one, and yes."

"What did he say?"

"Not much," she replied. "He introduced himself—his name is Shep Jameson."

"Like the whiskey?" I said.

"Yep, like the whiskey."

"That's sexy."

"Wait until you see him. He's got masses of wavy hair."

"What else did he say?"

"Well, he kept looking around, which was weird. It was almost as if he was looking for . . ." Her voice trailed off.

I held my breath. Someone? Was she going to

say *someone?* "You don't actually think . . . ?" I stammered.

I could almost hear her smile through the phone. "I guess we'll find out."

"What do you mean?"

"He asked for a book. I told him we didn't have it today but that it would be available tomorrow."

"Which book?"

"The Stephen Colbert one." Kendra was intentionally avoiding its title. The book had come out in October, but I still broke into hysterical giggles every time I saw it or even thought about it.

"You mean *I Am America (and So Can You!)*?" A laugh-squeak slipped out.

"Oh no, here she goes," Kendra murmured under her breath.

"Wait a second—we have that book."

"How do you know?" she asked innocently.

"Because two people donated their copies in the past week. One of them is probably still hidden in the circulation desk drawer. You stashed it there because it kept making me laugh and then forgot to put it back in the stacks. And come to think of it, so did I."

"Yep. I remembered about that copy today too. And I know about the other. But Shep Jameson doesn't. Fortunately, he didn't think to check the stacks. He took my word for it instead."

"Your sneaky, lying word?" I teased, but

gratitude softened my voice. “You did this for me, didn’t you? So he would come back?”

“Yep!”

“You’re such a good friend.”

“And you’re going to buy me rectangle pizza and Tater Tots in the caf tomorrow as my reward,” Kendra announced. “Night night!”

It was a fortunate thing my feast with Geraldine had been food coma inducing, or who knows how long it would have taken me to fall asleep? I dreamed of deep diving in a yellow submarine. Suspiciously similar to the color of a hard hat, in fact. Maddie (and Freud) probably would have had a field day with that one.

Needless to say, on Friday evening, my tuchas was glued to the chair and my eyes to the window by 5:20.

Nothing.

Mackie dropped by the library to pick up a book I’d recommended to her about the decadent Third Republic in France. I had slipped inside it a bookmark cut from a piece of a James Tissot painting—with a gorgeous, luxurious ball in progress and glowing chandeliers and women in gowns—and had written, “A little indulgence never hurt anyone.”

“Terabithia had a great week,” Mackie reported as I handed the book to her. “He gets bigger every time I look at him.”

I grinned. At least my ineffectual bedtime skills hadn't stunted his growth. The memory of his terrified face on the night of the snowstorm wiped the smile off my face.

She gently placed her hand on mine. "You okay there, Dodie?"

"Oh, yes, absolutely," I assured her. "I felt a draft or something."

"Okay, well, we'll be at Sullivan's this weekend if you want to stop by."

"And hang out with my little man? Of course I do!"

"She'll be pleased to hear it. She knew I'd see you today and told me to mention it. Terabithia's been teething, so she hasn't had a chance to call."

"No problem," I said. I was just happy to be invited whenever they wanted me.

After Mackie left, I checked the clock. Only seven minutes had passed. Still nothing. Could I have missed him? Nope. Because even though I had absolutely, positively been listening 100 percent to every word Mackie had said, I had also been checking the window over her shoulder.

By the time six thirty rolled around, I was feeling a little deflated. What if he had only been visiting Chatsworth, had blown town, and would never come back again? Possible, but it seemed pretty unlikely that a visitor would spend three days stalking a library and give up as soon as he heard the book he was looking for wasn't available. Not to mention, something told me he was the same guy from Wendell Wye's Bookshop, though I couldn't be sure since his hair had been covered. That would mean he'd been in Chatsworth for more than a month.

At six forty-five, before last call for checkout, the library door opened. As he headed toward the circulation desk, there was a faint unfamiliar smell—the clean scent from the kind of earthy, irregular Irish soap that's handmade. I was having trouble breathing. He smelled so good, like a robe you want to cuddle right into.

"Hey."

"Hi. May I help you?"

"That would be great. The librarian lady yesterday said the book I'm looking for would be here today."

"Okay. Do you think she put it on hold for you? If you give me your name, I can check."

"It's Shep Jameson," he said.

"Good evening." Ugh. Who was I, Count Dracula? "I'm Dodie."

"Am I too late?" he asked. "You're closing soon."

I tried to place the color of his eyes. A vision of a Eugène Boudin impressionist painting of the seaside arose in my mind, the waves bright blue green, more toward blue than green. "No, not at all." I smiled at him. At his hair, actually. First of all, because it was safer than trying to look into those eyes. Also because his hair was dark, full, and a little wavy but in a slightly shaggy way—just as I'd somehow known it would be. Not like a man who spends more on hair products than food. Now that the hard hat was off, there was no doubt that this was the intriguing-haired man from Wendell Wye's Bookshop.

Glancing back at me from time to time, he meandered around the stacks. He had obviously just showered, but I couldn't let myself think about that. I tried to think of something clever to write on a bookmark instead. My mind was completely blank. I took a bookmark cut from a colorful Richard Diebenkorn painting and simply wrote "Shep Jameson" on the back. For the next few minutes I pretended to read *Cook's Illustrated.* It would usually be impossible to distract me from an issue devoted to truffles, but somehow they couldn't hold my attention.

"Here's the book." I handed it to him when he came back to the counter.

"Thanks. Say, do you have any other suggestions?" He was standing right in front of me again. I raised my eyes slowly over the top of the magazine, savoring the feeling of excitement in the pit of my stomach.

"Sure. What kind of books do you like?"

He sucked in his bottom lip, thinking. "To tell you the truth, I'm not much of a reader," he admitted.

"Then what are you doing at a lending library?" I bantered, feeling proud that I was practically flirting.

"I wanted to see what all the fuss was about. Ever since I came to Chatsworth to work on the new mall construction, everyone has been talking about it."

"What do you think?"

"I think you'd better kick us out now, or you might end up with overnight guests." Shep was looking around the library at the few other visitors debating their options, which luckily prevented him from seeing that I had blushed all the way down to my toes. Overnight guests—holy pajamas! Or preferably, no pajamas at all!

"Right. Five minutes, everyone," I announced, pulling myself together.

"If anything comes to you for what I should read next, could I get a suggestion when I return this one? Maybe for a novel? I read *Don Quixote* a couple summers ago and thought that was really funny."

"Absolutely." There was going to be a next time! He wasn't just going to use the book drop outside!

I wanted to blurt out, *When will that be?* but I figured a little mystery never hurt anyone.

Seven

February 2008

My wallet had definitely taken a hit starting the library. Now I was beginning to discover that it wasn't cheap to maintain one either. The second round of bills was better than the first but not by as much as I had hoped. There were still plenty of expenses. Especially if I wanted to buy any of the fun extras that, in my mind, library visitors shouldn't have to live without. I wasn't sure that the donors behind the library grants I was planning to apply for would agree, but it didn't matter because I'd missed all the deadlines for the current year and would have to wait until the fall before the application process opened up again.

Digging into my own pockets, I always made sure to have a fresh supply of cookies from Billybee's Bakery on hand and plenty of hot apple cider to warm everyone up. Now that Elmira's mother had acknowledged the library was within walking distance, Elmira had practically become a fixture. She cheerfully offered refreshments to people as soon as they came in from the cold. Sometimes she showed up after school to help me reshelve books or tidy up or just to chat; often she would sit in a corner and lose herself in another book that was impressively advanced for her age. A smile would play about her lips when she was reading something funny, or her brow would knit in concentration when she was reading something serious. When she closed a book, she would clutch it to her chest. Just like I did.

"What did you think of that one?" I asked Shep when he came to return Romain Gary's *The Promise of Dawn* a week later. I had hoped to give it to him myself, but he'd come in on my night off, so Kendra had passed it along for me with a bookmark tucked inside that showed a glowy sunrise. I had worked up my courage to write the words "Welcome new beginnings" on it.

He laid it down on the circulation desk. "It was . . ." He trailed off, meeting my eyes. Tingles ran up my spine. His hand was so close to mine I could almost touch it. I imagined what his palm would feel like. Warm. His hand lingered on the book, but when he saw my expression, he jerked it away as though the book had burned him.

"Sorry," he said with a nervous laugh that sounded like a bark, "it's just that your eyes aren't blue anymore. In that sweater, they're sort of a greenish gold. They remind me of this painting I saw once . . . by some French artist. But I can't remember which one."

I took a slow, steady breath. "We need to get you something new," I rushed out.

“They call those kinds of eyes stormy, don’t they?” Shep murmured. I blushed down to my roots and was very grateful to find Diderot’s *Jacques the Fatalist and His Master* right at my fingertips.

“You’ll love this one if you liked *Don Quixote*,” I promised. “Almost as absurd and even more witty. It’s by a French philosopher who was one of the founders of the first encyclopedia.”

His tone completely casual again, he teased, “Is this what you give to all the construction workers?”

“No,” I replied, daring to speak as quietly and honestly as he had, “only the really special ones.” I handed it to him over the desk. It was only as he turned to go that I caught the guilt in his expression.

“You know, it’s funny. All anyone ever talks about is the madeleine,” Lula observed at the first session of our Foodie Book Club. “Personally, I’m more of a chocolate person, so the whole vanilla cakey thing never really did it for me. But beyond that, it’s really more about the tea Marcel dips it in. *Tilleul*, which people usually translate as lime blossom tea. But it’s not the same tree that grows the lime we’re used to, is it, Dodie?” She looked to me for confirmation.

My smile widened. I loved linden flower tea. In cafés all over Paris, you could order an *infusion de tilleul*—literally only the dried flowers, steeped in hot water, for a flavor that expanded on your tongue like petals opening, like those layers of the town that sprung out of the soaked pastry in Marcel's cup. When I was an au pair, I had treated myself to a cup of tea and a croissant any time I had a morning off.

"Is it, Dodie?" Lula repeated, a little more insistently.

I planted the feet of my head (erm . . . or whatever) back on solid Chatsworth ground and rushed to say, "Yes, that's right—it's linden flower."

"Linden flower?" Geraldine said. "What's that?"

"Young Marcel was very anxious, and linden leaves are thought to be relaxing, even sedative. Someone probably prepared the tea to calm him down. Isn't that sweet?"

"I should try that sometime with Deandra," Melissa said. "She wakes up soooo early. At this point, I would gladly grow a linden tree from scratch even for one weekend morning to sleep in."

"Well, linden trees grow about two feet a year, so you'd only have to wait a few more years before you could sleep in," Sam, our resident garden expert, said and laughed.

I would always have a special place in my heart for the madeleine dipped in tea, which had opened up Marcel's memory of his childhood town like a magical pop-up book. Of course, if I had a French pastry death match, the madeleine would lose. I'd probably trade for the peacock of the café dessert menu: tarte Tatin—deep amber caramel jellied around slabs of apple atop a thin, crispy layer of pastry. Sublime. The Foodie Book Club would mean a chance to share some of the lesser-known treasures to be savored too.

My stomach growled loudly. I knew I would love this group. It had been the first book club I'd dreamed up, soon after opening the library, because . . . well, if there's one thing I knew and felt comfortable talking about, it was food.

"Why don't you start a food-related book club?" Kendra had suggested when I was rhapsodizing about a dark chocolate and sea salt caramel eclair I'd eaten.

"You're so right. Books and food, two of my favorite things! What more could a girl want?"

One corner of her mouth quirked upward. I knew what she was thinking. Minutes earlier, she'd had to snatch an old picture of her baby nephew out of my hands. "Oh my gosh, look at those teeny, tiny fingernails!" I cried. "Can you even believe that little beanie with a whale embroidered on it and how mini it makes his head seem? I can't get over the fact that he's already two. His skin is so peachy. Is it as soft as it looks?"

Maybe my other favorite, babies, could be a part of the club too? Of course I didn't *really* want to do that; babies plus food plus books sounded a little too Hansel and Gretel-y.

It had taken me longer to get this book club together than the story circle because I wanted to make it just right—to pick a book that would generate conversation and to get the attendees excited about what was to come. Now, at our first meeting, all the members really seemed to be digging their teeth in. Not just metaphorically. I'd encouraged the ladies to start by keeping their food contributions simple, so Sam had made *Little House on the Prairie* hardtack, which actually tasted worse than it sounded. But it was the thought that counted!

Out of respect for Sam's efforts, I waited for everyone to finish the hardtack before I brought out a dish inspired by another otherworldly beautiful passage in *Swann's Way*. The ladies leaned forward to peer at the serving dish crowded with spears of asparagus snowed over with shavings of parmesan cheese. Sam grabbed the tongs.

As they munched, I read aloud:

"What fascinated me would be the asparagus, tinged with ultramarine and rosy pink which ran from their heads, finely stippled in mauve and azure, through a series of imperceptible changes to their white feet, still stained a little by the soil

of their garden-bed: a rainbow-loveliness that was not of this world."

A woman named Chloë, who owned a gourmet food store, sighed. I was sitting next to her. I planned to do so at each Foodie Book Club gathering. For one thing, she always listened politely, and although she didn't speak often, she had insightful things to say when she did. For another, she was French.

She also smelled amazing. Her perfume reminded me of one of my favorite streets in Paris . . . scents of Christmas and tea and tin.

"Ahem." Chloë cleared her throat gently, quietly enough for me alone to hear. I was leaning so close to her that my chair was about to tip over. I sprang back. No one else was looking at me. They were all thinking about purply asparagus. And as long and challenging as Proust's book was, each of the attendees promised to read a sample thanks to what they'd heard and tasted at the club.

Drat these glittery pipe cleaners! I was wrestling with a handful of them, trying to come up with a new project for my art classes at school, when Maddie called. She was up to speed on the Shep situation, or lack thereof.

There's nothing Maddie liked better than a challenge—especially when it came to men.

"Hey, I have an idea. How about I come next

weekend to brainstorm the next tactical maneuver for Operation Hard Hat? And to celebrate a certain someone's birthday."

"Don't remind me." I groaned. *You're being a spoilsport,* I scolded myself. "No, really, sounds great. That'll help get my mind off aging." I wasn't sure I believed that, but maybe saying it would make it true.

I had lots of reasons to feel cheerful. My friends. My family. My house. The lending library.

Still, when Maddie hung up, I shimmied the toile-covered box out from under my bed. I opened the top. I pulled out the calendar inside. For the second time since Maddie had broken the news, I marked a big *X* over another month that had passed, which meant that at the very most I had just fifteen months to get pregnant in time to give birth by my thirty-fifth birthday.

It wasn't helping matters that Shep hadn't returned to the library. I knew he kept up his impressive reading pace because he sent his friend Mike to ask me for a biography of Rilke, whose poetry I had told him I loved. I swallowed hard when I saw the request on the paper, trying not to read any sort of a message into his choice.

"Here you go, Mike." I gave him the Rilke book and three comics.

Mike smiled at me. He was a handsome man in his early forties with a baby-smooth face despite all his years working in the sun on construction sites. I had often seen him in the little town square on weekends chasing his children around while his wife, Lula, from my Foodie Book Club, stifled a huge won-the-jackpot grin behind her tabloid magazine.

"Shep's got a pretty poetic spirit himself for a construction worker," Mike offered, gesturing toward the flap of the book. "I don't know who this Rillkee fellow is, but Shep seemed pretty keen on getting to know more about him."

I giggled nervously, wondering if Shep had read any of Rilke's actual poems yet. Like the one where the bed is a rose. My mind flashed to a scene of me, Shep, and his scent tangled up in a bed of petals.

With a wink, Mike was gone, leaving me to my thoughts and to the sounds of the Watson twins, Joey and Sandra, fighting over who got *Are You My Mother?* and who got *The Poky Little Puppy*. Like the trusty library helper she was, Elmira went and resolved the dispute before I even had a chance.

Shep reappeared at the library the night before Maddie's arrival. He was wearing a coat and tie and dark jeans. My breath caught as I looked at him. I coughed to hide it. The expression in his eyes was unreadable: excited or frantic.

"Going somewhere fancy?" I teased.

"Yes, I . . . um . . . ," Shep stuttered, clearing his throat before he tried again. "I'm going to meet the parents of my . . . girl . . . friend."

I could feel my face fall. *Of course.*

He looked startled by my reaction. Trying to cover, I improvised. "Sorry, I've just been having these weird pains all day . . . in my spleen." Brimming with a tangle of emotions, including a whole lot of unwarranted disappointment, I found myself grinning somehow at my lame excuse. It made me think of Coco's appendix postcard.

Shep tentatively returned my smile. Then something flickered across his face that strangely resembled disappointment too. The two of us were a regular collection of mood rings. I replied, "Don't worry—I'm sure it's nothing. And that's great, Shep," I lied, wanting to hurry up the leaving part now. "So what can I do for you?"

He cast his eyes around the room as though he'd forgotten why he'd come. "I . . . um . . . I wanted to say that I'd come by tomorrow because I need to ask you for some new recommendations."

He had come to tell me that he would come back to ask me for some recommendations? "I won't be here tomorrow, but Kendra will be if you want to check with her," I suggested reluctantly.

Shep frowned and said, "Okay. When will you be back?"

"Tuesday."

“Are you going somewhere for the holiday weekend?” He was trying not to check his watch. I wondered why he was lingering. I decided to rescue him as graciously as I could.

“Yes. Are you meeting . . . them . . . at seven? You’d better run if so. It’s four minutes to . . .”

“You’re right. Well, bye, Dodie. Have a good weekend.”

“You too, Shep. See you.”

The next four minutes before I could close the library may not have been long enough for Shep to arrive on time, but they certainly felt very long to me.

Maddie honked her horn at ten as she pulled into the driveway. “Whoa there,” I said. “How early did you get up?”

“Do the math . . . if you can, birthday bookworm,” she replied through a gum bubble as she walked through the front door. “It’s not really that much earlier than I usually get up.” She flung her overnight tote beside the stairs. I had the same one, covered in pink flowers and green leaves. I smiled at her.

“Hey, travel husband.” She hugged me.

“Hey, travel husband,” I parroted, smiling even wider.

Maddie and I had decided years before that there were too many wonderful things to see and do in the world to wait around for a reasonably sane member of the other sex to do them with. Why wait to go to romantic spots—which of course were also some of the most special, magical, beautiful ones—until a love connection appeared? Our sisterhood friendships with each other were special, magical, and beautiful enough in themselves.

Plus we were good travel companions. We'd taken trips to Paris—which Maddie loved almost as much as I did, if that were possible—Spain, England, the Caribbean, and a bunch of other locations together. We'd watched sunsets the color of a Henri-Edmond Cross painting creep across the sky with palm trees swaying or *bateaux mouches* cruising or fountains darkening beneath them. We'd shared cheap hostel rooms that were way too tight for two people or way too big and full of random strangers talking at all hours. And I had never felt deprived by the absence of a male significant-other traveling partner. Whoever, wherever he was—and I did believe he existed, even if he wasn't a certain someone who was meeting his serious girlfriend's family—would make new memories with me in these gorgeous spots and in others. At least, I hoped it would turn out that way.

"God, you look smashing, Do," she exclaimed, eyeing me up and down. "Country life certainly suits you!"

I smacked her on the bum. "Very funny.

Kendra's in the kitchen, and she's dying to meet you. Get your tuchas in here."

"Only if you promise not to manhandle it the way you usually do. You haven't made a very good start," she teased, then swatted my own derriere as soon as I turned to bring in her suitcase, two other totes, and duffel from the stoop.

"Hi! I'm Kendra. I've heard so much about you."

"Maddie. Likewise! Great to meet you."

"Are you moving in?" Kendra deadpanned, cocking her head toward the bags in the entryway.

"Nope, I just couldn't trust that you would have anything of use here," Maddie sniped. Kendra looked a little taken aback. She'd see soon enough that my sister gave as good as she got.

"New York snob," I countered.

"Going on thirteen years," she replied, puffing up. "And, if I may remind you, you were one too."

"Was not!"

Maddie appealed to Kendra. "How many times has she complained to you that there's no good Malaysian food around here? Or that she wishes the community center would do a performance of *La Traviata*?"

Kendra grinned, looking at Maddie with amusement and me with affection.

"Screw you both." I laughed. I poured some syrup onto the beautiful banana chocolate chip birthday pancakes Kendra had made us, handing a plate to Maddie.

As the two of them bantered and traded funny stories, I was content to listen. I'd known they would hit it off; they reminded me a lot of each other.

I showed Maddie a bunch of my favorite spots in town. She loved Chatsworth. On Saturday, we drove to a couple little nearby Connecticut towns to poke around in their shops.

Naturally, I wanted to check out all the bookstores. Especially one called Gregorson's. The sign out front looked like it had been carved in the Middle Ages for an apothecary or blacksmith. I rubbed my hands together in anticipation. I *loved* places like this, little spots with a feeling of history.

The door creaked open, and Maddie and I were met by one of our favorite smells in the world—the scent of wood burning, eternal and primal. A delicious floral odor radiated from the bouquets drying in the corners of the room and hanging from old wooden beams that looked like they'd been transported from a barn. All the books on the few shelves had clearly been chosen carefully.

I ran my fingers over their spines as I walked past. Many of them were leather bound and stamped in gold.

My eyes fell upon a book down the row. Nestled in between an investigation into the New Deal and a copy of *The Canterbury Tales* was my favorite book in the entire world. A story so sad, so full of misunderstood love and longing, self-sacrifice, and beauty, that every reading of it left me uplifted and wrecked, devastated and motivated to be a better, more selfless person. It was a book written by Alexandre Dumas *fils*, and it had never been even as remotely famous as any of his father's work like *The Three Musketeers* or *The Count of Monte Cristo*. The story had served as the basis for *La Traviata*, one of the most popular operas of all time—and the one Maddie had just teased me about since I had dragged her to it two out of the ten times I had seen it at the Met. And yet the book had remained almost unknown—rarely translated and hard to find in the United States. It was *The Lady of the Camellias*.

I pulled it off the shelf. When I was thinking of my favorite books, I'd fleetingly considered lending this one to Shep; I had a copy at home that I treasured. I hadn't dared to. The story was so full of unrepentant ache that I feared it would give too much away. I was becoming afraid that if he discovered my growing feelings for him, it would be impossible for us to be friends. Would it be so bad to buy another copy of the book and save it, though? Just in case . . . in the future . . .

I opened it. The glue crackled a little in protest; the pages separated after being compressed for a long time on the shelf. On the very first page, written in a small hand that could have been from a decade or even a century ago, read the following words:

To S.

Love, D.

I breathed very slowly through my nose, carrying the book up to the counter. Seeing that I was finally done, Maddie set down the beach read she was skimming (last page first!) and announced, "My treat."

I didn't trust my voice, so I nodded.

"You already have this one. It's your favorite," she observed.

I squeaked, "Not this particular edition."

Maddie shrugged and said, "Let's go eat. Birthday pig-out!"

We shared a carbfest of wild mushroom pasta with goat cheese, butternut squash risotto with sage sauce, and triple-cream burrata mozzarella for dessert. Utter gluttony seasoned with Maddie's salty sense of humor.

After our late arrival home, we slept in. Maddie finally appeared while I was finishing the book review section of the paper at the kitchen table. "Mornin', sailor." I tipped my cup at her. "Tea?"

"Later," she said, rubbing her eyes. "Take me into the library!"

"Like that?" I joked. Her hair was giving birth to more hair, and her pajama legs were tucked into her fuzzy socks like pirates' pantaloons. "I mean, it is Sunday, and it is an extension of my house, but it's open today since it's a holiday weekend."

"Good point. I'm gonna go get dressed."

"Don't you want brunch first?"

"Are you kidding me? I want to see the library *stat!*"

I smiled as she padded back upstairs.

"Wow," she kept saying as she walked around the stacks, glancing at the full shelves. Not that it took very long in the small space. Still, she looked impressed. "You've really done it, Do!"

I threw my shoulders back like a proud mother hen. "Thanks!"

Lula's husband, Mike, and his cousin Ramon, who were on Shep's construction team, were asking Kendra if any new books had come in this week. My heart leaped to see Shep's coworkers there without him. Maybe he wouldn't be back before Tuesday. I couldn't think too much about whether he was timing his visits with my presence. It seemed too good to be true. I needed to remind myself that it didn't matter since he was taken.

Right as we were about to doze off that night, Maddie's phone rang. Her eyes lit up as she hit speakerphone.

"Guess who?" came a crackly voice.

"It's really hard to guess when I see a weird international number come up on my phone!" Maddie joked. With all her interesting global boyfriends,

I would think it wouldn't be that easy, actually.

"Hello, sis!" I said. "Where are you?"

"Benin. How's my favorite librarian?"

"Fantastic!"

"And how's your new man, Maddie?"

"Which one?" She smirked, then said, "Just kidding. I haven't had a date in two weeks!"

I had no response to that.

"Listen, girls, I'd love to chat more, but I don't know how long I've got the line for, so I wanted to share some news."

"Bring it on," Maddie said.

"Mark and I have decided to adopt."

My stomach jumped. "Really?" I said at the same time Maddie cried, "I knew it!"

"We're going to apply for an international adoption."

"Wow. A child that you met while you were there?" I asked.

"No, no, we'll apply through the system in Liberia. There are so many kids that need a home already waiting in orphanages."

"What does the timeline look like?"

"Probably up to two years. It could be longer because we're still here. It will be tough for us to get all the paperwork we need, not to mention do home visits, when we don't have a place back in the States yet. But we're going to dive in and do what we can."

"We're excited for you guys," Maddie said.

"Let us know if there's anything we can do to help you from here. Do is really good with paperwork, and I'm really good with BSing people to make them do what I want."

"Thank you! I very well may take you up on that. Listen, I gotta go. I want to call Mom and Dad and tell them too."

"Of course. Congratulations. That's a really big decision. I can't wait until we can talk more about it," I said all in one breath.

"Yep. Love you."

Maddie crashed right after the call while I crept downstairs and paced in my living room. I hadn't seen this one coming. Coco and Mark would be loving, responsible parents, and it didn't surprise me that they were ready to start a family when they got back. I wondered whether they had decided that adopting was the right way for them or if they'd tried to have a biological child and it hadn't worked out.

What if she became a mom before I did? Or at a time that was really hard for me?

I immediately felt like a creep. Instead, I would focus on how amazing it would be if Coco and I ended up having children of a similar age.

I called Kendra after Maddie left on Monday afternoon. "How did the rest of this weekend go?"

"The lending library was packed. I was trying to help everyone, and meanwhile our favorite voluble third-grade teacher, Benton, came on Saturday looking for a book on string theory—which I regretted to inform him we didn't have—and then he spent forty-five minutes trying to explain string theory to me and its relationship to time travel even though I hadn't asked."

"He's coming to the library now?" I asked. "Wow, he must really like you. He can't wait until the next school day to see you."

I could practically hear her rolling her eyes. "I think he enjoys torturing me in and out of school. He always comes by looking for some random book. Every time, I have to bite my tongue to avoid telling him to check the Chatsworth Library of Obscurity. But I know that's not very nice and that you would never say something like that to a library visitor."

"That's right," I agreed. "We want to keep them coming back even if we don't have the books they ask for."

"Well, I don't know if I really do want to keep Benton coming back. I feel like we get enough of his mug and his specs at school." Kendra paused, and even though I hadn't asked, she said, "He didn't show."

I sighed, knowing she meant Shep and unsure whether to wish he had or to be relieved that he hadn't and hopeful that he would soon.

"Listen, Dodie, I've got to hop off. Mackie's calling for some reason."

An hour later, I was in the library sifting through the comment cards envelope when I heard a knock on the sunroom door. Kendra was standing on the stoop with a fist full of tissues, the whole of it such a wet and soggy mess that it couldn't dry any of the tears that were streaming down her cheeks.

"What's wrong, Kendra?" I urged, shepherding her to the wing chairs and plunking a box of tissues next to her.

"It's Sullivan," Kendra said.

"Oh no, what is it?"

"She-she-she—" Kendra stammered, sucking huge breaths of air through each sob, "she's dead."

All the air disappeared from the room, and I swayed on my chair. "No," I managed. Kendra was pulling tissues out of the box and crushing them against her dripping nose.

She sent the box back my way as tears streamed down my face. "What happened?"

"It was an aneurysm."

"Oh God!" I cried. "Oh God, was she with Terabithia at the time?"

"No, Mackie and Jeff had taken him to the children's museum. She was supposed to meet friends for lunch, and when she didn't arrive, they called Jeff, and he went to her place and found her. It was too late, of course; it must have been over in a second. The funeral is tomorrow.

Mackie wanted me to let you know. She was too upset to tell you herself, and she only called me because Sullivan was supposed to come over this morning so we could catch up." A fresh raft of tears spilled over her cheeks at that.

I felt dazed, like it was all a bad dream. My friend. How could she be gone, like that? Poor Terabithia. Poor Mackie and Jeff.

After Kendra left, I called Mackie, trying to hold it together. I didn't expect her to pick up the phone. But she did.

"Mackie, I'm so sorry," I said.

She sniffled through a meek *thank you.*

"Is there anything I can do?" I asked. My stomach fell to my feet as I remembered the way Sullivan had winced in the light at the park. *Stop it,* I ordered. I knew from one of Benton's random, rambling monologues in the teachers' lounge that aneurysms were often impossible to predict, that sometimes nothing could be done to prevent them or save the person.

"No, I think we've got it all covered. The funeral will be at Eternal Rest at ten tomorrow, and the burial's at Azalea Cemetery, and afterward people can come back to our house for a bite."

"Please," I begged, "give me something to do."

She paused. "You know that banana-pineapple spice cake you make with the cream cheese frosting?"

"Yes, the hummingbird cake." It had been Sullivan's favorite. She'd said it was a strange combination of flavors that somehow totally worked. Then she'd smiled slyly in my direction, as if she had thought that also described me.

"If it's not too much trouble and you wanted to bring one of those . . . or anything really," Mackie said. "Your raspberry biscuits or those peanut-butter-pocket double-chocolate-chip cookies. Or whatever you want . . . I should go."

"Oh, yes, of course," I rushed to say. "Call me back if there's anything else you need."

Walking through the aisles of the supermarket picking up ingredients like a zombie, I wondered if Terabithia had started to miss his mother yet or whether he sensed at all that his life had changed drastically again. Back at my house, surrounded by bowls of biscuit and cookie and cake batter, I kept myself busy late into the night. My mind wandered between memories of Sullivan in art school, in New York, and in Chatsworth. I kept flashing back to the fear in Terabithia's eyes the night of the first snow, and it was like a knife in my heart—one that kept stabbing away until finally, after hours of turning over and over in bed, I must have cried myself to sleep.

Eight

The entire back seat of the car was covered with foil-wrapped platters of baked goods. "Maybe I did go a little overboard," I admitted, making an effort to smile. It hurt my face too much.

Kendra patted my arm. "People will be hungry," she said, and it sounded odd to both of us even though I knew she was right. There was something comforting about the sheer physicality of eating when grief turned the rest of the world so distant and immaterial.

Eternal Rest was almost empty when we arrived.

From the back of the church, I spotted Jeff's head with its wisps of white hair bowing over Terabithia's espresso-haloed one. Terabithia. I was almost afraid to see him because I didn't want to make the situation even worse. Mackie was receiving guests, dabbing at her red-rimmed eyes but with a brave smile on her face.

After Kendra and I kissed her on the cheeks and told her again how sorry we were, Kendra took a seat a couple rows back. I wanted to occupy Terabithia so that Jeff could fulfill his duties, and Kendra sensed that we shouldn't crowd the little guy any more than he probably already had been since the tragic event. She was still somewhat of a stranger to Terabithia, at least compared to me.

"Hi, Jeff," I said. "Hi, Boo."

Terabithia's lips turned up in a delighted smile. He raised his Goya-painting eyes up to me. "Dada!" he called me. It was close enough to *Dodie*. Besides, at a year old, he was a genius in my eyes for being able to talk at all.

"Hi, babe." I wrapped him in a hug and willed myself not to squeeze too hard. "Whatcha doin'?"

He held a shiny turquoise car up to me.

"Mooom moooom," Terabithia said for emphasis.

"Vroooom," I agreed, drawing out the vowels to make him smile. It worked. Jeff patted me on the shoulder, nodding his gratitude, and headed down the aisle to join Mackie.

By nine forty-five, every pew was full. Sullivan had scads of friends from growing up in town, and I suspected a lot of her portrait clients had come too. Was that . . . ? No, it couldn't be. But yes . . . I would recognize that hair anywhere. He turned, and our eyes met. His were full of concern. Did Shep know Sullivan? I didn't think so, but then again, Chatsworth was a small town.

At ten, the minister began the ceremony. Eternal Rest was a very open-minded, low-key church, a place where Sullivan had gone since she was a teenager. She had told me that she had never felt judged there and that the other churchgoers were from all walks of life, which was the way she had thought any kind of worship should be.

As I sat, feeling dazed by her absence, the minister's voice was soothing. But I was finding his words about it being "her time" and "God's way is bigger than our understanding" hard to swallow. The only thing that comforted me at all was his assurance that her "passage had been swift." It was so important to believe that she had not suffered physically, and even more that she hadn't had time to suffer mentally for even a moment worrying about Terabithia's future without her. My heart was like a big burning stone as I thought about that.

When the ceremony ended, everyone filed out. Shep hovered near the back, reading the church brochures on the table. I wasn't in any state to talk, but I couldn't exactly ignore him. Not that I wanted to.

"Can I help you with anything?" I asked Mackie.

"No, we've got it. You know where to go, right?"

"Yes. I'll see you there."

Shep turned and dropped the brochure in his hand. He came close. God, he smelled so good. "How are you?" His brow was furrowed.

"I'm . . . I'm . . ." I swallowed hard. My face probably already looked like a beet.

He gave me a spontaneous hug, pulling away quickly when my body went rigid with surprise.

I recovered myself and asked, “Did you know Sullivan?”

“Not really.”

“Oh. Then, do you know Mackie and Jeff?”

“I’ve never met Mackie. I’ve spoken to Jeff a couple times. I really came for—”

In a daze, I interrupted. “Are you coming to the cemetery?”

“For . . . ,” Shep continued, watching my face closely, “the funeral. I don’t think it would be right for me to be at the burial.”

“Please,” I found myself saying.

“Okay. I’ll meet you there,” he immediately agreed.

“What was that about?” Kendra asked as we pulled out and joined the line of cars.

“I have no idea,” I admitted.

At Azalea, Kendra and I stood across from Jeff, Mackie, and Terabithia, who were all holding hands. A neat rectangular hole parsed the space between us. Shep materialized behind me at some point. As the coffin was lowered, Terabithia looked up at Mackie, tugging on her arm. “Where Mama? Where Mama?” My knees quavered, but Shep’s arm was faster as he cinched me around the waist, and my head lolled against his shoulder. I tried to breathe as deeply as I could, willing myself to stand up straight and not draw attention. Kendra gently took my hand and squeezed.

Mackie had displayed photos of Sullivan and Terabithia all over the living room of her home, where a buffet table was spread with a crisp cream tablecloth topped with all our offerings. I carried Terabithia over to the table. He pointed at it with questioning eyes, then made the little grunt that was still his chief way of communicating besides gesturing wildly.

"Which one did I bake?" I translated. He watched me with wide eyes. "Let's make a plate of tiny tastes."

I put a bit of raspberry biscuit, a forkful of hummingbird cake, a sliver of mint brownie, and two bite-size peanut-butter-pocket double-chocolate-chip cookies on a plate for him. He still seemed to be waiting, and as soon as I looked down at him, he grunted in the direction of the peanut-butter-pocket double-chocolate-chip cookies on the table. I angled the plate I was holding so he could see there were already two on it. He grunted again, unimpressed. "Fine, then, three," I said. He waved his arms in satisfaction. I snuggled him into my lap on the couch, holding the plate tightly so he wouldn't kick it over with his bouncing knees.

He stuck his finger into the pocket of peanut

butter on top of a cookie, looking happy as the filling squished out. I gave him a bite of that one. Next he grunted at the cake, then went to smack it with his hand, but I was too quick for him. Somehow I managed to get all the teeny tasting platter into his mouth. Except for a few smears of icing that ended up on his overalls. And my sweater, skirt, and shoe.

Mackie and Jeff kept coming to check on us. About a half hour before the guests started to leave, they insisted I take a break and speak to some of the adults. I found it unusually difficult to make small talk; I had to force myself.

Mackie and Jeff pulled me aside on my way out. "You were indispensable today, Dodie," Mackie said. "We couldn't have done it without you." As if in confirmation, Terabithia attached himself to my leg. I picked him up and gave him a big, sloppy kiss on the cheek. He giggled, but then a cloud passed over his face. I wanted so badly to know what his little baby mind was thinking in that moment.

"It was my pleasure," I said, wiping my eyes with the back of my hand. "I want to help in any way I can. I hope you'll let me keep coming to see him?" As soon as it came out of my mouth, I worried that I was obligating them to me on a day that had already brought so many awful obligations.

There was no need. "I was so hoping you would

feel that way," Mackie said, squeezing my hand. "You come as often as you like."

A few days after the funeral, I tried to go into the library. Kendra was there with me, just in case I lost it. She was dealing with her grief by keeping busy. Benton was there, too, since apparently he made it his business to be at the library pretty much whenever Kendra was. After about an hour, I broke down.

"Dodie," Kendra said gently, extracting a book from my hands, "you're getting it all wet." She was right. I had dripped on a whole pile of books, in fact.

"Plus I don't think it's very encouraging for the library visitors." She gestured around the library. About five patrons were peeping over their books, trying to decide whether to approach the desk to check out.

"I'm sorry," I said. "I can't stop thinking about Sullivan. And Terabithia."

"Go be with him," Kendra urged.

"Yeah," Benton said, materializing from between the stacks with an armful of books to be reshelved. "We got it."

I raised an eyebrow at Kendra. She shrugged, smiled at Benton, and said, "Right. We got it."

After that, Kendra took a bunch more shifts in the library for me. She claimed she needed the continuing education hours and that it kept her mind off her sadness about Sullivan. I tried not to think about the fact that, unlike me, Kendra was a pro with an advanced library science degree. It should have been a comfort knowing the lending library was in good hands, but a little part of me was afraid the library might stop needing me. Keeping it going was more important than my ego, though, and I needed Kendra's help for that.

Over the next several weeks, I went to Mackie and Jeff's almost every day. I would rush home after work, change quickly, and head over, usually armed with presents for Terabithia or meals for everyone. "He's going to get spoiled," Jeff chastised, but I could tell that he didn't mean it, that it was only something you were meant to say when a child already had everything and was in danger of becoming greedy—hardly the reality in Terabithia's case.

"And you're going to make us fat," Mackie chimed in, patting her tiny waist. Unlikely. I was more afraid that what I cooked for them at night when I got home was all they'd been eating since finishing the dinners friends and family had brought for the first week after Sullivan had passed away.

My heart ached at the knowledge that there was no such thing as safe, no matter how much you loved someone. This thought made me hug Terabithia so hard he squeaked, looking at me with confusion. My eyes welled up, and before

I could help it, tears leaked out of them. His lip began trembling, and then he began to bawl too.

"I got him," Mackie said. "Go home and get some rest."

When my mom called to check on me, I was in hysterics. "I cried in front of Terabithia," I wailed. "I'm supposed to make things easier, and instead I'm making them worse. I'm going to be such a terrible mother."

"Oh, Dodie." She sighed. "Don't be so hard on yourself. You care. That's what good mothers do. And besides, no one knows what to do at times like these. It's senseless when someone so young dies. You have to process it in your own way. And try to go easy on yourself."

March 2008

About two weeks later, I was sitting upstairs in my room organizing pictures of Terabithia into an album for Mackie and Jeff. There were a few recent ones of Sullivan in there; I'd had to snap most of them surreptitiously since she had hated pictures of herself as much as she had loved them of Boo.

It was seven o'clock in the evening, and the library was closing. I walked to the window. I could see the tops of the heads of a few children and their parents who were leaving. A couple of the firefighters were there, too, joking about something, one of them punching the other in the arm. I saw Elmira unzip her backpack and put in two books. She still clutched one in her other hand, and she began walking with it open in front of her. Walking and reading. A smile played across my lips. I missed the library. I missed the people. I needed to go back.

Shep was waiting for me to unlock the sunroom door when I arrived home after school the next day. He hadn't ever come so early. He was shifting from foot to foot. Jefferson Hendrow, the little boy from story circle, whispered, "Mama, why is that man doing the pee-pee dance in front of the library?" as I walked by. I dissolved into laughter.

Since Shep hadn't heard Jefferson, confusion flashed over his face.

"Hey," I greeted him. "Come on in."

"Thanks," he said, following so closely behind me that I had to stop breathing to avoid taking in some of his delicious, soapy scent. I didn't think throwing myself onto the lips of an unavailable man in front of Jefferson Hendrow and his mother would be a very good idea.

Once Jefferson and his mother were occupied in the children's section, Shep followed me to the circulation desk. "How are you? Is it getting any easier?" he asked, pushing his watch up and down on his arm. I tried not to look at his wrist.

The last time I had, I'd broken out in a cold sweat.

"It's been a challenge," I admitted. "But I decided it was time to come back, and I'm trying to focus on the library."

"Oh, I'm sorry I brought it up," Shep said awkwardly. "Of course, of course."

I shook my head. I hadn't meant to be rude.

He cleared his throat. "So, Dodie, do you have a new recommendation for me?"

I nodded, thinking of the white paper bag upstairs that contained the copy of *The Lady of the Camellias* that I might never have the courage to give him. Two copies, actually. I had lovingly nestled my own worn copy into the bag, too, sap that I am.

"Here you go." I handed him *Bleak House* instead. I had saved Dickens until I knew his tastes pretty well; Esther Summerson was one of my all-time favorite characters—and, I secretly admitted to myself, the book was nice and long.

As much as I loved seeing him regularly, the little reflection and distance I'd gotten over recent weeks made me think it might be helpful if Shep didn't come to the library quite so often. That and the fact that during our weekend together, Maddie had said the exact words, "Maybe it might be helpful if Shep didn't come to the library quite so often."

I couldn't imagine hurting his feelings by

suggesting in any open way to cool it on the visits, so this was the best I had come up with. Well, the best I'd come up with for keeping him away had actually been Thomas Mann's *The Magic Mountain*, at a shorter but far denser 720 pages, but I wasn't sure a novel about a tuberculosis sanatorium would leave the door open for future romance if he were ever single again.

Shep frowned when I laid it on the desk.

"What's wrong?" I asked.

"Nothing, I just . . . it's going to be a busy week at the site, so it'll probably take me a while to get through this book."

"You might be surprised," I said. "It's a pretty quick read." I wasn't doing a very good job with this. "But it's probably ideal if it takes some time." Oops, I hadn't meant for that last part to be audible.

"Why would that be ideal?" he said quickly.

"Because . . . it's a book you should savor," I covered. "Something I think you'll enjoy," I added, because his frown had gotten a little deeper.

"I've been enjoying finishing the books quickly," he said, gazing right at me.

I swallowed, fighting very hard against the urge to look away. "Oh yeah? Why is that?"

"I guess I like . . . this library," he said. "And you have very good taste."

I'll say, I thought, wanting to kiss him badly enough that I *had* to look away.

"Thanks," I replied, both desperately hoping for him to leave and desperately wishing he would stay.

"Okay, Dodie, I'd better head out," Shep said after another long pause.

"Bye, Shep." He was still frowning, so I couldn't help myself; as he was leaving, I said, "Maybe you can find a way to get more reading done this week than you think."

He turned around, and a slow smile spread over his face. "I hope so," he replied, and then he was gone. I smiled to think of the bookmark I'd dared to hide deep in the pages. "Hope is one of the most priceless riches."

A few hours later, I closed the library and reshelved all the books that had been returned. The scent of Shep lingered in the air, mingling with the delicious smell of pages and pages of books still to be read. I sat down in the squishy chair and read the comment cards and breathed it all in until it was time to drag myself off to bed. My first day back and my spirits were already feeling a little lighter thanks to my beloved library. It really did help.

Nine

April 2008

My other salvation was school. I was no longer sleepwalking through the day; I was back to running around like a chicken with my head cut off.

"Could you pass the glue stick, Miss Fairisle?" Jonah Brownlee asked me. A construction-paper frog—an impressively realistic replica of the poisonous blue tree variety—hung from his fingertips. I handed him the glue, and he swept it over the little tab at the back that would make it stand up straight in his diorama.

"Should Eve's hair be longer?" Schuyler asked, pulling on my sleeve.

Wow, that was some surprising anatomical detail for a third-grade art project. These kids obviously had access to films that I hadn't at their age. Or nudist colonies.

"Yes, definitely. Do you want some more corn silk?" I rushed to say, pushing the shoebox of it over to her. "And how about one of these miniclovers for Adam?"

"Miss Fairisle, Miss Fairisle," came Cameron's voice from the other side of the room, so urgently I was afraid he might have maimed himself with the safety scissors. “What do you think?” he asked as soon as I got over to his work space. “Does it say *Fosse* to you?”

I peered inside the diorama. It was clearly the work of a child who’d grown up with show business parents and had inhaled a lot of glitter. I loved it.

“Amazing!” I definitely hadn’t provided the metallic stretch fabric he had swathed his dancers in. He must have brought it from home. I grinned to think of the kids being so invested in the project. Day three, and the dioramas were shaping up.

“Miss Fairisle, are there any more antique lace doilies left I can cut up?” Lavinia asked.

“Miss Fairisle, Miss Fairisle, could you take a look at this . . .”

On it went until the end of class and the end of the day. Being that busy was a relief. It took some of the weight off my shoulders before I headed to Mackie and Jeff’s house. It also helped me concentrate until the moment I pulled into my driveway each afternoon, heart leaping into my throat. It wasn’t right to feel this way about a guy with a girlfriend.

And it certainly wasn’t right the way hope washed over me after his friend Mike visited.

“Hey, Dodie,” he greeted me after he’d gathered up an armful of comics to check out. “How’s it going?”

"Oh, you know, hanging in there. How's everything with you?"

"Great. The kids are finally getting good grades, and it's made Lula and me veeeery happy." There was a devious twinkle in his eye. Too much information, but I didn't begrudge anyone else just because it had been . . . sooo . . . very . . . long . . . for me.

"Nice! Um, how are things going at the mall site?"

"Okay. A little tense on the job. Shep's been on edge a lot lately," Mike said.

"Is everything all right? Is he okay? I mean . . . um . . ." I seriously had to rein in my concern. Mike was studying my face as if he knew something.

"Yeah, yeah, he's fine. I think he and his girlfriend have been fighting a lot."

Holy Hanukkah present in April! I thought, and then, *Shut up—that's not nice.*

"Apparently she said he acted really detached in front of her parents and accused him of being emotionally limited," Mike continued. "Like, she doesn't think he'll ever . . . sorry, Dodie, I didn't mean to make you uncomfortable. I will can it. Always say too much, Lula tells me." His sly smile told me that the gossip hadn't been an accident, though. Oh, gosh, did Shep know how I felt about him? And that was how Mike knew? I had to play it cool.

"Nothing to worry about," I reassured him, slipping bookmarks I'd written for people into the books I had set aside for them. "I'll forget we even had this conversation."

Except that was about as likely as being the victim of a land shark attack. Poor Shep. I hoped things would work out for the best . . . whatever that meant for him. I couldn't help thinking, though, about the passion I saw smoldering in his eyes when he talked about books. That didn't seem very emotionally limited to me. What Mike had said about Shep's poetic spirit echoed in my mind too.

It was important to remember that Shep was still taken, and I needed to resolve to meet someone available. Would it hurt anyone if I allowed myself two little weeks, maybe three, to indulge in the memory of Shep's soapy smell as he followed me into the library or the way his Boudin-ocean eyes became almost an Ingres black blue when something in a book particularly affected him? Okay, maybe I would give myself a month for good measure.

The following Monday, I was reading bits of the love story between Kitty and Levin out loud to Chloë from a recently donated copy of *Anna Karenina*. On the bookmark slipped inside was one of Monet's haystack pictures, the light all golden and periwinkle, and I had written, "The quietest love stories are the best to be savored."

"Convinced to give it another try yet?" I asked. "Oh, no, Joey," I cried out, peering over Chloë's shoulder, "could you please color on the construction paper instead of in *How the Grinch Stole Christmas*? And Sandra, I think that plant has enough water now. Thank you for being such a good helper!"

Chloë did not look convinced. "Suicide by train? How very undignified." She sniffed, but she held open the book for me to stamp anyway.

Oh no. Irish soap. My heart started to pound. I peeked out from under my eyelids.

"Hi, Dodie. Do you have any of these?" Shep pushed a little list toward me, where he'd jotted down friends' recommendations.

"Did you finish *Bleak House* already?" I asked.

"No, but I think that one will take me a while. I'm going to multitask." He flashed a smile at me that flambéed my underwear.

I scanned the list, trying not to wonder what he'd been up to over the weekend.

"I don't have these here," I said. "Except I just finished reading this one, *The Elegance of the Hedgehog*, and it's on my nightstand. It will make you laugh, and it will break your heart. I don't usually do this, but I could lend you my own copy if you promise to take good care of it."

A lot of the books in the lending library were indeed mine, so it was somewhat of an arbitrary distinction. Maybe I liked the idea of having a sort of secret with him. Judging by the look on his face, he seemed to like it too. Almost, I would say—if I hadn't been so out of practice with men—as though he was wondering what my nightstand and the rest of the room looked like.

"Would you mind holding down the fort here?" I asked. "I'm going to go grab that book, and I'll be right back."

"Here you are," I said, passing the book to him, wishing again that I'd had the time to choose the perfect bookmark and quote to go with it.

As soon as he left, I started to wonder if I'd made a mistake. Both of the main characters were female, one of them an odd recluse and the other a twelve-year-old suicidal bookworm. It might not be his thing at all.

But when Shep returned at the end of the week, the dark circles under his eyes were gone. He looked relieved, lighter. "I really want to thank you. This book was so moving."

"My pleasure."

"Listen, could I take you out for dinner this weekend to thank you properly?" he offered.

Holy Knights of the Round Table! "I'm not sure . . . I mean, maybe it would be better if . . ." I was trying to be cautious even though every fiber in me was shouting, *Say yes, you idiot!* He might still be with his girlfriend. Or grieving, if things had ended recently.

Then again, maybe not.

"Okay," I finished before he could rescind the invitation.

He said nothing, but his sudden huge grin flooded my chest with excitement. There would be time on Saturday night to find out where things stood.

Before I closed up the sunroom library for the night, I hung some drawings a few kids had made that day for the bulletin board. They might as well have been Monets to me. Like some lovesick schoolgirl, I kissed every book before I reshelved it. They were my babies, after all. And they smelled sooo good.

Kendra came over on Saturday to do double duty. As a volunteer for kids' story circle in the library, her rendition of *Animal Boogie* nearly brought the house down. As my wardrobe consultant afterward, she showed the patience of Job while I tore apart my entire closet and dresser looking for the perfect outfit.

"That's it," she finally breathed when I put on a pearl-purple silk top with a gray skirt that swung out over the knees. I was pretty sure the top had been one of the first things I'd tried on, but I was also pretty sure she was right. The outfit made me feel comfortable.

"Go get 'em, girl. I'll let myself out," Kendra said, sifting through my belts. "Oh, and Dodie?"

"Yes?" I said.

"You might want to hide that," she suggested, pointing to a copy of *Parenting* magazine that had slipped out from between two fashion glossies.

I reddened and, stuffing it into the bottom of the trash can without meeting her eyes, said, "It's really weird. They sent me a free subscription when I signed up for *Elle Decor*."

"Uh-huh," Kendra said.

Shep rang my doorbell right on time. When I opened the door, I gave him a quick smile. I couldn't look him in the face again as he stood beside the car door. Or as he drove. I couldn't manage it until I had no choice but to make eye contact because we were sitting across from each other at the restaurant. I was way too sure that my schoolgirl crush would be stamped across my forehead.

The menu gave us something to do. I glanced at Shep's sexy wrist as he handed back the menu and promptly forgot what I'd ordered. *Get a grip,* I told myself. *It's only a wrist! And you have talked to this man less than a dozen times.*

"So," Shep said.

"So."

Before I could launch into a stream of chatter to fill the silence, Shep began. "So I used to be really afraid of heights when I was a kid. Terrified. My brothers gave me so much hell about it. There was this low bridge over a creek near where we used to go in the summers in Massachusetts, and they all jumped off it, and that was still too high for me even though you could almost touch the water with your feet if you sat on the edge of the bridge. Then I figured I had better get over it if I wanted to work in construction, and so I started offering to take the jobs up on the scaffolding, and it scared the crap out of me the first few times until I realized it was all in my head. Not vertigo or anything. Just, you know, that I must have thought I was supposed to be scared. And now it doesn't seem any different to me. It's sort of like when . . ." Shep stopped abruptly. "Sorry," he said. "This is totally unlike me. I never talk this much."

"Oh really? I do all the time!" I joked, trying to put him at ease. Oh no. Would he be insulted that I agreed he was talking a lot?

"I guess I'm . . . nervous," he admitted.

I breathed in and out five times, slowly and deeply, through my nose. Then I said, "Me too." His hand was so close to mine I could almost touch it. Then—I'm not sure how—I *was* touching it.

"So what brings you to Chatsworth?" I asked, finally able to meet his eyes.

"You heard about the new outdoor mall they're building, right?"

Yes, I had. At first I had grumbled about it. I had already become protective of Chatsworth's charm, and I didn't like the idea of chain stores—high end or otherwise—changing the face of it and competing with the family-run stores on Main Street. Sullivan had told me to stop being a snob. "The more, the merrier." She was probably right. I knew that was the site where Mike and Ramon worked. And of course I liked it even better now that I knew it had brought Shep here.

"So do you have a specialty? I'm not really sure how that works," I admitted.

"I pretty much do everything, but I love the details like carpentry and tile and working with those people toward the end of the process. If there hadn't been so many of us kids going to college in my family, I would have tried to go to architecture school afterward. I love fixing things up."

"What kinds of things?"

"Boats." He grinned.

"Boats?"

"Yep. I grew up in New London, a five-minute walk from the water. At first I helped out as a kid to make some extra cash, but by high school I got really passionate about it, and now it's a big hobby."

"Is it weird being in Chatsworth then?"

"Well, we're not exactly landlocked here. There's a boat workshop near the water about twenty minutes away in Eagle Ridge, and it's only a half hour to the coast."

"Sure. But don't they say that once you live by the water, you always want to?"

"That's definitely true. In theory, this is a temporary job in Chatsworth anyway."

Oh, mud. So anything that happened between us had an expiration date on it. I swallowed my disappointment. "How long do they expect the mall to take?" I asked as casually as I could manage.

"Probably about a year. But I could always sign on to another project in the area if I like it here as much as I think I will," he added.

That was enough of a hopeful thought for me.

When he walked me to my door at the end of the night and said softly, "I'd like to return that book to where it came from," I surprised myself by agreeing. I hadn't had a man in my room since I was with Daniel years before.

Shep looked around eagerly when we got there. The curiosity on his face made me smile. He placed the book on the nightstand next to the little bud vase I'd filled with forget-me-nots in the hopes, I realized, that I might find myself in this exact moment.

Shep glanced at the bed. I stifled a nervous giggle, trying again to breathe slowly through my nose—but in a sexy way—to calm myself down. It had been so long since I'd kissed anyone I really, really liked. He was looking at me like I was an ice cream cone. That was encouraging.

But there was something pricking at me, a fear. "Shep, I have to ask. I thought that you had a—"

"Dodie," he interrupted, his voice low. "When Sullivan died, everything became so clear. I wanted to be by your side. There was no other choice for me, no other person. Knowing how sad you'd be . . . that's why I was there that day."

"For me," I murmured, even though a part of me had already suspected. "But how did you know?"

"I know Sullivan was one of your closest friends and the reason you're here in Chatsworth. This is a pretty small town, and about four people told me that when I asked about you. Also, you have that picture of Terabithia on the desk of the library. And I always see you looking at it. It didn't take much to put two and two together." He gazed around the room, his eyes resting on four other pictures of Terabithia mixed in with photos of my family.

I blushed.

"You're really beautiful when you blush."

Now my cheeks were on fire. I felt a twinge of sadness—any thought of Sullivan and Terabithia would probably cause that for quite a while—but it faded as I met Shep's eyes again.

After wrapping his arm around the small of my back, he tugged me in so that our bodies were pressed up against each other. His soapy smell was even more intense up close. I could hear my pulse pounding. He kissed me tenderly on the cheek and, finally, trailed down to my lips.

In the weeks that followed, whenever I wasn't at school, the library, or with Terabithia (or on the phone filling in a cheering Maddie or a very enthusiastic Mom and Dad), Shep and I were more or less inseparable.

For the most part, my life before Shep had been simple and delicious like a coffee ice cream and hot fudge sundae. Now, thanks to him, it was an even more brightly colored and brightly flavored sorbet sundae with lots of things in it that not only tasted good but were good for me. Not like flax or anything. Maybe pineapple in season. Mango too. Somehow familiar yet exotic. But most of all, more irresistible and more delicious!

Still, I wondered about what had happened with his ex-girlfriend Quinn. He never mentioned her. Of course it wasn't hard to find out the basics in a town this small, especially thanks to Mike's loose lips at the checkout desk. Apparently, she was from Derbyshire, and they had met over the summer at a party on a boat. I asked him about her once when we were falling asleep on one of the first few nights we spent together.

His face tightened, but he said lightly, "We were in different places and wanted different things."

"Like what?" I asked. I sensed his reluctance

to talk about her, but I was already worried about how strong my feelings were.

Shep sighed. “Quinn wanted a baby, and I was nowhere near ready to have a child with her.”

I nodded, thinking, *Did he feel any differently now, one month later? Was it her? Or would he feel the same way now no matter whom he was with?* I had a feeling I wouldn’t like the answer to any of those questions.

Ten

May 2008

I had seen Trey Parks admiring Melissa Boyd at the library a number of times before, a slow smile on his face as she read to her daughter, Deandra. Today they were reading *Moo, Baa, La La La!* A total classic.

"You two know each other, right?" I asked him. I would have introduced him to her, but I had seen them making small talk a few weekends earlier.

"Yes, we're in a night class together on bookkeeping at Eagle Ridge Community College."

"That's nice. So . . . have you hung out after class at all?" Being the town librarian had clearly emboldened my nosy side.

"We've had coffee a few times." *But,* his face said, *I'm clearly stuck in the friend zone.*

The week before, at Foodie Book Club, Melissa had told me—over truffles and spiced hot cocoa inspired by *Chocolat*—that her divorce had been really messy and she was much more interested in chocolate than men at the moment. But now Trey and I both watched as Channing Robison, one of the investors in the mall project, tapped her on the shoulder and asked her a question. She laughed. Ugh, he was flirting with her. He had a ridiculously handsome face and a ridiculously large ego to match. Melissa seemed to be responding.

Trey was no longer smiling. He looked as though he had missed out on the annual crop of Cadbury Mini Eggs. (That had happened to me once, and I'd had to send out an all-points bulletin to my art school friends across the country. Thankfully, my buddy Jenny Doig in La Habra, California, had come upon a CVS employee trying to hide a whole box for herself and had managed to wheedle a few bags.)

Trey was not ostentatiously handsome like Channing, but he had kind eyes and a sweet, boyish face. He was serious and steady and always offering to help unpack book deliveries or fix the clogged toilet in the bathroom or change light bulbs simply because he was a nice guy who liked to be helpful (and because he was a big fan of the library). He reminded me of Gabriel Oak from *Far from the Madding Crowd*—overlooked by Bathsheba Everdene in favor of the dashing, selfish Frank Troy.

Trey left before seeing Melissa give Channing her number. Kendra did notice, however, with a grimace in my direction.

When we were closing up, I told her, "You know how people request books they want added to the library on the comment cards? I'm thinking about taking that a step further and starting a year-round Secret Book Santa."

"How would that work?"

"I'll keep a wish list at the checkout desk, and then when people see a book on the list that they have, they can donate it anonymously. That makes it more of a treat for the giver and the receiver, don't you think?"

"Yes, I do. When are you going to start it?"

"Well, maybe I will kick it off with a couple discreet donations myself this week and get it going before summer starts."

"Such as . . . ?"

I leaned in closer. "I was going to give Melissa a copy of *Far from the Madding Crowd*." I raised my eyebrows at her.

She gave me a wry smile back. "Maybe I should secretly donate a copy of *Emma* to you."

"What do you mean?" I feigned innocence.

"You know exactly what I mean. Are you about to create a matchmaking mess?"

I laughed. "Of course not. I just don't want Melissa to miss out on Trey; he's a gem. Whereas Channing Robison is a lump of coal."

"Very shiny coal with cheekbones that could cut diamonds," she noted.

"And an ego that could smother a canary."

Kendra rolled her eyes. "I think we've taken this mining metaphor one step too far."

"I agree. What do you think of the Secret Book Santa idea, though? Seriously."

"I love it. You should also encourage people to donate books they overhear someone saying they want to read so people get surprises even if they aren't signed up on the wish list."

"Definitely!" I would have Elmira decorate the wish list sheets. My spine tingled at the thought of the donations and how the receivers would feel when they got the books they wanted . . . or a book they needed but never even knew they wanted.

My relationship with the library had started to deepen the way that comes from knowing your loved one well. Each time, before I entered, I would stand in my kitchen and peek through the sunroom door. The faint lemony scent that had been there when I moved in had now been fully replaced by the smell of old paper. Each hand that touched a book, that gently flipped the pages or pressed them down so the spine would lie flat or even bent the paperback around itself . . . each of these acts of devotion would release the delicious secret scent inside.

The Chatsworth Library, meanwhile, was completely on hold. Geraldine had told me that funding for repairs had run out before they could put in modern heating and air-conditioning. With school ending and summer vacation on the way, it didn't seem as though anything would happen before the fall.

• • •

"You all right?" I asked Shep. He was staring out the window in the library, head cocked to the side like he was listening for something.

"Oh, yeah, sure." He quickly looked away.

I shivered, doused with a cold wave of déjà vu. This wasn't the first time Shep had acted twitchy lately. Or the second. After weeks of being nearly inseparable, my time with Shep suddenly became more rare once summer hit. It was always really busy for him. He loved boats like I loved books. He even built little ones. (Little as in for a couple people, not as in the toy variety.) There were his trips to go sailing and his work on a new boat he was thinking of selling, plus my shuttling from Mackie and Jeff's to see Terabithia and trying to keep up the lending library. Now that it was summer and I didn't have school, I had extended the hours to 10:00 a.m.–7:00 p.m. Monday through Thursday and 10:00 a.m.–3:00 p.m. on Friday and Saturday.

"Is something wrong?"

"Nope. Should I wear my khakis on Friday?"

Okay. Guess he didn't want to talk about whatever was bothering him. It didn't seem worth pushing it; our relationship was still too new. I wouldn't be the nosy nag no matter how curious I was. Most of our time together was as delicious as anything I ever could have dreamed up in all my rom-com-inspired fantasies, so it seemed better to let him open up when he was ready and in the meantime enjoy every second we spent together.

Shep and I had planned a Friday-night fancy date—a wine tasting and gallery tour followed by dinner at a new French restaurant called L'Epicure. A few of the old stores on the main street of Chatsworth had closed as leases went up, and in the past few years some new owners from Boston and New York had opened art galleries, turning a part of the town center into a little cultural destination. It had already been that way when I had arrived last year, but I had barely visited any of them yet.

I took extra time getting ready, straightening my hair before curling it and donning a new rose-colored dress with the most divine little darts near the waist and the faintest hint of ruching on the sleeves.

Shep's eyes lit up when he saw me.

"You look beautiful," he said, kissing my cheek, lingering to take in my perfume. I kissed his neck.

"So do you," I said into his collar.

"You ready?"

The first gallery had artful black-and-white photos of wild animals. The second had bright Miró-style abstracts. The last had breathtaking panoramic views of various places in South

America so vivid you could almost smell the fires burning on the pampas or feel the air grow colder as you rose higher in the foothills of the Andes. Shep looked utterly rapt.

Over caramelized figs with Gruyère and balsamic drizzle on puff pastry at L'Epicure, Shep said, "What a coincidence, seeing those amazing pictures of South America tonight."

I felt a chime of fear remembering his vacant look over the past few weeks instead of his kindled-from-within one now.

"What's that?" I asked cheerfully anyway.

"Those photos of South America. The Amazon. It's my dream to go there. Just think of what I could learn about building boats."

"That would be amazing," I agreed, silently subtracting the dengue fever and oversize bats that could carry you off into the jungle before you could scream *help*.

"I want to make it happen soon. Wouldn't it be amazing?" Shep asked. He was clearly not listening since I'd just used the same word.

"Totally," I assented.

"So you would go with me?"

"Oh, um, sure," I said, conjuring up visions of being tangled in the sheets in a bed with one of those diaphanous (but still highly protective) mosquito nets.

"You know what would be even more amazing?" he steamed on.

"Hmm?" I said, sopping up the last of the balsamic drizzle with a piece of brioche.

"Living there for a few months. You know, having a home base, being able to travel and see all the natural wonders . . ."

I froze. A few months? Not just for a vacation? Shep continued listing pros until he noticed my nineteenth-century-photograph posture.

"Do?" he asked quizzically.

"I wouldn't want to leave my family . . . or . . . or . . . Terabithia . . . ," I stuttered, afraid of crushing his dream for us. But I couldn't help it.

"Oh, yes, of course," Shep backpedaled. He looked like a kid who had gotten pink bunny pajamas for Christmas instead of a Red Ryder BB gun.

My stomach sank. Shep's heart was somewhere else—somewhere I couldn't follow him. *He's going to leave,* I thought. *Just when I finally found him, he's going to leave.*

Eleven

June 2008

Mackie's eyes were red when she opened the door to me a few days later. I had become accustomed to it in the two months since Sullivan's death and never said a word, just gave her a hug. I missed Sullivan so much, too, but I didn't want to add to her parents' burden.

"Dada! Dada!" Terabithia was shouting my "name" from the other room. It was the come-hither shout, not the here-I-come shout.

"He's playing with blocks. Go on ahead, and I'll get us some lemonade," Mackie said. The phone rang. "Excuse me."

Each time I built a tower of blocks, Terabithia would giggle and clap. Then, with a twinkle in his eye, he'd sweep the tower with his arm, sending blocks cascading across the mat.

"Yes, yes, I understand," Mackie was saying, her voice level even though I could see her wiping a tear away as she stood in the door watching Terabithia. "I'll speak to Jeff about it, and we'll be back in touch in a day or two. Okay, thank you. Bye-bye." Mackie stared at the phone for a long time after hanging up.

Why was Terabithia grunting now? Oh, because

in my distraction I had stopped stacking blocks for him to knock over. He was like a pint-size foreman bent on destruction.

The sounds of pouring and the clink of ice cubes filtered in from the kitchen. Gripping a glass of lemonade, Mackie sat down on the couch and watched us, sipping quickly. Boo's round little arms pushed off the ground, and he toddled over to her, reaching for the glass.

"Oh, honey, I'm so sorry," she exclaimed. "How rude of me to forget all about you two."

She returned with a sippy cup of milk for him and a tall glass like hers for me. Condensation sparkled on the sides, and a few torn mint leaves lazily circled the ice. We all drank in silence except for the occasional click of the cup against Terabithia's new teeth.

When he was bathed and tucked into bed, I asked Mackie gently, "What's going on? If you want someone to talk to about it . . . I mean, besides Jeff . . ."

She waved my concerns away. "I'm happy to tell you; I consider you part of our family now."

Wow. Part of their family.

"Jeff and I aren't young like we used to be . . . obviously. I mean, we're in pretty good health—knock wood—for our age . . . but full-time care for a baby . . ." She paused, then started again. "We're in our midseventies. He needs a hip replacement in the next year, and he'll be recovering for more than a month. His angina has gotten worse, and the doctor says he has to find a way to reduce his stress levels. And with my eyesight being what it is, I can't drive anymore. The fact is, as much as it guts me to say it, Terabithia would be better off in a household with younger caregivers. I haven't slept more than three hours a night since Sullivan died. First, I was up all night worrying about how losing her would impact Boo. Then, after a few weeks, I started to worry about the impact on him if he stayed with us; if, in a few years, our health worsened when he was still much too young to know how to take care of himself but when it might be too late for him to find a set of parents who would look after him if anything happened to us. We don't have forever to wait. We have to make the hard choices for Terabithia. Babies are much more likely to be well adjusted if adopted before the age of two."

My heart stopped. I tried to breathe slowly through my nose. Adopted?

Seeing the horror in my eyes, Mackie burst into tears to my even greater horror. "I know, just the thought . . . of . . . Ter—with other people."

Now I was crying, too, looking at Terabithia's door with panic as though someone might already have snatched him away. Deep down, I had known this was a possibility based on Mackie's and Jeff's ages, but I hadn't been able to bring myself to think about it. How could I? Terabithia was going to be sent far away where I'd never see him again.

After a few eternal minutes, Mackie blew her nose and said in a more collected voice, "I don't know what Sullivan would have wanted us to do. I never thought . . . I never thought my daughter would die before me."

I held up my hand, jumping to my feet. "I'm sorry. I can't talk anymore right now. I'll call you tomorrow." I gave Mackie a quick hug, then sprinted away without missing the look of surprise and hurt in her eyes.

I had to get out of there. I didn't want to say something I would regret. Like, "How could you think Sullivan would want her baby to end up with strangers?" I knew it was unfair. But I couldn't help feeling that way.

I called Mackie the next morning. After Terabithia grunted for the phone twice and playfully hung up both times, I got Mackie long enough to say, "I'm so sorry for last night. I was being selfish and, frankly, panicking at the thought of losing him. You and Jeff are doing the right thing."

Did I really believe that? For the rest of the weekend I wasn't able to stop thinking about what she'd told me.

• • •

"Let me handle that," Shep offered when I dropped the sixth book in a row while we were reshelving. "I'll finish that stack." Watching his wrists while he made quick work of the rest momentarily distracted me.

"Hey, Do," he said later when we were washing dishes. "Why don't we switch? I'll wash, you dry?"

"Why?" I asked, savagely swiping at some intractable Indian curry in the bottom of a bowl.

"Because it seems like you have a murderous vendetta against your dishes, and I'm sure you would actually like to keep them."

I paused. "I'm angry," I admitted . . . to him and to myself for the first time.

Shep's eyebrows rose. He looked like I'd announced, *I'm a yellow-bellied sapsucker,* as though he knew what that was but had no experience with what to do with one.

"Who are you pissed at?" he asked, rescuing the dishes from me. I plopped onto the couch.

"Mackie and Jeff."

"Why? You don't blame them, do you?"

"I get that they're worried about what kind of life Terabithia will have with them, but they're not that old. I mean, yes, I know that Mackie has vision issues and Jeff has a hip problem and angina, and I know that they'd be ninety or so when he goes to college"—*Whoa,* I thought, *ninety!* I was losing steam as the words came out of my mouth—"but that's seventeen years away! And how could they imagine letting anyone else raise him? Knowing that his new parents might not let Mackie and Jeff see him as much as they want? Knowing they will probably miss his first day of kindergarten? His first soccer game? His first—"

Shep interrupted, seeing me regather steam and knowing from experience that I could keep going for quite a while. "I hear you. And you're right. They've probably thought of all of that. So look at it this way, Do: think what a *selfless* thing they'd be doing. Setting aside how much they'd miss him so that he could have a safer, fuller life with someone else. It's an impossible gift to imagine."

I put my head on his chest as soon as he sat down. "But they're the only family he knows," I protested. "Besides me, of course." My words echoed in my mind. An idea was dawning. I thought of the calendar under my bed, which was now crawling with the red *X*s I'd sneaked in once a month since December.

Besides me.

Of course. It was the solution to all my problems—my grinding-to-a-halt reproductive system, my aching desire to have a baby—and maybe to Mackie and Jeff's problems too.

Dodie to the rescue!

• • •

After my initial anger-fueled resolution wore off, logic started to set in. Was I sure I could do this? To be a mother by myself? On a teacher's salary and with a library to take care of? I was already stretching each month to keep it going and had pretty much ruled out the possibility of taking a real vacation for another year or so. When I looked into the expenses typically associated with adoption—the home visits alone would cost in the thousands—I wondered if I was biting off more than I could chew. While Shep was downstairs watching baseball, I headed upstairs and called my mom, looking for a dose of reality.

"What did you like least about being a mother?" I asked.

She was silent for so long I thought the line had gone dead. "Mom?"

"Yes, darling, I'm trying to remember."

I waited.

"You know, all that seems so silly now. I mean, sure, there were times where Maddie had terrible colic or you had reflux or Coco would throw a tantrum and roll around on the supermarket floor, but there were so many joyous times. The first time your hair was long enough for a ribbon—you were quite a baldy for the first couple of years. It was more like peach fuzz," she reminded me. "And the poems you used to write in school, and Maddie's contrite little face after having to walk the blacktop as punishment. And the way Coco used to run to pet Kirby after doing something wrong, as if showing the dog affection proved she was still a good person." She laughed.

This was not helping.

"What about the times we were sick or injured, when we fell out of our cribs or skinned our noses or had terrible strep throat?"

"Yes, those were awful times," she agreed. "And when your father left, of course . . . it was hard to go through that and even harder to watch you all going through it. We had some really lean years, and sometimes I felt like I was barely holding it together. Still . . . I was lucky that you were such great girls and that Walter came along when he did."

"It can be so scary being a mother, can't it?" I pressed on.

"Definitely." She was quiet for a moment while I tried not to choke on the ache I felt at the thought of losing Terabithia.

"Then on the other hand," she countered, "that fear, that vulnerability, reminds you of the depth of your love because it shows you how much you have to lose."

"Oh, Mom." I sighed.

"It's okay, honey," she murmured.

Spooned into Shep in bed that night, I listened

to his even breathing. A branch tapped on the window. It sounded almost like hail. It hit again, loudly. Shep startled awake. *I don't ever remember a branch doing that before,* I thought as I trailed off into sleep.

A short time later, I sensed him slipping back under the covers. His body was rigid.

"You okay?" I asked drowsily.

"Yeah," he grunted.

"Was it a branch?"

"No."

"Was it hail?" Sleep was falling away from me like a robe.

"It was nothing, hon."

"You sure?"

No answer. Now I was stark awake. I went to the bathroom. Out the window, I glimpsed a flash of brown: a nosy night bird trying to spy on us, then winging away under the trees.

By the time I finally fell back to sleep, light was beginning to seep into the darkness.

What made my mom such an incredible mother? I asked myself many times over the next few days. It was too hard to try to parse it that way, like separating water molecules from the ocean. There had been so many moments where she showed me what it meant to be joyous, full of wonder and kindness.

"Oh my gosh, Walter, pull over, pull over!" she

had cried on one trip home from Maddie's soccer game, craning her neck to see the full ground-to-sky arc of a rainbow miles wide, its ends disappearing into the trees far away to each side of us. It was vivid, Rainbow Brite–like. She was smiling from ear to ear.

Then there was the time we went to Atlantic City. After playing the quarter slots side by side for a while, I left her at an Elvis one and moseyed into the next aisle to the Lucky Horseshoes. A handful of quarters later, I returned. My mom was standing in front of the machine wheezing with laughter and pointing. Quarters poured out, repeating that delicious pinging noise you think only happens in the movies. I looked up at the King gratefully. *It figures,* I thought, cracking up at the sound (or lack thereof) of my mother's infectious laughter.

We swept the coins into a bunch of plastic cups, feeling like celebrities as a crowd gathered.

"How much?" I asked her.

"Eight hundred quarters! Two hundred dollars!" she cried. She paused, her voice growing serious. She could buy herself a new bag or a fabulous dress. Instead, she said, "I'll tell you what. Why don't I get you your own hotel room so that Walter's snoring doesn't keep you awake?"

A week passed since the restless night with Shep, and he had been quieter than usual with circles under his eyes to match mine. I didn't know what was going on in his head. Maybe making dinner at home would give us the chance to open up, even if, truthfully, I didn't want to talk about myself at all.

"It's zucchini-lemon pesto pappardelle." I set it down in front of him and held the grater over his plate. "Parmesan?"

"Hit me," he said, rubbing my hip and smiling up at me.

A mound of snow descended onto the pasta. I let it pile up the way he liked. Then I started grating cheese over my own plate.

"Do," Shep began, "I was wondering, how are you doing?"

"Fine. How are you?"

"No, really, how are you? I feel like we haven't talked much about it since you told me and both of us have been so . . . busy . . . but I know you must be having such a hard time with the news that Mackie and Jeff might—"

"Don't say it!" I cried, putting up my hand to stop him.

He took it gently and kissed the palm. "Give Terabithia up for adoption," he finished.

"I'm sad about it," I allowed.

"I know," he said, wrapping his arms around me and squeezing just the right amount. I felt the soft, strong pressure of his lips on the top of my head, once, twice, three times, like some sort of good luck charm. "Talk to me about it. Tell me what you're thinking."

My spine stiffened. I couldn't tell him the truth. He would think I was crazy if I confessed that I was considering trying to adopt Terabithia with no savings, a small enough income for one person, a library that wasn't even a year old, and only babysitting experience before Terabithia. How could I talk about how much I wanted Terabithia without admitting how much I craved a baby in general? It wasn't hard to guess how my (unbelievably amazing) boyfriend of only a few months would react to that revelation. I decided to keep it to myself.

"Terabithia has been through so much. To lose Sullivan . . . so young . . . totally out of the blue . . . and he can't even communicate. We don't know what he's thinking or what to do to help him or how to make it better because how do you make that better? I wouldn't even know how to make it better for anyone. It's so senseless. And this means that although he may find some loving new parents"—I flinched as I said the words—"he's going to lose Mackie and Jeff. Even if they get to see him now and then, it's not the same. It's like this whole adjustment he has to make again. More loss. The way they love him—the fact that they want to keep him but feel they can't in order to give him his best chance at a great life—it guts me."

Shep nodded. “What about you and how *you* feel about Terabithia?”

I knew what he meant. His words, the look on his face, filled me with . . . love. He really *saw* me—saw through me and realized there was something I was holding back. The heart of the issue. Terabithia. Not Dad too.

I knew I had to tell him about Not Dad eventually. But a part of me was afraid that if he knew I’d been abandoned before, he would leave now instead of letting me think he was in it for the long haul.

I shook off these dark thoughts and looked into those beautiful oceanic eyes, so full of the earnest wish to hear me out. I couldn’t tell him about Terabithia. Two months together. It was too soon, too much of a risk.

“I’ll be all right. I just really adore that little guy,” I said in as light a tone of voice as I could.

Shep nodded, like he didn’t believe me but wasn’t going to push it any further. I gave him a big hug and said, “Enough about me. What I really wanted to talk about tonight was you. You seem preoccupied. Is everything okay?”

“Yeah, I guess I have been distracted lately,” he acknowledged, gazing off into the distance . . . not even realizing he was confirming it.

“What’s on your mind?” I asked, terrified that he was going to answer, *An apprenticeship in boatbuilding on the Amazon River*.

He picked at a thread that was starting to wear loose on his jeans right around the knee. "Nothing particular. Work stuff mostly."

That meant something other than work stuff. "Is everything okay at the site?"

"Yeah. Some of the guys are getting on each other's nerves. It happens a lot in the summer. It's so hot out there sometimes—we're baking in the sun, and people get kind of pissy over stupid things."

"What else besides work?" This was excruciating. I hated conflict even more than I hated those scary caveman-style BBQ turkey legs on steroids they served at Disney World. I got straight to the point. "South America?"

"South America?" Shep repeated, confused.

"When we were at L'Epicure, you mentioned . . ."

"Oh," he said, as if remembering something that had happened in the distant past instead of weeks ago. "Oh, yeah. Who knows what I was even talking about? Sometimes I get these crazy ideas, like escape fantasies . . . this week I was reading about the Viking Ship Museum in Oslo. Anyway, never mind. You want to see if there's anything good on TV?"

I nodded, happy to be released. As I sank down into the perfect space under his arm, something didn't quite fit. Had Shep dropped the South America idea because I'd told him about Terabithia's possible adoption? Or had he really forgotten so quickly? Because there was something even bigger on his mind? What was he trying to escape from? For someone as evasive as I was these days, I had the sneaking feeling my own questions had been avoided. My fear of the answers was apparently stronger than my desire to find out because when Shep started stroking my hair and eased me back against the couch, I let it all go.

After I closed up the library on Saturday, I spent the afternoon with the O'Reillys.

"Mackie, you're so quiet today," I pointed out while playing with magnetic tiles with Boo. Mackie had barely even glanced in my direction since I'd arrived. "Is everything okay?"

She gave me a tight smile. "Yes, actually, there's been some good news on the adoption front."

My heart sank. *So soon? No news could be good news on the adoption front,* I thought. Then, *That's so selfish of you. Think of Terabithia!*

"Oh, really? And what's that?"

"There's a couple who's interested. Jeff and I are meeting with them on Monday. Dodie, are you all right? You look really pale."

"Yes, I, well, it's hard to think of . . . no, I mean, it's really, it's really—" God, was I going to burst into tears? No, I was not! I swallowed hard and squeaked out, "Promising."

"We thought so too," said Mackie, looking about as miserable as I felt.

"What do you know about them?"

"Let's see: the husband teaches paleontology at Fairfield University, and the wife works at a nonprofit that specializes in microfinance in third-world countries." Mackie handed me a photo. "That's Jed and Eileen right there."

He seemed fit, like a runner, with tidy, close-cropped hair on the sides and more height on top. His eyes were kind. His wife had a mumsy haircut, but she didn't look mumsy. There was something about her mouth that seemed tart, maybe even cruel. I was about to air my concern when I noticed Mackie's expression.

I . . . I couldn't do it. She looked so . . . hopeful.

"They seem like they'd be nice, right?"

Something inside me cracked a little as I whispered, "Sure."

After an awkward moment, I offered to come on Monday. "Give you and Jeff a second opinion? Er . . . um . . . third opinion? Or watch Boo so you and Jeff can focus?"

"Thanks, dear, but that's all right. It might be better if there aren't too many of us so Terabithia doesn't get overwhelmed. Besides, he's so enamored of you he probably wouldn't pay a scrap of attention to Jed and Eileen."

"You're going to introduce them to Terabithia?" This was all moving so . . . fast . . .

Mackie's brow furrowed. "You think it's too soon? Maybe Jeff and I should meet with them first, now that you mention it . . ."

"Good idea," I said solemnly. If Jed and Eileen met Terabithia, they'd be goners. But I was so sick of my sabotaging self by then that I had to get out of there. "Well, listen, I should be heading home, but let me know how it goes on Monday, okay?"

"Of course I will."

"Out of curiosity, what time is your meeting?" I asked. Mackie was looking at me strangely. "I want to make sure not to call you then and interrupt," I explained.

"They'll be here around three thirty."

I gave her a hug. "Good luck."

On Monday after school, it was a particularly nice day for a drive. The quickest route home would sort of take me past Mackie and Jeff's. I couldn't help but notice that it was 3:07. *Maybe I'll just sneak a little peek at Jed and Eileen,* I thought. Only a teeny one.

It was best to be unobtrusive. I didn't want to screw things up, after all. (Okay, well, I sort of did, but I wasn't *actually* going to act that crazy.) To be extra careful, I parked my car down the street, hopped the fence over the neighbor's yard, and slunk around the back of Mackie and Jeff's house. I situated myself right under one of the living room windows in a flower bed, careful not to trounce any of the plants. Jed and Eileen were two minutes late. *Ha! Nice first impression,* I thought, pulling a book of short stories out of my purse. Might as well make use of my time.

A moment later, a blue minivan pulled up in the driveway. *Space for a kid,* I noted begrudgingly.

I couldn't see Jed and Eileen entering the house without leaving my perch and risking being spotted through the window, so I waited three torturous minutes while they made their introductions in the hall, and then Mackie and Jeff showed them to the living room couch. Jed was wearing a pale-blue-and-white-checked shirt and sky-blue pants. Eileen had on a long dress with a collar and flared sleeves. She looked like an escapee from a Laura Ashley cult. *That doesn't mean anything. You, of all people, should know not to judge a book by its cover.* I was going to be impartial, to make myself proud, I resolved, pushing aside the thought that spying on their meeting was not exactly . . .

What? What in the Henry Higgins?

Mackie leaned down and picked up Terabithia, who must have been in his exersaucer. It took everything in me not to bang on the window and yell, “I thought you weren’t going to introduce them!”

Jed’s and Eileen’s faces were only partially visible, but their posture made it clear: they were melting over Terabithia.

I reconsidered: Eileen’s mouth didn’t seem cruel after all. She might just not be very photogenic. I couldn’t deny that her eyes seemed kind too.

Nooooo . . .

After a few more minutes, while I alternated between feeling terrible and feeling reassured, Mackie turned, and Terabithia was now facing over her shoulder. Looking directly at me. Or at least at the top of my head and my eyeballs. He grinned. His mouth dropped open. I couldn’t hear through the soundproof glass, but as his jaw opened and shut twice, I knew he was saying “Dada!”

Ooooops. That was my cue. I ducked down as quick as a wink and crawled around the back of the house.

“Dodie, is that you?” Jeff called as I was about to vault the neighbor’s fence.

My face burned. “Um, yes.”

“Is everything okay? We weren’t expecting you today.”

“I was going to visit Terabithia, but then I remembered about—” I stopped before telling the lie. Of course I hadn’t forgotten about Jed and Eileen's visit. I came clean. "I was spying on Jed and Eileen," I confessed, ashamed.

Jeff's brow knitted. "They're about to leave. Why don't you sit in the kitchen, and I'll send Mackie in when they're gone?"

"Okay."

When Mackie came in, I tried to hold my tongue. "How did it go?" I asked, but then the words slipped out: "I thought you weren't going to introduce him."

"Well, we weren't, but then we would have needed a babysitter, and—"

"I would have been happy to babysit."

"I know you would have, but . . ." Mackie raised her eyebrows. "More to the point, what were you doing standing outside the window? Why were you spying?"

"I couldn't wait to find out what happened, but I knew you'd said it would be too many of us for me to come, so I thought I would . . . observe."

"Dodie . . ." Mackie trailed off, then stopped herself. "I know this is hard for you too."

"Mackie, I don't think I can bear the idea of Terabithia being somewhere else. I'm sorry—I know it's even harder for you as his grandparents than it is for me—but . . . I really want to adopt Terabithia myself," I blurted. "What do you think?"

Mackie blinked quickly twice. "Wow, Dodie. Wow. That's . . . that's a lot to take in. We've already started down this path with Jed and Eileen, for one thing. And I don't know if . . ." She trailed off, then seemed to think better of whatever she was going to say. "Let me talk to Jeff about it and get back to you, okay?"

"Of course," I said. But what I was thinking was, *Really? You know me so well. You've seen how much I care about him. What else do you need?* Then again, it was unfair and impatient of me to look at it that way. This was the only child of their only child. And there would never be another now.

Twelve

July 2008

“Hey, Dodie?” Geraldine said. “I’m looking for *The Good Thief*. It was a *New York Times* Notable Book last year. Do you have it?”

“Yeah, it’s in Fiction,” I said.

“No, it’s not,” she corrected me politely.

“It’s by Hannah Tinti. Did you look under *T* in Fiction?”

“Yep. No sign of it.”

“Hmm, I don’t think anyone took it out, at least not while I was here. Let me check, though.” I pulled a stack of library cards off the corner of my desk. Thumbing through them, seeing the dark-red date stamps—some from the lending library, some from other libraries where the books had lived in years past—made me smile.

When I realized that there were eleven more stacks of library cards nestled in the drawer, I stopped smiling.

“I can’t find *Netherland* either, even though I know Lula returned it last week,” Roberta added. “Do you know if someone checked it out again?”

I didn’t. I flipped uselessly back through the library cards. I’d thought my loosey-goosey system of stamping and collecting the library cards and then roughly remembering who had which book had worked fine. Apparently not.

"Here," Elmira said, materializing with a book in each hand.

"Hey, Elmira. I didn't even know you were here," I said.

"I got here about five minutes ago. Anyway, I heard your conversation, and I found those two books you were talking about. One was on the random book table, and one was misshelved in Narrative Nonfic." She handed them to Roberta and Geraldine. I stamped their cards and gave them back the books, feeling a little miffed at my own confusion.

"Thanks, Elmira. What would the library do without you?"

She beamed like the winner of a sweepstakes. My heart twisted in my chest. It took so little to make her happy. *So* little. And still, that emotionally celibate mother of hers kept letting her down. She had put Elmira in summer school even though her grades were some of the best in the class. That way, she and her equally lovely husband didn't have to be bothered entertaining Elmira when they could be lounging by the country club pool with her little brother tucked into childcare there. Or, in the case of Elmira's father, yelling at office underlings on his cell phone by the country club pool. "Maybe we need a better cataloging system," I mused.

"Or a cataloging system, period?" she joked.

"Yeah, I guess so," I conceded. "Any ideas?"

The spark in her eyes reignited. "What if we created an online catalog? And got a bar code reader? I can google how to link them. I know you don't really like using the electronic one, but it would make stuff a lot easier here."

"You're probably right. But I would still want my stamper."

"No one's taking away your stamper," Kendra said as she walked in and sat on the edge of the circulation desk. "Hi, Elmira. Trying to convince Dodie to enter the twenty-first century?"

"The stamper's not going anywhere," I announced.

"But it'll be obsolete once you have everything set up electronically."

"No, it won't."

"Explain," Kendra directed me. Elmira looked uncomfortable, like her little soul was warring between my romantic vision of a library and the practical reality of modern tech-savvy times.

"It's like . . . well, it's like . . . the United Kingdom," I sputtered.

"How so?" Kendra humored me.

"The bar code reader is . . . um . . . Parliament. It's a balanced system. It makes sense. It's more . . . newfangled. But there's still room for the . . . um . . . monarch."

“So the stamper is the queen of England?” Kendra clarified.

“Right.”

“Which one?” she asked.

“Maybe QE II. Although I don’t know, Victoria’s always been a favorite . . . it’s so hard to choo—”

Kendra and Elmira were cracking up. Oh. She was making fun of me. They both were. I blushed, tightening my grip on my stamper protectively.

“Anyway.” I changed the subject. “Elmira, would you be willing to help me out with getting the electronic catalog set up?”

“Yeah! Can I start now? I don’t have to be home for another hour.”

I pushed my laptop her way. “Sure. Do you want to start by entering in the names of the books, and then we’ll figure the rest out later?” I got her settled at the table with a glass of cold water, and she started typing away, listing books from memory. It was a relief to give her something to do, a reason to be out of her house. I was equally glad to be focusing on the library rather than what Mackie and Jeff would say to my spur-of-the-moment confession and offer. I read a few pages of the Zen master Thich Nhat Hanh’s *Being Peace* and tried not to fixate.

A few endless days later, Mackie called and asked me to come over.

"Jeff and I talked in detail about what you asked," she said when we were seated on the couch. "And we're honored that you would think of adopting Terabithia. It means so much to us. And it would have meant the world to Sullivan. But right now, we feel that we need to continue to explore Jed and Eileen's adoption."

I swallowed hard. "May I ask why?"

"Well, we know your intentions are good, but this is a huge thing to ask of someone. Jed and Eileen have been very forthright about the fact that they tried for ten years to have children and couldn't, and they want to be parents more than anything. They have been preparing for a child for a long time now. For the child's care, for school. They are ready to dive in. Whereas are you sure you want a child?"

"Yes," I said fervently.

"But do you want one right now? Are you ready?"

I frowned. *She's asking about money.* And I couldn't honestly say yes right then and there. Things had been tight. I was covering my bills and the library's, but barely.

Seeing my expression, she continued gently. "Do you want to do this on your own? You're in a new relationship. Hopefully it will work out. But think of the pressure it would put on that relationship to introduce a child. And if it doesn't work out—not that we have any reason to think it won't—are you prepared to be a single mother?"

"Sullivan did it."

"That's true. That's what she chose. She knew that it might make it harder for her to meet someone and that for the foreseeable future she would be putting Terabithia's needs before her own. Is that what you would choose?"

I was silent. It was a lot to consider. And obviously I hadn't thought through every aspect. But I certainly would now. One thing was clear, though: Mackie and Jeff were not going to wait around for me to figure it out. They were moving forward with Jed and Eileen. And it would be wrong of me not to be supportive of that choice. Especially for Terabithia. I sighed. "So what happens now?"

"We're going to start the adoption paperwork."

"Oh. Wow. That's a good thing, right?" I said through clenched teeth.

"Yes, I think so."

"Well, good then."

There was an awkward pause. She cleared her throat.

I let her off the hook. "I should go. Thanks for your honesty."

"Thank you for loving Boo and for such a generous offer," Mackie said, patting my shoulder. I gave Terabithia a hug and headed home.

As I was pouring myself a big, fat glass of

wine, Anoop rang the bell. He had a huge grin on his face.

"Anoop, I am so happy for you!" I said with my first real smile in days. "I've been hoping to be here when you delivered the mail so I could congratulate you."

"Thank you, Ms. Fairisle," he said. "She is a lovely girl, and I am lucky she said yes."

"So modest. She's a lucky girl herself. Your smile is evidence of that."

Anoop was shaking his head. "The smile is for you. The postcard is for you." He handed it to me with relish, and then hopped down the stairs two at a time.

The front was a sketch of a plane. Aside from my address, the back had only two words: "Coming home!"

"The great Coco returns!" I told Shep over pineapple shrimp fried rice that night.

He grinned. "Awesome! When?"

"A couple weeks from now."

"I can't wait to meet her and Mark."

"What do you think about meeting the rest of my family? Will you come with me?"

Shep nodded, dumping more rice from the pan onto his plate and mine. "Of course."

A shiver of excitement washed over me. This was a big deal. "Yay!"

"I know! I can't wait to get out of town."

Huh. That wasn't what I was expecting him to say. Although it was true for me, too, after Mackie's response. "Really? Chatsworth's summer charms not doing it for you?"

"No, it's not that. I don't know—it's been stressful lately."

"At work?"

Shep's face did a weird twitching thing. He paused for a little too long. "Yep, at work."

"Is something else wrong?"

"Nah, it's just dumb stuff." He waved his hand dismissively.

"Well, if there's anything you want to talk about, I'm here," I said, fishing a little bit.

Shep gave me a hug. "Thanks, Do. I'm good, though, really. And excited about the homecoming weekend."

Maybe it was my relief that he'd said yes to coming with me without even thinking about it. Or the idea that it wouldn't be fair to send him into my chatty family without knowing our history. It was time to tell him about Not Dad. "Shep, you know how whenever I tell you a story about Dad's kindness, you always smile at me and say I'm a chip off the old block?"

Shep smiled. "You are."

"Well, I'm not really a chip off his block."

"Sure you are. And you're modest just like him too."

"No, really. Dad is not my . . . I mean, Walter is not my real dad."

Shep's eyes widened.

"He's my stepdad."

"Oh." He was watching my expression carefully. "So, who's your real dad?"

"He left when I was four."

Shep didn't respond for a full minute.

"Are you mad?" I asked.

"No. But I'm surprised you didn't tell me sooner. Why didn't you say anything before?"

"I don't know. I guess I didn't want you to feel pressure when things were new with us."

"What do you mean, pressure?"

"Pressure to stay . . . so that you wouldn't hurt me."

Shep actually laughed. "Do, that's not a thing."

"Sure it is. You're a nice guy, and if you knew I'd had this feeling of abandonment before, you might stick around even if you were not that interested."

"What, like forever? No. That's definitely not something I would do. Or anyone else I know."

"So you *are* interested?" I joked, already desperate to change the subject.

"Not really. I'm just here for the pastries."

I swatted him.

"I do have some questions," he said. "Have you seen him since he left?"

"No, he's not in our lives. Hasn't been."

"Did you ever want to go talk to him? See what he had to say for himself?"

"Not really. I was already rejected by him once. I don't need to relive that feeling."

Shep looked pensive, as if he was adding things up in his head. "That must have done a number on you."

"Yeah, it did. It's hard for me to trust anyone I'm in a relationship with," I admitted.

Shep took my hands. "That's understandable. But you can trust me. And you can talk to me about anything, too, okay?"

I was silent. Maybe I should tell him about Terabithia. No. What was the point now? "Thank you."

"Yeah, sure. Now tell me more about the house you grew up in. Will there be awesome boy band posters on your walls? Will I be put in my own room, or will your parents let us share your canopy bed?"

"You sure it's a good idea to leave Shep with Maddie right after introducing them?" Mom asked, glancing into the den, where it looked like the two of them were having a Biggest Hand Gesture contest.

I grinned, stirring the hot spinach-and-artichoke dip until the cream cheese got all melty. "It's not as if I have a choice. I can't get a word in edgewise. Once Shep commented about whether the Yankees always faked crappy play at the beginning of the year to throw off the competition, Maddie was off and running about the Red Sox being bums . . . I was not about to get in the middle of *that*. They were making each other laugh, so I don't think it will get violent."

The doorbell rang. "Co!" I cried, hurtling to the front hall and flinging open the door.

"Do!" she shouted. "Mad!"

Soon Coco was in my arms. My baby sister! Through happy tears I could see that her hair was the longest it had ever been; it almost reached her waist, and it was thick and streaked with sun. When I finished hugging her, I threw my arms around Mark. His hair was longer too. Dad had come to join the crowded hugging party. Shep stood in the doorway from the den, smiling and letting us have our moment.

"How are you guys? Tell us everything!" Maddie demanded as we all headed for the couches.

"So you're Shep," Coco said, her eyes glimmering as she looked back and forth between us.

"That's right. Great to finally meet you both."

Later, as Shep and I watched Coco and Mark at the party, he murmured into my ear, "She looks different from the pictures you showed me. They both do."

Coco was gesturing with a drink. Her

bright-blue dress showed off the color of her eyes, and her hair was pulled off her face with two bobby pins. The high heat in the room had caused a few tendrils to escape. Mark's hand was resting gently on her back just above her waist; their connection was palpable even though neither of them was looking at the other.

Coco caught my eye and winked. I attempted to wink back. Watching her stifle a laugh at my ineptitude, I noticed that around her beautiful eyes was a set of tiny new lines radiating outward from the corners. Mark had a matching pair. The lines were so fine that they would have been imperceptible to anyone but a family member. Nonetheless, they were there, telling stories we had not yet heard of their experiences out in the jungle. Shep, my mother, everyone was right. They had changed.

There was something else too. Before their trip, Coco had always had a way of being charming and meek at the same time. When she told a story—and she was a great storyteller—she always gestured inward, toward her body, as if trying to hold in a secret or—more likely—as if ever so slightly embarrassed to be the center of attention.

Now, even though her shoulders sagged a little with jet lag, she swept the air with her fingers, making big circles outward as she described the terrain in this or that country or this or that person they had helped. It was Africa that had given her this new sense of confidence. It was also Mark.

He cocked his head to listen to what my dad was saying. Mark was an excellent listener. When Coco looked up at him and smiled, it seemed as though they were sharing a secret. My breath caught in my throat.

"You okay?" Shep asked. I nodded. I had almost forgotten he was standing right next to me.

"Yeah, I'm good," I said hastily, my voice rising an octave.

I missed Terabithia so badly. I thought about how he would reach up toward the windows until I lifted him and he could play with the shutters, babbling, "Wow wow wow wow," each time he opened and closed them. How many more times would we get to do that? How many more times would I get to make him giggle until he got the hiccups?

That night, the guys slept in the bedrooms while Maddie, Coco, and I had a sleepover on the couches downstairs. But first, we feasted on the leftovers—mostly the sweet ones.

"These petit fours are amazing," Coco said, putting one in her mouth from a plate with half a dozen more on it.

"They are," Maddie agreed. "What's in them, Do? Crack?"

"I think it's the almond. I used marzipan in between the layers and then apricot preserves."

"I think it's also not having had access to this level of indulgence in ages," Coco added.

"So, what now?" I asked her.

"Back to our lives here," Coco said.

"You think everything will be different?"

"Of course," she replied, smiling. "We're going to be parents."

"Wait, is there news?"

"Nothing concrete yet. Just moving through the stages we could while we were away. Next up is home visits and, hopefully soon enough, a referral."

"What does that mean, a referral?" Maddie asked.

"When they connect us to a particular child. And send his or her picture."

The three of us sat there in silence thinking about that for a moment. What it would be like to see the child—their child—for the first time. An image flashed in my mind: Sullivan, looking at Terabithia's picture for the first time. My mind could conjure up that picture easily, but what I couldn't imagine was what she had felt, the swelling of love and recognition. *Yes, that's my baby,* she might have thought. *I can't wait to go get him.* My stomach felt like lead. I pasted on a smile, though. I was excited for my sister—and for their future child.

Coco didn't seem to notice anything was amiss. "What about you and Shep?" she asked. "Have you guys talked about a timeline?"

"Not really. He definitely wants kids, but I don't think he's in a rush to have them." I remembered what he'd said about Quinn. Definitely not in a rush to have them.

"I meant marriage, but okay. Have you told him about what you want?"

"No. I don't want to put unnecessary pressure on things right now."

"But you see a future there, right?"

"I do."

"And do you think he does?"

"I really hope so."

"Well, don't wait too long to find out if he's serious," Maddie advised.

I flushed with annoyance. Who was Maddie—queen of the permanent present—to give me relationship advice? I forced a smile. "Don't worry, I won't."

On the drive home, I thought about Coco's adoption plans. It wouldn't be easy for them, but there was no question that they were ready for it. They had each other. And more important, in this case: they had Mark's aunt's money. *That's a horrible thing to think,* I reminded myself. But it was also a fact. They had spent very little on their humanitarian trip. Mark's inheritance meant they would have the means for the adoption costs as well as to raise a child. Mackie had only hinted at it, but talking to Coco made it clear: I couldn't do this without a lot of money. And I didn't have much to spare.

Elmira and I were chatting at the circulation desk when she noticed Mackie and Terabithia coming through the door. Elmira clapped her hands. "I finally get to meet the baby!"

I grinned at her; she sounded much older than she actually was sometimes. I couldn't believe they hadn't met before, but Mackie usually brought Terabithia on Saturday mornings, when he was in good form before he needed his nap. Elmira typically came after school and had to do chores on the weekend before she could sneak away.

"Hey, Boo." He held out his arms to me and toddled over. "I'd like to introduce you to a friend of mine. This is Elmira."

"Hiiii," he crooned, reaching out to touch her hair.

She shook his hand. "Hi. Nice to meet you."

He blinked a slow, decisive blink. I kissed him on the nose and brought him to his favorite corner, where the tubs of board books sat on the low shelves underneath the bulletin board.

"Want to find your book?" I asked. A big, gooey smile spread on his face. I squealed inside as his four little white bottom teeth appeared.

“Hand me that tub,” I said to Elmira. She put it on the floor in front of Boo. As usual, he rifled through for a minute, then grabbed the tub by its sides and turned it over so the books crashed to the floor. Nothing doing. “More!” he ordered. Elmira passed me the next tub. Again, he dumped them out on the floor.

“Fog! Fog!” he chanted, waving his arms like he was about to take flight. There, peeking out from the bottom of the pile, was his all-time favorite: *The Piping-Hot Frog Book.* Each time after he left, I buried it at the bottom of the tub to make the hide-and-seek more fun for his next visit.

Then we would read the book. Today, Elmira did the honors.

“It’s our luck that you moved here and that you’re taking such good care of us,” Mackie told me. “And I don’t simply mean with books.”

I plastered a smile on my face. “Thank you. That’s very kind of you.” Somehow, the words seemed hollow, like some kind of consolation prize, even though it was the kind of thing I would have longed to hear before Terabithia came along.

Thirteen

August 2008

Shep had planned a surprise trip for our six-month anniversary. (Well, the six-month anniversary of our first meeting. He said he couldn't quite wait for the anniversary of our first date . . . and who was I to argue?) I wasn't even allowed to pack for myself because he had been so determined to keep the details a secret. I wondered if I would end up wearing lingerie around on the street somewhere. My only request had been that he not take me camping, although he was already well aware of my feelings on the subject. It wasn't that I didn't like being physically active in the outdoors. I really did. It was more that I liked to be physically active in the outdoors and then take a shower. And go to the bathroom in a real bathroom. As often as I wanted.

I switched my cotton pajamas with pink whales on them for a pink sundress. When I got downstairs, he looked as excited as when he was about to go sailing on a brand-new boat. The car was already packed, and two bowls of oatmeal—the good kind that took a half hour to prepare—were steaming on the table, topped with trickles of brown sugar and a handful of blueberries.

"Happy anniversary, honey," Shep said, kissing me on the cheek.

"Happy halfiversary, Shep," I said, feeling like Hanukkah had come early. We ate our breakfast in silence, holding hands. There had been a shift lately. Ever since going home with me, he seemed lighter, more present again.

There was no picnic basket in the back of the car, which meant that we were going somewhere with delicious food. Even though I had just eaten, I was excited to find out what would be next.

"Shoot, Shep, I'm sorry," I said when I woke up more than an hour later. "I didn't mean to fall asleep."

"That's okay. I like my surprises to be really successful."

"Well, this one will be, because I have no idea where we are."

At that moment, we were turning into the driveway of an inn. My eyes scanned for a sign. "There isn't one," Shep told me, reading my mind. "But in about two minutes, you'll know where we are."

The reception area was dressed in nautical blue with honey-colored rafters and crisp white moldings around the windows. We were near the water!

"Welcome to the Inn at Mystic," the frosted-haired woman behind the counter greeted us, smiling warmly. Her face was naturally tan, her cornflower-blue eyes (the color of a Constable sky) gleaming as if our visit was her delight.

"Mystic!" I cried, throwing my arms around Shep. He *loved* Mystic. I had been dying to visit ever since he started telling me stories of all his wonderful childhood memories going there with his brothers and his mom and dad. He hugged me back, one of his special Shep hugs that made me forget about the reception lady. She had the discretion to be rifling through some papers in a file on her desk, unable to stifle a grin.

"Hello," Shep said to her. "Jameson. Shep Jameson." He stuck out his hand. The woman looked vaguely surprised at his friendliness but recovered and shook hands with him.

"Here you go." She proffered our keys on a blue-and-white grosgrain ribbon. "Have a nice day. Please let me know if you need anything."

"Thank you," Shep and I said in unison.

I pushed open the door to our room and gasped as I caught a view of the harbor through the windows directly in front of me. "Shep!" I cried, racing to press my nose against the glass.

"Look, Do," Shep said as he discovered the rest of the room. "A fireplace!" I clapped my hands and knelt in front of the hearth, imagining its warmth radiating over us later that night. Shep had disappeared through two doors to explore the bathroom.

"Honey, get in here," he called, his voice sounding far away.

"Not till you're done," I joked, rounding the corner and stopping dead in my tracks. "Oh! My! Goodness!"

Shep was nodding with a wicked smile on his face. A deluxe whirlpool sat on one side of the bathroom, beckoning for bubbles to cover the gleaming white marble and for us to slip inside. "We could just . . . ," Shep suggested.

I gave him a huge smooch and found the superhuman restraint to say, "Mmmm . . . we'll have plenty of time after it gets dark."

"What if I don't want to wait?"

I caved. "Hmm, maybe you're right."

Then Shep was the one who looked reluctant. "No, you're right—we should go," he agreed. "I can't wait to show you the town."

He unzipped the bag he'd packed for me—which was sitting on a gorgeous antique canopy bed with jacquard pillows and a cotton bedspread with swirly patterns and million-thread-count sheets—and threw me a light sweater. "Let's go!"

The weather couldn't have been more picture perfect; it was cool and crisp and salty. Shep shared stories from family vacations in Mystic as we stopped into the places he loved, like the toy store and nautical souvenirs store and fudge store. (Okay, we more than just stopped in there.

The owner let us sample every flavor, and we still ended up buying a pound for ourselves and half a pound each for about sixteen of our closest friends back in Chatsworth.)

We managed to find room to eat lobster rolls at a restaurant overlooking the water. The thing is, you've never had a lobster roll until you've been to New England. They used these hot dog buns that were flat on the sides, buttered and grilled them, then filled them with succulent meat tossed in just a little mayonnaise with some spices and sometimes a bit of chopped-up celery. Real lobster rolls celebrated the beautiful simplicity of the crustacean—it was so good you didn't need to dress it up. I ate every single scrap of mine plus my shoestring fries and most of Shep's.

The next surprise he'd planned was a half-day trip on a tall ship. We turned our faces up to the sun, full of salt and lobster and the sea air we were sucking in as if we couldn't get enough.

What was weird was that as we were coming back into the harbor, the sun still high above us, Shep looked a little green around the gills. Shep *never* looked green around the gills. Definitely not on a boat. (As opposed to me, who did feel a little woozy if we were ever anchored and rocking on the swells for more than a few minutes. In fact, I'd been concerned about going out on the choppy water the day after a storm, but Shep had assured me I'd be fine.) "You okay, honey?" I asked him. "You look a little funny."

He shook himself. "I'm fine. Maybe that lobster roll was too much, especially with all those fries."

Now I was genuinely worried. First of all, Shep had a stomach of steel. Second, I had eaten most of Shep's fries. He knew I had. Something was fishy besides our location.

I twisted around looking for a crew member to flag down for a bottle of water, figuring Shep might be getting dehydrated. Everyone else had deboated, and the nearest crew member was tying a rope around the thing that you tie a rope around to keep the boat from floating away from the dock. "Stay here for a second. I'll get you some water," I said, but when I looked over at Shep, he had already moved. He was still right next to me except he was now on one knee.

I sat back down. I started breathing very, very slowly. Shep took my left hand in both of his and said, "Dodie." Just like that, like a sentence, with all the certainty in the world.

"I'm obviously not one for big speeches, but I think we understand each other without me having to say what I feel. You know more about me than anyone else in the world now—my good parts and my bad parts—and I hope you'll get to learn everything else over the rest of our lives. And I know you, all of your good parts and—lucky son of a bitch that I am—the fact that you're pretty much the best person on the earth and hardly have any bad parts, only enough to make you human in everyone else's eyes except mine.

"Along with each day since I met you, the times I've spent at Mystic with my family have been some of the best ever. I couldn't think of a more perfect place to ask you to make this the new best day of my life and to ask you to spend the rest of your life with me."

He reached into the pocket of his peacoat and pulled out an antique-looking purple velvet box. By this point, I had stopped breathing through my nose and was trying hard not to faint dead away.

"Do," he said, opening the box toward me, "will you marry me?"

"Holy crap!" I gasped, and then I said it again! I hugged him so hard that he had to pat me on the back to release him.

"Yes! Yes! Yes! Yes!" I cried over and over as he slipped the ring onto my finger.

For the rest of the afternoon, we soared around in a daze like giddy kids. We got big cones of coffee whirly-twirly with chocolate jimmies and considered calling our parents, deciding to wait until after dinner so that we could savor a few hours of the little bliss bubble around us before our families very good-naturedly inserted questions of when and where and how into it. I reveled in the unfamiliar pressure of the ring around my finger as Shep—my fiancé!—held my hand.

He'd chosen an old-fashioned seafood restaurant for dinner. "I'll have two dozen oysters, the baked stuffed shrimp . . . and could you leave us the dessert menu so we can mull it over?" Shep requested.

"The salt air will do that to you," our waiter said, but I suspected it didn't have anything to do with the salt air.

"You don't look so green around the gills anymore," I teased him after I'd ordered the clam chowder and the broiled scrod.

"Nope," Shep—my fiancé!—concurred. "And besides, I have to make up for my fries you ate before."

All that food and a summer fruit crisp later, we headed back to the inn. I couldn't wait any longer to call my parents. "I wish there was a way to conference in my sisters," I said.

It took my dad several rings to pick up. They were probably driving home from dinner and a movie with their friends, a Saturday-night ritual. "Hi, honey," he said. "How was your day?"

"Dad, I'm engaged!" I yelled through the phone, loudly enough that my mother could hear from the seat beside him. My mom said, "Yay, Dodie and Shep!" as if we'd just won a contest. Which, of course, we felt like we had.

My dad's voice was deep and warm. "I'm so happy for you two. Give Shep a handshake for me." I was going to do a hell of a lot more than that when we got back to the inn, but not on my dad's behalf.

"Give him a hug from me!" my mom trilled. "Pass me the phone, pass me the phone."

Dad resisted. "I want to hear the story too." I could hear the rustling as they debated it.

"Guys," I interrupted, smiling, "why don't you call me when you get home, and then you can each get on one of the phones and hear the story at the same time like usual?"

Maddie was out, so I reached her on her cell phone. She freaked. Coco and Mark practically hooted with joy. I thought I heard them giving each other high fives. Super cheesy and adorable.

Then Shep called his parents. His father said, decorously but earnestly, "That's great, son," and his mom cried and asked to speak with me to tell me how happy I made Shep. Then he called all his brothers. My parents called back, and I told them the story. Well, except for the "holy crap" part. Shep and I had already agreed we could omit that from the official history but that he was welcome to use it as leverage when we were married if I ever insisted he accompany me to a chick flick instead of watching the big game.

Then I gave him his halfiversary present: the copy of *The Lady of the Camellias* I had bought with Maddie before Shep and I even got together. "This is my favorite book."

"Oh, wow, really? The librarian's favorite book? I've seen this in your reading pile but wasn't sure if you had actually gotten to it yet."

"I reread it every so often."

"I can't wait to read it too."

"It's beautiful, but it's really sad. So maybe not right now when we're celebrating our engagement!" I laughed.

"You were beautiful and sad when I met you," Shep mused, stroking my hand.

"I was."

"Are you happier now?" he asked.

"Much." I paused. "I miss her, though."

"I know you do."

"Sullivan would be so pissed at me if she knew I was talking about her right now, of all times, instead of enjoying this moment." I couldn't help but smile.

"Yeah, and she'd be right."

"So let's stop talking and get in the Jacuzzi!"

I insisted on driving home on Sunday—partly because Shep deserved a rest after all his great planning . . . partly because I'd deprived him almost entirely of sleep for two nights.

Propping my hands right up on that steering wheel also gave me a great view of my sparkly ring. Shep had chosen a Victorian princess ring.

A beautiful little diamond nestled in a bed of ornate leaves, the whole setting dainty enough not to look silly or showy on my finger. He could have proposed with a pipe cleaner ring for all I cared. But it did mean something that he had chosen what I would have desired most out of a thousand different styles and settings.

"I can't believe you kept the secret. I had literally no idea," I said. "Where was the ring all that time?"

"I didn't let it out of my sight," he grinned. "It was in my pocket."

"You know I used to get seasick. How did you know I wouldn't throw up on the boat?"

"I didn't."

"What if I had?"

Shep laughed. "I probably wouldn't have proposed to you right then."

My cell rang. "Hey, Mackie. Did you hear the news through the Chatsworth grapevine? I was about to call you."

"You heard the news?" Mackie asked. My brow furrowed. *Huh?*

"About our engagement," I stumbled on. "Shep and I are so excited."

"You two are engaged?"

"Yes!"

"That's . . . that's great," she said, as if coming to. "I'm really pleased for you." There was an odd tone to her voice. My stomach flipped.

"Is everything okay? Are you and Jeff all right? How's Boo? I can't wait to tell him the news!"

"Yes, yes, we're fine. Give me a call tomorrow, would you? I should go. Congratulations. We're really pleased for you," she repeated before hanging up.

"Do?" Shep asked, glancing over. "What's going on?"

"I don't know. She sounded weird."

"What did she say?"

"That she's really pleased for us . . ."

"That makes sense."

"And something about having news."

"Oh, do you think it's about Terabithia being adopted?"

"Maybe," I replied, my voice cracking.

Shep patted my hand. "That would be good news, right?"

I was silent.

"Right?" Shep said more insistently.

"Yes!" I said, so loudly we both jumped.

Mackie had said "Call me tomorrow," but there was no way I could sleep until I knew what was going on.

"Dodie, hi. Sorry about before."

"That's okay. Was there . . . anything you wanted to tell me? I was afraid maybe you had news and I cut you off."

"There is news, actually," she said slowly.

My heart stuttered.

"Jed and Eileen have decided to move forward with the adoption. They've already completed the series of home visits, and they're starting the final paperwork, which means that in three weeks the adoption will be official, and Terabithia will be . . ."

Mackie and I were both sniffling. She never finished her sentence.

Terabithia will be . . . theirs.

Terabithia will be . . . gone.

After I forced out a congratulations and Mackie pretended to appreciate it, I hung up the phone and sat staring at it until Shep pulled it out of my hands.

"It's going through?"

"Yeah."

He squeezed my shoulder. "It'll be okay."

"I know," I said, standing up to look him in the eyes. We had a lot to celebrate, I reminded myself. Then Shep leaned down and whispered, "We're getting married," and it was hard not to smile. He stroked my hair, and I melted, tipping my face up into the kiss of my future husband.

I'd been staring at the ceiling since early morning, changing positions every so often in hopes that I would fall back to sleep. No dice. I gave Shep a kiss on the cheek, and after spending a few delicious seconds remembering what it was like to be in bed with my new fiancé (!), I threw on a dress and headed into the library. The book I wanted was *The Crimson Petal and the White*. I reread the scenes I was looking for, scenes in which the heroine of the story cares for a little girl who is not her own. Granted, her name was Sugar, she was a prostitute (but with a heart of gold!), and she'd kidnapped the child. No one realized how good of a mother she was when really she was better suited for it than the girl's parents or anyone else in the novel.

I heard a tap on the window. "She's in there!" There was giggling and what sounded like a squeal. I stood up.

"There's the new fiancée!" Kendra and Geraldine cried in unison through the window. "Open the door!"

I smiled. "Come on in!"

The two fell on me in a group hug.

Kendra was grinning ear to ear, toting a bag. "We thought this called for a celebration before you start a wedding diet," she joked, knowing I couldn't stay away from caloric food for very long. "It's from—"

"Billybee's!" I cried.

"Of course you'd recognize the green stripes on the bag!"

I moved the *Lord of the Rings* trilogy someone had left on the table to make space for our impromptu party. Kendra pulled out a bowl with plastic wrap over the top. They had bought an entire banana pudding! Shalom, breakfast! She threw a plastic spoon at each of us, and we dug in.

"Are you so excited?"

"Of course!"

"What's wrong?" Geraldine asked.

"Nothing! I'm just a little in shock."

"Yeah, I can see how a curly-haired, blue-green-eyed, sexy, book-loving, manly man becoming your husband might do that to a girl," Kendra teased. "Not that we didn't see it coming."

"Really? Cuz I didn't."

"Well, you've been really preoccupied lately with another little fellow," Kendra pointed out.

I wondered if she had heard the news yet from Mackie. I studied her expression. Guess not.

"So have you thought about when?" Geraldine asked, dropping a chunk of banana on the table, spooning it up, and downing it.

"Ew," Kendra said.

"What? Ten-second rule."

"I'm thinking next fall," I answered.

"Fall weddings are so romantic!" Kendra crooned.

My friends stayed for an hour, chatting about what style my wedding would be and how we could incorporate books into the centerpieces. My thoughts kept wandering.

I wasn't sure why I hadn't told them about Terabithia. I still didn't quite believe it myself.

I spent the rest of the day picking at the banana pudding and stressing about the fact that Mackie and Jeff had taken Terabithia to get some paperwork done for the adoption, which meant one less day I could see him out of the short three weeks or so I had left.

When Shep came back over after basketball with the guys, I tried to cheer up and jabbered a bit about wedding plans. Pretty soon, he caught on. "Do," he said heavily, "I know you're excited about our engagement. We'll have time to celebrate that. Right now, it would be crazy to deny you're grieving. We have months and months to plan the wedding. For now, focus on Terabithia. You should spend as much time with him as you can."

"Thank you," I murmured, throwing my arms around him. And maybe it was how considerate he was being. Or the fact that now we were supposed to do everything together, including making decisions. It had been long enough. "Shep, there's something—"

My cell rang from somewhere in the couch cushions. "Sorry, just a sec." I dug it out. "It's Coco. Mind if I get this?"

"Yeah, go ahead," he said, reaching for the remote and instantly tuning me out in the way that so many people (besides me) have when watching sports.

"Hey—" I started to greet her.

"Her name is Sianeh! And I have her picture!"

"Oh my gosh. Oh my gosh. The referral came through?"

"The referral came through!"

"Send me her picture *immediately!* I'm putting you on speakerphone so I can go to my computer."

"Do, why don't you have a smartphone?"

"I know, I know. But just please email it. And tell me more."

"She's the cutest ever! Wait till you see her. I can already tell she's a sweet baby with a fiery little personality from the picture. She's six months old and from a village in central Liberia."

"Does this mean you can go meet her?"

"Yes! The adoption agency is going to help us start making our arrangements. Do, I can't believe it. It's all happening so fast. I will be meeting her in a matter of weeks!"

"Yeah, it seems like you started the process such a short time ago. Doesn't it take a lot longer to get a referral?"

"Usually, yeah. Liberia has tended to have shorter wait times than, say, Ethiopia, but it still seems superfast."

"Why do you think that is?"

"I'm wondering if it's because of some of the people we met when we were there. I don't know how much influence they have, but the day before we left, we definitely ended up at a lunch with some people who were pretty high up in the government there."

"Wow. How did that happen?"

"You know how Mark's gramma Bessie was Liberian? She used to tell Mark's dad and his aunt Rose all these stories about the poverty there and how she would always try to send money back to her family after she came to America, even in the beginning when she and his grampa Kambili had almost nothing. Rose studied abroad in Monrovia during college. She used to go back to Liberia every few years, and she started donating a lot of money to Liberian charities when she got really rich."

I was clicking like crazy while she talked, trying to get the picture to download and open.

Finally!

Oh, my heart. Staring out from the picture was . . . Sianeh. I saw immediately what my sister meant. Sianeh was looking at the camera with her head cocked a little to the side like she was saying, *Gotcha!* to the photographer instead of the other way around. There was the hint of a smile around the corners of her lips, and her eyes were warm but serious with a gaze that seemed strong and direct for a six-month-old. My sister's forever daughter. My future niece.

"What does Sianeh mean?"

"Sweet journey," Coco said quietly, her voice breaking.

Fourteen

September 2008

"Hi, Mackie."

"Am I on speakerphone?"

"Yes, sorry, I'm driving." I was on my way home from school.

"Oh, okay, be safe. Do you want to call me back?"

"No!" I blurted. "I mean, not to worry, I do this all the time. I'm almost home anyway. Is everything okay?"

"It's fine, it's just—Jeff and I need to go to the bank and get some of Sullivan's paperwork out of the vault there. Do you think you could come here and watch Terabithia till dinnertime?"

I was supposed to open the library. Kendra was on vacation, visiting her mom in Florida, or I would have asked her to fill in for me. Geraldine was at a class for her library science master's. It wouldn't hurt for me to miss one afternoon, I decided. I'd nip home, put up a sign, and then head to Mackie's.

"Sure, I'll be there in about twenty minutes."

By the time Mackie and Jeff returned, I had already fed Terabithia some pasta with sauce and cheese. It was all over his bib, his face, and his fingers. He was waving his spoon around, saying, "Yummy basta Dada, yummy basta Dada. Bissia more! Bissia more!"

Mackie bent down and kissed his 'fro. "Are you having a good dinner?"

"Yeah," Terabithia said.

"You're such a natural with him," Mackie observed as I put another few pieces of penne in front of him.

My heart leaped. Even the slightest hint that they saw how strong the connection was between us gave me hope. Unfounded hope, probably. But still, I couldn't help it.

"We picked up his passport from the bank vault," Jeff told me. "Sullivan had to get one to bring him over here from Ethiopia. Of course, it makes sense. It's just, you don't think about a baby needing a passport like that, do you?"

"Can I see it?"

"Sure." Jeff pushed it across the table, avoiding pockets of sauce and cheese.

I opened it. Boo was looking slightly up, probably above the camera to where Sullivan was holding a toy or making a face to get him to smile. His eyes sparkled. He looked happy.

A wave of jealousy at Coco's situation hit me. She could look at the picture of her child, and it was a beginning. Here I was, looking at a picture of Terabithia, trying to prepare myself to say goodbye soon.

How was I going to get through the next few weeks?

Elmira came up to me after school, her eyes wide. "Is the library going to be open today?"

"Yes, something came up yesterday at the last minute." I was irritated, but I hoped she hadn't heard it in my voice. It had just been one day. Was that such a big deal? I mean, shop owners and other volunteers had conflicts all the time. And I'd put up a sign.

"Okay," she said, taking a deep breath. "Good. Because I need some books for my project on—" She stopped, afraid that she was holding me up. I guessed the expression on my face wasn't my friendliest. "Well, anyway, I'll see you there," she finished.

As she walked away, Benton was coming toward me. He probably wanted a full report on Kendra's vacation. Which I didn't have. I'd missed a call from her while at Mackie and Jeff's and had been too tired to call her back when I got home.

"Hi, Dodie."

"Hi, Benton."

"Everything okay at the library?"

"Yeah. Why wouldn't it be?"

"Oh, I stopped by yesterday and saw the sign.

Wanted to make sure nothing was wrong."

What was this, the Dodie Fairisle Schedule Inquisition? "The library's fine. And I don't know how Kendra's vacation is going. I'm not in charge of everyone and everything in this town. So don't bother asking me," I snapped and turned away.

"But I didn't ask—" Benton protested.

I locked myself in the teachers' lounge bathroom and splashed water on my face. What was wrong with me? Why was I being so mean? On the other hand, why couldn't people cut me a little slack?

Mackie, Jeff, and I were laughing so hard we couldn't catch our breath. Portraits for Little Ones had had a cancellation, so we'd scooped up the slot for a big farewell photo session with Terabithia. To remember him by, at this age, when he was still here with us. And probably, in my case, to gaze at while shooting for the world record in therapeutic ice cream consumption after he was gone.

The photographer had brought out a big stuffed bear. It faced Terabithia, looking at him placidly. Terabithia was hamming it up, looking back at the bear, sitting on its lap, touching its nose, saying, "Hi, Bear. Smi-yuh, Bear. Cheese, Bear. Peez, Bear!" The bear did not seem amused, but we were.

"Oh God!" I exclaimed when the photographer went to change the scenery to a big ABC block Terabithia could sit on. "It's already four thirty!" It would take me at least ten minutes to get home if I left right away.

"Go, go ahead," Jeff urged. I kissed them and Boo on the cheeks. Boo started crying as I left, crooning, "Why Dada leave?"

Major chest pains.

I raced home, but it was almost five by the time I got the sunroom unlocked and ready for visitors. A handful of friends waited on the front steps.

"I'm so, so sorry."

"It's okay, Dodie," Mike said, patting me on the shoulder as his daughter slipped past me and headed for the crayons and construction paper.

"No problem," Marvela Jeffers agreed, placing her knitting books on the counter to renew them.

I felt a twinge of guilt. Maybe other hopefuls had come by and hadn't been able to wait. But as more people streamed in and the chairs filled up, that sunny buzz of library love pushed away the darkness falling outside the windows, and it seemed like everything would be all right after all.

The date was fixed: Eileen and Jed were going to take Terabithia on October 3. *Not take. Give a new, loving home,* I kept reminding myself. It wasn't very helpful. I contemplated some drastic scenarios including Boo-napping. I couldn't go through with it. I wished I'd had a chance to adopt Boo myself. I felt like I'd abandoned him in some way. And Sullivan too.

Strangely, what occupied my thoughts when I wasn't stressing about Terabithia were memories of Not Dad right before he left. One day, when I was reshelving in the library, the window caught my eye. It had been raining off and on all day, and the trees were suffused in that green freshness that the gray light always brought out. I always thought of those days as English countryside days. I touched my finger to the pane as if I could feel the drops of rain that trembled on the other side.

It reminded me of something. I closed my eyes and saw myself in a green rain slicker with a hood and matching green-and-yellow duck boots. My arm was aching from stretching upward so far; Not Dad was very tall, and his hand was in mine.

"I'm taking you somewhere I know you'll like," he said. My heart was beating like a little bunny's. I *never* got a day with him all by myself! And now he had a surprise for me too!

It felt like we walked forever. I was sure it was only a few blocks, but time and the distance stretched as it always did when you were small and didn't know where you were going.

I watched the ducks on my feet as we crossed the street and met the sidewalk.

"Look up," he said.

Perched next to the sidewalk was a tall red rectangular thingy. A telephone booth! Like the one in my book about the little girl in London who saved dogs from mean owners! I ran up to it, peeking in all the rain-clouded little windowpanes. The paint was so *red.* Tomato red. Fire engine red. Happy-day-with-good-surprises red!

He pulled the door open for me. Then I could see what the rain had hidden—inside the booth, on almost every surface, books were lined up. Near the bottom were picture books, many of them turned on their sides so they would fit on the narrow shelves. Most of the other shelves held books for adults—lots of paperback novels, a few books with hard covers and pictures of fancy-looking men and women on the spine, even some cookbooks. I clapped my hands with delight and turned in circles inside the space, marveling that someone had done this, had made a library in a little phone booth for everyone to use!

It began to rain hard, and he was standing outside since only one of us could fit. Drops bounced off his umbrella. "Time to go."

I made an effort to remember all the turns we took to get home. Maybe he would take me back there. It was good to know how, though. Not that I would go by myself at four years old, but in case Mom didn't know where it was. He was barely speaking to Mom anymore. Something bad was happening between them that I didn't understand.

Three days later, he was gone.

My front doorbell rang, shaking me from my reverie.

"Kendra! Welcome back."

Her smile seemed strained. "Hey, Do." She kissed me on the cheek.

"Want a cup of tea?" I offered.

"Sure." She set her purse down on the living room couch.

"How's your mom?"

"Great," Kendra said. "She's taken up Krav Maga."

"Uh . . . what?"

"It's like this Israeli form of self-defense. Martial arts, you know."

I definitely did not know.

"She showed me how to choke an attacker with his own T-shirt." She smiled.

"That sounds . . . helpful."

"Well, my mom's only in her late fifties, and she lives in Boca, but she wants to be prepared for when she's an older lady."

I wasn't quite sure what to say to that. "Did you get some good beach time?"

"We mostly went to the pool. There's a swim-up

bar in her complex. I've never been hit on by so many men in AARP."

I laughed. "That must have been a big ego boost."

"Yeah, it really was."

"Here, let's take our tea into the library," I said, handing her a cup.

We headed for the two wing chairs in the corner, and I pushed back the stack of books on the table to make room for our saucers to fit as well as a plate of chocolate chip cookies that I'd picked up at the store since I hadn't had time to bake in eons. We both sipped in silence for a few minutes, lost in our own thoughts.

"Dodie, there's something I want to talk to you about."

"Sure. What's up?"

"Mackie told me the adoption is going through."

"Yeah. I know."

"Why didn't *you* tell me?" she asked.

"It's only been a few days."

Kendra squinted at me.

I felt my face color. "I . . . I . . . guess I didn't want to believe it," I whispered.

Kendra threw her arm around me and squeezed. "I know how close you've gotten to him. It must be really hard for you."

"Thank you."

"You have been really distracted."

"I don't think I've been that distracted."

"Hmmm . . ."

I frowned. "You think I've been distracted?"

"Did you know I've been dating someone recently?"

"Really?"

"I'll take that as a no."

"I'm sorry, Kendra. Who is it? God, Motor-mouth Benton must be in a tailspin." I felt a twinge of guilt at how curt I'd been with him about her.

Kendra didn't smile at my joke. "He doesn't mind, actually."

"Tell me about this new man!"

"Not right now. There's something else serious I want to talk to you about."

"Okay." My stomach turned.

"It's this place." She gestured around the sunroom.

"What about it?"

"Well, I ran into Lula at the store the other day, and she mentioned that she's come here a couple times with the kids on weekdays after school and it's been closed."

"There was actually only one weekday when I had to close and one where I opened an hour late."

Kendra ignored me. "When I was in the library at school the other day, Cameron mentioned that he and his dad had tried to come on Saturday, but it was all locked up.

"And I didn't have very good service where I was this weekend, but when I got back, I saw a message from you that said"—she reached into her purse and called up the text—"Can't make it to the library. Will you take over for me today? Thanks a mill." She raised her eyebrows expectantly.

When I had gotten back from Little Duck Park, I had seen with horror that the library was still closed. I had no idea Kendra was going away again right after coming back from Florida. I had assumed she would be around because she always had been. Of course, once I had realized what had happened, I was hoping that the fickle gods of text messaging had eaten my message and that Kendra would never know about my slipup.

"I shouldn't have assumed," I admitted.

"No, you shouldn't have. If I had known ahead of time, I would have tried to work something out—even though I can't promise I can drop everything an hour beforehand. And as it turns out, I had no idea. Neither did anyone else in town who schlepped over here with their hopes up."

I thought of Elmira's anxious face the day I had yelled at Benton. This place was her escape. Because of me, the library had been closed on two days with no explanation and had opened late on another day, all in one week. That was not good. I had been treating the library as a privilege, subject to my schedule, when I had opened it as a right the people of Chatsworth had come to depend on.

"Oh, man," I groaned. "I feel terrible."

Kendra gave me a sympathetic smile. "Listen, it happens. However . . . to make sure it doesn't happen again—"

"Oh, it won't! I'll make sure it doesn't."

"How will you do that? These are Terabithia's last three weeks here."

The hairs stood up on the back of my neck.

"If anything," Kendra barreled on, "you're going to be busier than you have been. You're going to want to spend all your free time with him. Not here in the library."

"That isn't true. I can do both."

"Well, you haven't been doing both very well lately from what I can tell. No offense," Kendra said.

I bristled. "Listen, it was three times. I've been rushing home after school, opening this place up no matter how much I want to get into my pajamas or go to the gym or bake banana bread with cream cheese frosting or slob around on a weekend. It's time consuming and expensive, and it's not like I'm getting paid to do this like you are. I wish everyone would get off my back!"

Kendra was quiet while I steamed. After a minute, she said, "Okay. That's all fair. And I know you don't need me to remind you that you chose this. It is a lot. Whether you realized how much you were taking on in the beginning or not, you're in the thick of it now. And it's obviously getting to you. I've never seen you so . . . well, so pissed before."

"I don't think I've ever been so pissed before," I agreed miserably.

"Well, the main reason I am here is to tell you that despite what you seem to think, you don't have to do this alone. I have an idea. I want to help you in a more official way. Let me take over the library for you for a while. I love helping out here. I would be glad to do it."

My mouth hung open. I closed it. "You think I need someone to take this place over for me entirely?"

"Honestly, yes."

"Listen, I sincerely appreciate the offer, but it's not necessary. I'd love to have you keep helping out, but I'm not going to turn the library over to you." I knew she was being nice, but the idea made me feel like throwing up. *My* library. I couldn't have anyone thinking I was failing. I couldn't let the people of Chatsworth down that way. Or myself.

"Why not? It would be totally temporary. Until after Terabithia, um . . ."

I put my hand up before she could repeat it. "Thanks, Kendra. I'll definitely think about it."

"I'm not kidding here, Dodie. This is important."

"I'm aware of that. That's why I set it up and have worked so hard to keep it going for the past year."

"Don't get upset again. I'm only trying to help. You can ask for more help, you know."

"You're already helping. I appreciate the fact that you take a couple shifts a week."

"That's not what I meant," Kendra said, looking at me from the side. "There are other ways I can help."

Did she mean money?

"What do you mean?"

"Well, I could make a financial contribution."

"Thank you, but no." I couldn't possibly take her money. It would complicate our friendship.

"Why not?"

"I want to do this on my own. I have to. For this place to be sustainable. Otherwise it's—no offense—a Band-Aid."

"Dodie, this isn't just about time or money. Something's up with you. I know there is. It's not just Terabithia. What else is going on?"

It didn't matter now if I told someone. The pressure of months of keeping it in was like air inside a balloon that kept getting pumped up further. It was ready to pop, and as soon as Kendra stuck a pin in, the secret burst out of me: "It *is* about Terabithia. I wish I was adopting him!"

I had said it out loud! A feeling of relief rushed over me. Someone else knew!

"I know."

My eyebrows lifted.

"I mean, I figured. Dodie, you are such a deeply caring person. And I know how much you loved Sullivan. But this isn't just a library. Or a job. This is a human being. It's forever."

"Of course it is, and it would be. That's what Sullivan would have wanted. Something permanent. And I feel like crud that I can't offer Terabithia that, or Mackie and Jeff. I feel like a failure."

"Why? How is this your fault?"

"I guess it's not. But I feel like, I don't know, if I had worked a few jobs and saved more money instead of going to art school . . . or if I had spent less time reading . . . or . . ."

"Come on, Do. How could you have known this situation would come up? How can you blame yourself for trying to do what you love or for trying to figure out what you want your life to be?"

I knew she was right. But that didn't change anything. Disappointment flooded my chest. It was exactly as I had thought. Telling someone hadn't helped. It only meant that someone else knew I had failed.

"What does Shep think about it?"

I looked away.

"He thinks it's not the right time, doesn't he?"

"Well, I haven't exactly told him . . . ," I admitted.

"What?"

"I haven't told him I was thinking of adopting Terabithia."

"Why the hell not? I mean, he's your fiancé, right?"

"Yes, but . . ."

"Were you seriously going to spring on him the idea of another person becoming part of your family at the last minute?"

"No. Even if it worked out, he would have had at least a few weeks' notice."

Kendra looked like she wanted to shake me. "That is bonkers. Beyond bonkers. A few weeks? That's nothing. This is a child."

"I know." I swallowed hard against the bitterness as tears slipped from my eyes. "But it doesn't matter anymore, anyway." It was over.

During the next few weeks, I made a concerted effort to be perfect about the library schedule, but I couldn't return all the smiles aimed at me by the relieved visitors. Resentment tightened my chest. This huge event was happening in my life, and I wasn't spending as much time with Boo as I wanted because I was expected in the library.

Although, a little voice tempted me, if I stopped being so full of pride—if I was even a little less full of pride—I could have handed the keys over to Kendra. For the first few days after we talked, she offered again to take more shifts. When I turned her down for the third time, she stopped trying. I knew she would only come now if I asked her. But I couldn't. I had to know whether I could juggle all the things in my life—a job plus a library plus a fiancé plus a baby (who wasn't even living with me, so it didn't fully count).

When I added all those things up in my head, it sounded crazy even to me. I was exhausted. I tried to put on a brave face for Shep when he came over after work to help me reshelve and tidy up the library or carry boxes of newly donated books to the front desk to be cataloged. Later, when I felt his hand on my hip as I started to drift off into a troubled sleep, the warmth would spread through me, and I would find the strength to stay awake long enough to remind him how much I loved him. The truth was we were barely seeing each other during the daylight, and when we were, Boo's imminent departure sat heavy between us. I should have been the happiest bride-to-be in the world. Instead, the thought of adding one more thing to my plate made me want to scream with terror.

Only a few more weeks, I would tell myself, but the idea of what would happen at the end of them was definitely not a comfort.

Fifteen

October 2008

October 1 came. Then October 2.

"Are you sure it's okay for me to show up tomorrow morning?" I asked Mackie, my voice trembling as I changed Boo into his pajamas.

"Of course," she said, patting my shoulder. I couldn't bear saying goodbye to him one single day sooner. "We'll see you at nine. Jed and Eileen will be here at ten."

At ten! I opened my mouth on the verge of asking if I could come at eight. Or seven. Or five.

At home, Shep put on *Never Been Kissed*, figuring it would cheer me up. It didn't. I was exhausted and wired at the same time. He tucked me in before hopping in the shower. I twisted and turned in my bed, trying to get comfortable, to shut my mind off, but memories of Terabithia streamed through like water. The sound of his laughter at his debut party. His fingers dipping into the peanut butter pocket on the cookie after Sullivan's funeral. Sitting cross-legged on the floor of the lending library while he dumped over the tubs until he found *The Piping-Hot Frog Book*. Pushing him on the swings, from our first trip to Little Duck Park when he was an inert little lump to now when he would pedal his legs to go higher and higher. Some part of him was mine, but after tomorrow he would be beyond my reach. I sucked in lungfuls of air, trying to steady myself with the reassuring scent of Shep's soaking-wet hair beside me. The hours crawled.

At eight forty-five the next morning, I was in my car.

"Do you want me to come with you?" Shep's voice was gravelly. He might have sounded like my very own Dark Knight, but he looked like a sexy angel with the sheet only covering his delectable bottom half.

"No, you sleep. I'll come straight home after," I promised.

"Okay. We'll go eat our faces off at a big brunch."

My hands were shaking as I turned the key in the ignition. I tried focusing on the music on the radio. I should have had Shep come with me. Or Kendra. I didn't know if I could do this on my own. No, I had to—for Boo. For Mackie and Jeff too.

I pulled into the driveway at 8:59 and rang the doorbell. No one answered. That was strange.

Mackie and Jeff came down the stairs.

I panicked. "Where's Boo? Did they come early? Is he gone already? Oh my God, he's gone, and I didn't get to say goodbye."

"No, he's here. I put him back down; he was so sleepy this morning I could hardly wake him in the first place."

Something was definitely up. Mackie and Jeff seemed really calm. Too calm. "Have a seat, Dodie," Jeff said.

I cut right to the chase. "What's happening with Jed and Eileen?"

Mackie and Jeff exchanged a look.

"What, are they coming? Not coming? What's going on? Please tell me. I'm going to explode." My voice escalated higher and higher, but I couldn't seem to do anything about it.

"They're not coming . . . because Eileen is pregnant."

I swayed on my chair. "What? I thought—I thought—" I stammered.

"They couldn't have children?" Jeff said.

"Yeah."

"So did they."

"Oh my gosh . . . that's . . . um . . . unexpected. So what does that mean for the adoption?"

"They haven't decided for sure yet," Jeff said. "But they're not likely to go through with the adoption now."

"Really?" Relief washed over me like cool water.

"They don't feel they can support two children right now, two babies. Especially an adopted child—even though Terabithia's pretty well adjusted here now, it could be difficult for him to move to a new home again—and a newborn baby. It's financial too. They make a good enough living, but it would be really tight with two young kids."

I searched Mackie's and Jeff's faces. "Are you okay? I mean, this must be a huge blow for you."

To my astonishment, Jeff and Mackie started laughing. It was nervous laughter but genuine nonetheless. "We're relieved as all get-out," Jeff admitted.

My mouth dropped open. "Does that mean he'll be staying with you?"

Mackie frowned. "No, we still think it's best if someone younger than us adopts Terabithia. I guess we weren't quite ready yet. We're grateful for a little more time with him."

"Me too," I said so forcefully that Mackie and Jeff laughed again.

If ever there was a sign from on high, this was it. I tried to stop myself from saying anything. It wasn't the right time. But I couldn't keep my mouth shut. "Please consider me. I'm sorry—terrible timing, right? But think about it. Please."

Mackie rubbed her forehead and gave me an exhausted smile. "If we are going to seriously consider this, we would have to treat you like any other adoption candidate. Well, not like any other—there are some things that we already know for certain, like how much you love children, especially Boo, and how great and caring of a mother you will be."

My eyes teared up. They knew this about me?

"On the other hand, we have to make sure it's the best situation for Terabithia. That he will be safe and well cared for and a top priority for the person or people raising him. So we would have to ask you the hard questions, the invasive questions. About relationships and marriage and finances and thoughts on education. Are you up for that?"

I was nodding. Of course. I had to be thinking of all those things now. All those things. A lot of things. But that's what was typical when you had a child. You had to divide your resources—attention, money, time—and always make sure your child felt loved and cared for.

And I had to tell Shep. I knew I should have told him before we got engaged so he didn't feel like he was stuck. But I had always found excuses—that I was afraid of failing, that Jed and Eileen were adopting Terabithia. Now the way was clear for me. "Can I stay until Boo wakes up?" I asked.

"Of course."

"Dodie, what's happening?" Shep asked when I walked through the door. "I got your text. I can't believe the timing."

"Shep, I have something to tell you. I want to

adopt him myself," I blurted. "I can't go through this again knowing he might be far away forever." I wish I hadn't been so blunt after waiting this long to tell him, but there was no time to waste now.

Shep was silent as too many agonizing seconds passed. "But that's not a reason to try to adopt him yourself."

"That's not the only reason," I said. "I love him."

"Of course you do. But are you really ready to take care of him?"

"Yes," I said without thinking.

"To be his mother?"

"Yes. I know I can do it."

"I'm sorry, but how do you know? From babysitting?"

I didn't like the tone of Shep's voice.

"Tons of first-time mothers don't have anywhere near that much experience," I pointed out.

"That may be true. But from what I can see of my nieces and nephews, being a parent is pretty much all-consuming. And you have the library . . . and your job . . . and . . ."

"I want to be a mother more than anything," I said.

Shep blinked, then leveled his gaze at me. "More than you want to be my wife?"

"What is that question supposed to mean?"

"You said you want to be a mother more than anything. And you and I are engaged. So does that take precedence over everything? Is that why you've been putting off setting the date with me?"

"No, it's not. I mean, I haven't been putting it off." Even as I denied it, I knew there was some truth to what he was saying. Part of the reason I had said *next fall* was because it was far off enough that I didn't have to worry about the specifics yet. Still, I couldn't believe that's what he was focusing on right now. "Are you asking me to choose?"

"Are you asking *me* to choose?" he shot back. "This is the first I'm hearing about your wanting to adopt Terabithia. What about my feelings on kids in general? Or right now? Or adoption? Or Terabithia? Do I get a say in this?"

"Of course," I said. "I didn't want to assume that you would be on board with it."

"Okay, well, but if that's true, what if I'm not? What does that mean for us?"

It was a fair question. One I hadn't really allowed myself to think about. And his anger—which was obviously growing the more the timeline added up in his head—was totally reasonable too. "Are you?"

"That's not the point. What does it mean for us if I'm not on board?"

"So you *are* asking me to choose. You or Terabithia?"

Shep sighed. “Dodie, I’m not asking you to choose. Not yet. I’m not promising that I won’t. I’m trying to understand this news you’ve dropped on me. I mean, how long have you been considering this?”

I squirmed. Should I tell him that it had been a glimmer of an idea since right after Sullivan’s death? “A while.”

“And when were you planning on telling me?”

“When it was a little more concrete.”

“As in, irreversible?”

“No, of course not. Listen, Shep, I don’t know if Mackie and Jeff would even consider letting me move forward.”

“But you’ve talked to them about it?”

“Yes,” I admitted. “I said something when Jed and Eileen first met him. But they made it clear they couldn’t really consider it. Now maybe they can.”

“You talked to them about it before you talked to me?”

I nodded. It sounded so bad when he put it that way.

“Did you bring it up again today?”

“Yes,” I confessed. “But I knew I was going to be talking to you about it before anything would happen.”

Shep stood and walked a full circle around the room, rubbing his hands through his hair.

“I can’t believe you didn’t tell me. Here I am envisioning the rest of our lives together, and you’re thinking of introducing a child into the mix but don’t even mention it? Why?”

“Honestly, because I was afraid you would react this way. It’s pretty clear you’re not happy about the idea.”

“I don’t even know how I feel about it. I need more than five minutes to react. I need to process it.”

“Okay,” I said. That was a reasonable thing to ask. But what scared me was that I felt a hardening inside already. Like I was steeling myself for him to disappoint me and maybe even leave. It wasn’t reasonable for me to expect him to say immediately, *I’m in*. Some part of me had thought he would, though.

He gave me a perfunctory kiss on the cheek. “I’ll call you tomorrow.” It would be the first night we had spent apart in months.

“Okay,” I repeated. As soon as the door shut, I called Coco and left a message. She would give me her honest perspective. Hopefully with some reassurance. And I could finally tell her I was planning to adopt too. She was getting ready to leave for Liberia, and I knew her hands were full. But this was an emergency. Three hours later, after I’d reorganized all the pretty blank journals I’d been buying at museums, I gave up waiting and climbed into bed.

• • •

The next day, Shep finally showed up in the late afternoon unshaven and with circles under his eyes that matched my own.

I made peppermint hot chocolate, and he stood in silence watching me stir. I tried not to think that he kept glancing at my ring as if he was wondering whether he should have given it to me.

When we sat down, he bit his lip and said, “I’m not sure, Do.”

I tried not to panic. “About me? About us?”

“No, I’m sure about us. But I don’t know if we’re ready for a child. If I’m ready.”

“But I’m ready.”

“I know you . . . are.”

Was that a you-think-you-are pause?

“So what does that mean?”

“I honestly don’t know. I guess I need more time to think about it.”

“Okay.” Despair clutched at my throat. Somehow, through all the time I had delayed telling him, it hadn’t fully registered that he might give up on us because of what I wanted. It would be his right. “I don’t want to lose you, Shep.”

“I don’t want to lose you either.”

But this is *me,* I thought with all my might. *This is who I am and who I want to be.* Instead, I said, “What can I do right now? Do you want to put the engagement on hold until you decide?"

Anger flashed through his eyes. "No, I wasn't thinking that."

I backpedaled. "You need time to process this. We don't have to decide anything right away. Let's see how things go, and we'll figure it out from there." I owed him the time since I had certainly taken plenty of my own before telling him. I felt sick to think of the choice I might have to make soon.

Coco called the next morning. Before she could speak, I couldn't resist sniping, "Well, somebody is very busy." I had really needed her calming, listening ear—and it had been almost two days.

I heard a stifled sound before Coco tried to speak. "Do-o . . . I—the . . ."

I could barely understand her through her sobs. "Coco, what's wrong? Is it the baby? Is she all right?"

Coco heaved a few more times, then managed to say, "The . . . baby's . . . fine. But her parents have decided to take her back."

Oh, no. No no no no no.

"Are you sure?" I felt sick to my stomach. On the one hand, if the baby's birth parents had changed their minds and were certain they could take care of the child, well, I could understand that. But my poor sister. And that poor child. All the months of waiting. All that time the baby was at the orphanage. And with international adoption, the child wouldn't have been assigned to a family here unless the parents had officially given up their rights.

"Yes, I'm sure. The birth father and mother reconciled after years apart, and they want to start over. The agency has told us that we could fight it and that we might win based on how far into the process we are since they forfeited their legal rights. But how could we?"

"Coco, I'm so, so sorry," I kept repeating. I couldn't ask her what was next. Grieving, obviously. I thought of the picture she had shown me of that sweet baby girl. Sianeh. I could only imagine how many times she had looked at it.

She cried, quieting little by little.

"What can I do?" I asked. "I can hop in the car and come see you?"

"Thanks, Do. I appreciate it. But I think Mark and I might need to hole up for a little while and grieve."

"Of course. I'm here when you're ready. Maddie and I can come cook for you guys and pamper you—or just cry with you—when you're up for some company."

"Thank you. Will you call Mom and Dad and Maddie and tell them?"

"Yes. Let me know if you think of anything else that would help."

"I wanted so badly to . . ." Coco started to cry again.

I waited, but that was all. "I know, Co. I know."

Maddie unleashed a giant torrent of swear words when I told her. "Poor Coco. Do you think some cheese would help?" she asked.

"What?"

"Let's send her and Mark a cheese basket."

"Um . . . okay. Not a bad idea, actually."

"Are you going to go visit her?"

"In a few days. She and Mark need some time to themselves first."

"Well, let me know when you and Shep are going, and I'll meet you guys there."

"I . . . don't know if Shep will be with me."

"Why the hell not? He's your fiancé."

He still was . . . at least for now.

"Do, what's with the silence?"

"Shep and I are having some problems."

"Are you fighting about the wedding?"

"No. It's about Terabithia."

"Is he acting jealous because Terabithia is staying? Because if he is, I will crush his—"

"No!" I interrupted her. "We're just having some . . . growing pains," I said. I really could not bear the thought of telling her about my plan to adopt Terabithia and how Shep had reacted to it. Not right now, and not when Coco was in so much pain.

"I'm here if you want to talk about it. Seriously. No more bodily harm threats. Just a gentle, completely partial listening ear."

I smiled. As much as I loved Maddie, I didn't know if she would even understand why this was so important to me. I couldn't put this on Coco right now. And the other person I wanted to talk to the most about it, the one who would understand more than anyone else, was Sullivan.

Sixteen

Whether I would have Shep's help and support or not, it was time to put Operation Adopt-a-Boo in motion. Now or never. As soon as he headed to work on Saturday, after an oddly cordial breakfast at Marvel Betty's, I took my place at the circulation desk, got out a pen and paper, and started doing calculations.

The library expenses continued to be higher than I expected. As it happened, people still needed toilet paper. Even though I was baking far less often, there were other costs due to wear and tear now that I hadn't had to worry about in the beginning. I figured I still needed about $1,000 a month to cover those expenses. Add that to my living expenses, the adoption attorney fee, enough money to provide for Terabithia for at least a few months, and the portion that I would be paying toward the wedding venue, which I really needed to book *stat* to ensure Shep and I could get married in the fall. I tabulated a little extra for unforeseen adoption expenses. The total came to . . . $11,023. What the Sam heck?

I did the calculations again. First by hand. Then on my old-school Texas Instruments calculator. Then on my phone. Then on the internet. I had forgotten to carry a one. Eesh, $12,023, then.

That was a lot of money. I would find some way, though. I had to be resourceful.

Two weeks later, Kendra shanghaied me at the library. She had been wandering the aisles deciding on something to read. She set *Love the One You're With*, *Twilight*, and *Atonement* down on the desk to check out.

"Hold on," she said and dragged a chair over to the circulation desk so she could speak quietly. Uh-oh. Was I in trouble?

"What's the deal with the jam?" she asked. "Because you're going to have to come up with something better than that."

"What jam?"

She raised her eyebrow at me. I silently pleaded the Fifth. She sighed. "The jam you're obviously trying to mass-produce . . . alone."

"I'm not—"

"Cut the crap, Dodie. I heard you talking to Chloë at Foodie Book Club, and you've been showing up here with pieces of raspberry stuck in your hair, not to mention you smell like Marie Antoinette's garden half the time."

I sighed.

"And . . . ?" she prompted.

"I was making raspberry-rose jam. Chloë said she would sell it in her gourmet food store. I'm trying to make some extra money. There are a lot of expenses right now."

"Sure," she said. "With the library and all."

"Right."

She paused for what felt like a whole minute. "Does this have anything to do with Terabithia?"

"It might."

"Please tell me you have talked to Shep about it if you are even remotely considering . . ." She trailed off, glancing in both directions to make sure we weren't overheard.

"Yeah, I did."

"I'm assuming from your expression that he didn't respond the way you'd hoped?"

I shook my head. "If . . . theoretically . . . I still wanted to explore that possibility I mentioned . . . ," I began gingerly, "do you have some kind of creative expense-paying ideas up your sleeve?"

"Nope." Kendra shook her head.

My stomach sank. I couldn't believe how much even the suggestion of it had raised my hopes—or my increasing desperation, if I were honest with myself.

"I'm not wearing sleeves," she replied, a grin breaking through as she flapped her poncho sweater thingy around for effect. "My big idea for financing whatever the hell crazy scheme you're cooking up is actually right behind you."

I turned around. There was nothing behind me except the painting of the two mermaid sisters that I had been steadfastly ignoring since the library opened.

Except it *wasn't* the painting of the mermaid sisters. It was another old painting of mine of a girl looking down at the sleeping dog whose head was in her lap, her face etched with love. Eek!

"I'm c-confused," I stuttered. "Did you get rid of the mermaids and swap this in this morning?"

"Nope. I put this one up yesterday."

"What happened to the mermaids?" I asked in spite of myself. I didn't want to look at them—had managed not to look at them for months and months even though they were literally over my shoulder—but it was a little sad to imagine them going back under a cloth in my attic.

"You're kidding, right? Jesus, you really don't pay attention. The mermaids have been gone since before Mother's Day, Dodie. I sold them to Mike. He wanted the painting for a present for Lula."

"Did she like it?"

"I guess so because she's bought two more of your paintings since then," Kendra said levelly.

I gripped the edge of the desk. "Where did she see them?"

"On the wall behind you."

"So there have been . . . other things up besides this one?"

I was starting to piece it together—the petty cash box that seemed like an endless cup of sweet tea miraculously refilled each time I got up to go to the bathroom (which was pretty often when you were drinking an endless cup of sweet tea). Most people had a problem with someone sneaking money out of petty cash. Apparently, I had someone sneaking it in!

"Yes. Four, as a matter of fact."

"Four?"

"Four. Have you not heard people talking about them? When I sit here, people ask me all the time who are they by—are there more? Maybe no one asks you because word's gotten around that you're a secretly talented artist who hates to talk about it," she suggested.

I was shaking my head in disbelief. "Thank you," I said even though there was a knot in my stomach. Thinking about those mawkish and sentimental pieces being paraded in front of the Chatsworthians' eyes . . . Or, heaven forbid, on their own walls.

Kendra shrugged modestly. "You should really think about doing a show . . ."

No way. Not on Charles Darwin's life.

". . . sell a bunch of pieces at once . . ."

Over my unconscious body.

"I've been selling them for about two hundred dollars, and you have a few bigger ones up in your attic, so I figure you could make a few thousand dollars."

Not a chance in Helena Bonham Cart—

"Seven grand, maybe even eight or nine . . ."

Okay, fine. Problem solved. Probably.

• • •

My paintings hung on the walls of the library on the night of the art sale. Aside from the possible earnings, it was exciting to bring together my love of art and my love of books. Maybe in the future we could hold children's art exhibits or invite illustrators in to talk about their work. First, I had to make a heap of money.

Fortunately, the chief fire marshal was in Jamaica. As deputy fire marshal, Anoop blessed the gathering at the beginning when it was only Shep, Kendra, Geraldine, and me, and then he announced that he was taking his fiancée to a showing of *He's Just Not That into You* and wouldn't be back to check on the occupancy level at my house.

"This is amazing, Do," Shep said, kissing my hair. He was putting on a supportive face; whenever he assumed I wasn't looking, his mouth sank into a frown, and I knew he was thinking about what I hoped to do with some of the proceeds.

"Eight thousand dollars!" Kendra and I were screaming on the phone the next morning. Every single painting had sold. I was so much closer to my goal. Coupled with my salary, some savings, and my birthday money, I might be able to prove to Mackie and Jeff soon that I was on the financial footing I needed to be.

"Do, you ready for breakfast?" Shep called up the stairs.

"I've got to go, guardian angel," I said to Kendra. "Thank you so much for believing in my art and forcing me to sell it."

"You're welcome. But Do? Take it slow, okay? You'll need a lot more saved up before you can reasonably tell Mackie and Jeff you are ready."

"Of course."

Seventeen

November 2008

Kendra hadn't been kidding. Within a few weeks, the $8,000 was already disappearing more quickly than I cared to think about.

I needed a get-rich-quick scheme. What else could I sell from my attic besides paintings? No, wait . . . what if I went back to painting? The art sale had given me enough confidence to think I could do it again.

I headed to my trusty old Robshaw's Hardware and Art Supplies. Mr. Robshaw helped me select paints and canvases and an easel that I put in the corner of my study overlooking a big oak tree outside.

The first time I stood in front of the empty canvas, I felt a flicker of excitement remembering how much I had loved painting, how the hours had flown by as colorful brushstrokes turned into animals and people.

An hour later, I was still staring out the window watching the sunlight shape-shift between the ice-glazed branches.

Okay, maybe the problem was that I needed a subject to paint instead of trying to come up with something out of my head. Over the next few days, I gathered a bunch of my favorite photos from my travels and tried to paint pictures of the people in them. The grizzled accordion player on the street in Montmartre, Paris. The children playing chase in the Campo de' Fiori in Rome. I couldn't seem to begin.

I forced myself to try. The brushes felt like lead in my hand. I didn't want to paint. I had to, but I didn't want to.

Shep would come over to keep me company. "Will you sit in the living room?" I asked him on the first night.

"I can't sit here?" he asked, pointing to the comfy chair in my study on the other side of the room from my easel.

"No, you're too distracting," I said, kissing him lightly. But the truth was it was too much pressure having him in the room.

After a few hours, he came upstairs to check on me. "How's it going?"

"Pretty well," I lied, inching the canvas away from his view.

"Can I see?"

"Not yet. I'm pretty protective about my work in progress."

That wasn't true either. Sullivan and I used to look at each other's paintings all the time. But that was a different situation. A different time. Before . . .

I missed her so much. And I loved the idea of painting again for Sullivan. For Terabithia. But so far, I didn't seem to be able to do it.

Coco and Mark held Thanksgiving dinner. It was the first time any of us saw them since the adoption fell through even though we'd all offered or threatened multiple times to come.

"Let's just wait until the holidays," Coco had said to me. "We're doing okay. I promise. You can all come then."

"Are they sure they want to do that to themselves? Right now? I asked Coco, but she keeps insisting it's fine," I had told Mom the week before.

"I had the same thought," my mom had replied. "And that's why it's good that we're all only staying until Friday morning. She told me it'll be a welcome distraction and remind them of all the things they're grateful for."

And when we arrived, we saw that they'd gone all out. There were two kinds of turkey in progress—basted and baked golden brown, and fried crispy and golden brown. It wasn't the bird but the roasted potatoes with garlic, rosemary, olive oil, and sea salt that my sisters and I were prepared to fight over, though.

My mom and I sneaked into the kitchen and made her traditional foods—good old green bean casserole with cream of mushroom soup and fried onions on top and garlicky mashed potatoes—as well as some of Shep's family's favorites, including cheddar-and-beer stuffing and chunky cranborange sauce.

Shep and Mark and Dad were in the living room telling stories about their own Thanksgivings growing up. I caught Shep's eye through the doorway and smiled; he waved a thumbs-up in my direction.

"Is Shep behaving?" Maddie stage-whispered. I shot her a look.

"How was he misbehaving?" Coco wanted to know.

"He really wasn't. We've been having a difference of opinion lately on some wedding-related things"—sort of true, though not so much wedding related as marriage related—"but we're okay. How are you holding up?"

"Better. We're going to wait until after the New Year to start the process again."

"Do you get kicked to the back of the line?" Maddie asked.

Mom and I shot her a look.

"What? Is that an offensive question?"

"It sounds like you're asking if they're getting kicked to the curb," I pointed out.

"Well . . . I mean . . . they kinda did."

Coco managed to laugh. "I know what you meant, Mad. And the answer is I don't know.

This happens so rarely. It's a pretty in-depth process to put your child up for adoption, and then there's that lag time of several months. So I don't know what kind of precedent there is."

"I'm so sorry about Sianeh, Co," I said. I wanted to tell her in person.

A pained look crossed her face upon hearing the name. "Thank you."

"I can't imagine what you're feeling."

"I suspect you can, at least a little bit," she replied. "You've probably had to face some similar feelings about Terabithia's adoption. It must be so hard to imagine saying goodbye to him."

My mom and my sisters were all looking at me as if they knew what I was trying to do. "It is," I admitted. "It really is. And Coco, you're going to be an amazing mother."

Her eyes filled with tears. "I hope so."

We heard the bing of the turkey in the oven. Soon our plates were heaped with piles of steaming stuffing, creamy green beans, turkey glistening in skin slotted with feathery herbs, and a crowning of potatoes the golden brown of late-summer sunshine. We took turns saying what we were thankful for. And then—after a wait that always seemed too long but that made everything taste better—it was time to eat.

• • •

"Such a bummer for them, huh?" Shep said when we were eating leftovers back at home on Sunday.

"It really is."

"They seem to be holding up pretty well, though."

"Yeah."

"Did you know that Mark invested a big chunk of the money he inherited so he can put it in a 529 savings plan for their future kid?"

"No, but that makes sense." What was a 529 savings plan?

"They also made sure they were in a good school district before they moved into their house."

"Yeah."

"They've done a lot of planning."

Shep wasn't the most subtle.

"So you've been thinking about it more?"

"Do, I never stopped thinking about it. But I don't know what the solution is. I'm not ready. You're not."

"Hold on," I said. "I'm working on it. So I've had some setbacks. But I've got a nice long holiday break starting on the fifteenth. I'm going to use the time to paint."

"Uh-huh."

I got up from the table. Daniel hadn't thought I had the talent to be an artist. And now it seemed like Shep didn't think I was ready to be a mother.

Or he didn't want me to be one. Hurt and anger rose up in the back of my throat. "I know I can't make you want to do this with me. But you could at least believe in me."

I slammed the door of my bedroom behind me. A few minutes later, I heard the much softer closing of my front door.

Eighteen

December 2008

The day after Thanksgiving break ended, I was heading out of school when I saw Elmira through the window of the principal's office. Her mother was with her, which was the first sign that something big was up. The second sign was that Elmira's face was as white as paper.

"What's going on?" I asked the receptionist.

"She was caught stealing," he confided to me in low tones.

"No, I mean Elmira Pelle." He must have thought I was talking about someone in the waiting area.

"Yep, that's the one. Snuck into her teacher's room and stole a bunch of books. They found them in her book bag."

What the deuce? This did not sound—in any way, shape, or form—like Elmira.

The principal looked up and saw me standing outside the window gaping. When he caught my eye, I gestured to myself. His brow furrowed, but he waved me in.

"What's going on?" I asked.

"Elmira stole several books from her teacher."

"That doesn't sound like—" I stopped. It would

be better if I listened first. "What do you mean?"

"Ms. Larezzi is writing a paper for a journal about Louisa May Alcott, and Elmira is doing a report on *Little Women*, and we found Ms. Larezzi's books in her bag."

"Elmira?" I asked. "What's this about?"

"I was just borrowing them. You know I'm a really quick reader, and I was going to put them back tomorrow. I didn't think she'd need them, and I really did for my project."

"I thought you were using the books we have in the lending library on Louisa May Alcott. Why would you need Ms. Larezzi's books?"

Elmira wouldn't look in my direction. That's when it hit me. My lending library had been closed a lot lately. Her mean-girl mother probably wouldn't drive her to the Derbyshire Library or the bookstore. Elmira hadn't been able to get the books she had needed, so she'd borrowed them from her teacher, who happened to be about as charming a woman as Leila Pelle was.

It was my fault. Elmira had turned to a life of crime because of me!

I recovered my speech for her sake and took her mother and the principal aside. "Listen, Elmira has a spotless record. I can vouch for the fact that she's been an invaluable help to me at the lending library and a model student. I'm sure this was a misunderstanding and she meant to ask for the books. Or borrowed them and was going to return them right away. Can't we look the other way this once?"

Leila Pelle's mouth was set in a hard line. "I don't think that's appropriate. Expulsion is too severe, but I think she should be punished for her actions. We'll do that at home, of course, but she needs to associate her punishment with this place as well to be sure it never happens again."

"It won't!" I cried.

"Well," the principal mused, "our other options are suspension and detention. That means someone will have to look after her or pick her up late."

A red flush was creeping up Leila Pelle's neck as her desire to discipline Elmira warred with her complete reluctance to have to change her schedule. "Isn't there some sort of probation you could put her on instead?" she finally asked.

"Yes, we could do that," the principal replied, turning to Elmira. "We'll give her three months of probation. If there are any other violations, we'll have to consider a more serious punishment. Do you understand, young lady?"

Elmira nodded. Her hands twisted in her lap.

"Let's go," Leila Pelle ordered. "We'll talk about my punishment in the car." She marched Elmira out the door.

I felt sick to my stomach as I drove home. I headed around the back, unlocked the door of the sunroom, and sagged into a chair to reflect on what had happened. Elmira had trusted me, and I was no better than her mother. Kendra had been right. I wasn't doing a very good job. It was almost a certainty that Elmira wasn't the only person in Chatsworth who needed the library and had come to find it closed. These people had become my friends. I knew them by name. I knew some of their troubles, and I knew which books might make them feel better.

The library had taken on a life of its own. It was a place where people connected. Sometimes, those conversations alone were enough to make a person leave with a smile on her face or walk a little bit lighter. But I had been so wrapped up in my drama with Terabithia that I hadn't fully recognized the miracle that I had created . . . until it was all on the verge of falling apart.

I was in danger of losing the library. And Shep. I couldn't be there for Terabithia—financially or otherwise—unless I closed the library for good or gave it to Kendra. That was not something I could live with. My library was my baby too.

A few days after the Elmira incident, I was playing with Terabithia at Mackie and Jeff's after school, and my eyes closed. Only a few seconds later, I felt a gentle tug on my arm; Terabithia's little face was pinched with worry. "Dada?" he said carefully. "Is you okay, Dada?"

I gave him a big hug and said, "I'm sorry!"

and went on building train tracks for him to tear apart. Falling asleep while Boo was awake scared me.

Mackie was napping on the couch in the living room. It seemed as though every time I looked at her, there were new worry lines on her lovely face. Even in sleep, her hands were clenched in her lap. Jeff was standing by the counter in the doorway to the kitchen. At first I thought he was reading a magazine. Then I realized he was supporting himself on the counter with one hand, the other pressed against his chest.

"Jeff, are you all right?"

His breath was coming in short bursts. I grabbed a chair and sat him down, then reached for the phone and dialed 911. "I'd like to report an emergency at 121 Merryton Road. I think it's a heart attack."

Mackie appeared at the door and rushed over to Jeff. The dispatcher gave me some instructions. Jeff swallowed an aspirin as Mackie held his hand. "Everything is going to be all right, my darling," she soothed.

Terabithia's waking wail greeted the ambulance. "You go," I told Mackie as the EMTs came in. "I'll take care of Terabithia."

"It's okay, Boo," I lied, trying to distract him with his favorite talking octopus toy.

The sirens quieted. The hours crawled. They had gone to the hospital around 11:00 a.m. A little after 7:00 p.m., when I had put an exhausted and confused Terabithia to bed, Mackie called.

"How is Jeff? What happened?" I asked.

"He's going to be okay. He had a minor heart attack, and they put a stent in."

"Oh, gosh!"

"He'll be here overnight. If you don't mind staying another few hours, I'll plan to stay until they kick me out."

"They're kicking you out? Do you want to stay with him overnight? There's no rush. We're fine here, and Terabithia is sleeping away."

"There's really no space for me to stay in his room even if I wanted to."

"Is Jeff resting?"

"Yes. He looks peaceful now; he was in such pain before."

"Good. Come get some rest when you can."

Mackie got home at nine, her face gray with fatigue. I gave her a hug. "Are you all right?"

"Yes, I think he's going to be fine."

"No, I meant are *you* all right?"

"Oh, me. I'm okay. But exhausted. I'm going to go check on Terabithia. I'll be back in a minute."

"What is that amazing smell?" she asked, peering over my shoulder. I was stirring a pot on the stove. Took a little taste. Needed more salt.

"I made vegetable soup. Just from bits and pieces in your refrigerator. I hope you don't mind."

"No, that's sweet of you. I hope you won't be offended if I only have a little. I don't have much of an appetite. I think I need to go to bed."

Hint taken. "Is there anything else I can do for you all?"

She shook her head.

"I'll come back tomorrow and watch him while you go to the hospital. You don't have to rush. I'll take care of Boo for as long as you like," I said.

There was an awkward pause. "Thank you. My sister will be here first thing, so there's no need. Jeff will probably get discharged in the morning, but I know you have school, and there's no telling how long we'll be."

"Okay, well, if you need me, let me know, Mackie. And call me if you need anything during the night."

Shep had taken on a second shift a month ago, so I knew he still wouldn't be home. I needed to see him. I needed to make things right after last night. *He is doing this for you,* I reminded myself. *For the wedding and probably for the engagement ring he gave you.* I sank into the couch and flipped on the news. "There's been an accident at the construction site at Trumbull and Sheldron in Chatsworth where the new outdoor mall is going up. There's no word yet on whether any of the workers sustained injuries, but you can see where the crane smashed part of the newly built walls of the Thai Tower restaurant."

"Oh my God, oh my God," I kept mouthing over and over as I dialed Shep's cell. No answer.

"Honey?" Shep said from right behind me, scaring the daylights out of me. I hadn't heard the door close.

"You're okay!" I exclaimed.

"Course I'm okay, but are you?" He pulled back and looked at my ghostly face. "What's going on?"

"Oh, Shep, I saw there was an accident at the site"—obviously news to him based on his expression—"and then you didn't pick up, probably because you were walking through the door, but I was afraid, and after we fought yesterday—"

"Calm down, Do—I'm fine," Shep soothed, stroking my hair. I took deep breaths while he called the foreman. Apparently no one had been hurt. I filled him in on Jeff.

"I have the day off work tomorrow, Do. Maybe it would be a good idea for you to take the day off too."

After he made me a cup of almond tea, I started feeling a little more like myself. Miraculously, I managed to find a sub for school the next day, which was as rare as a winning lottery ticket.

Shep and I cuddled and watched TV for a little while longer before we headed upstairs to crash. I had barely been around for Shep, and when I was, my mind was somewhere else. *I have tomorrow off,* I thought, drifting toward sleep. We could have breakfast together and not be rushed. We could go for a walk and get some fresh air. We could do anything we wanted.

But the next morning, all I wanted was not to give up on Terabithia. I just couldn't. I slipped out of bed, careful not to wake Shep, and padded down the hall to my study.

And sat down in front of the easel.

And sat.

And sat.

I had to admit that my painting renaissance was not going to happen. I had tried and tried. I didn't have it in me anymore. Maybe I was too tired. Maybe I was trying to force it, when my painting before had come from passion and not necessity.

Maybe I had come to terms long ago with the fact that my place in the art world involved googly eyes and glitter paper instead of gallery openings and towering canvases.

Maybe I was just a different person than I had been, one who now had stars in her eyes for a real baby instead of for mermaids or little girls with puppies or turtles on lily pads.

There was no use denying it: no fairy godmother was going to materialize with the miracle I needed.

Shep poked his head in the door. "Do? You all right?"

I sighed and turned the canvas to face him.

"Nothing, huh?"

"Nope. I just really want—"

"I know," Shep murmured. "But not like this. I know how much you love him, and you are going to be an amazing mother someday. But for you to drive yourself crazy trying to scrounge up the money . . . that's asking too much. Sweetheart"—Shep took both my hands in his—"here's the thing. The reality is that Coco and Mark have the means to give Terabithia a life that's not in our power right now. It's not fair, but I think deep down you know it's the truth. Have you thought about talking to Coco?"

"No," I practically yelled. "I mean, no. They're already back on the list for a referral. It would be way too weird for her. She knows how I feel about Terabithia. It's not like we're swapping My Little Ponies." The words were pouring out of my mouth. I felt hot and cold.

Shep clasped both my hands to steady me. "Think it over, Do." He paused. "We'll have kids one day, when we're ready. We can adopt from Ethiopia if you want."

"They won't be Terabithia."

"That's true," he agreed. "They won't be Terabithia."

Shep didn't want to leave me on Saturday morning, but he had to go to the site. Even before the accident, the mall project was running behind schedule. They'd brought in a new crane and were trying to make up for lost time. I hoped they weren't rushing things.

A little after eleven, as I was getting to the part in *Love Actually* where Jamie and the whole town of Marseille went to the restaurant where Aurelia worked so he could awkwardly profess his love to her—and she revealed she learned English for him, which was soooo romantic—a knock on my door interrupted my brain-candy film fest.

"Dodie, it's me."

"Hey, Kendra, what's up? It's good to see you. Come on in."

Kendra's face was a funny shade. Kind of purple, actually.

"Have a seat," I invited her. "Let me get you some . . . um . . . some crackers and jam."

"I don't want any goddamn crackers and jam," Kendra seethed. "I want to know what in the name of ever-living hell is going on with you."

This was bad. I knew this was really bad. I'd seen Kendra this mad exactly one time ever. Now.

"Um . . . what do you mean?"

"Do you know how long it's been since you've returned my calls?" Kendra asked.

"No."

"Are you aware that I've left you eight

messages in the last twenty-four hours?" she demanded.

"No," I said meekly. "I haven't been looking at my phone. Yesterday was a really hard day for me. And lately I've been busy—"

"Doing what?" she said, glancing at the paused movie, her voice arctic. "What could be so important that you couldn't hear my news? It certainly can't be the library occupying all your time . . . I know you closed it early for the holidays, though I don't know why . . ."

"What news?" I asked, but she shook her head as if to say, *Not a chance till you give me a proper answer*.

It spilled out. "I have been trying to figure out how to adopt Terabithia."

"Still? We talked about this months ago. I thought by now you had figured out that it was a completely crazy, impossible desire."

I was silent. I couldn't fight this fight anymore—not with Kendra, not with Shep, not with myself.

"I can't fix the mess you've made with Shep or the library. You have to fix this yourself. For your own self-respect. Figure out what you want, and if you're going to close the library for good, just do it and don't keep everyone's hopes up. Eventually, they'll reopen the Chatsworth Library. Look, I've got to go. Benton's waiting for me."

As she turned the knob to let herself out, my eyes caught on a huge, clear, shining rock on a platinum band on her *ring finger*. I grabbed her hand. "Kendra? Is this what you wanted to tell me?"

"Yeah, I was planning on it. But now's not the time. You've got bigger fish to fry." And with that, one of my best friends, newly engaged to a man I didn't even know she loved, walked out the door.

"Hey, Coco," I said, flopping into one of the wing chairs in the sunroom for a long overdue phone conversation. "How was your day?"

"Fine, how was yours?"

I sighed.

"What's up?"

"Nothing really. Have you and Mark adjusted to being home?" I'd barely brought it up before. The truth was I felt uneasy on the phone with her. Shep had suggested what I'd been thinking but hadn't been able to admit: that there might be a solution right in front of me. An excruciating one but a solution nonetheless. After a little small talk, my jealousy would rear up, and, hating myself for it, I would find an excuse to get off the phone. This time, I was definitely going to try to listen for as long as she wanted to talk. I had obviously been sucking at that lately; my conversation with Kendra was all the proof I needed.

"It's been weird," she said. "It's the little things that remind me of how long we were away. I watch TV and it's as though the people on it are speaking a different language. But I love nursing, and being back on the floor has helped a huge amount. And there's also Mark. He makes everything so much easier. It's amazing having a partner, isn't it, Do? I mean, I can tell that Shep is so solid. It must be great having him there for you, knowing you can depend on him. It goes without saying that he knows he can depend on you in return. I mean, you're nothing if not dependable."

There was a huge lump in my throat. "Thanks, Co, and . . . um . . . I'm really sorry. I have to jump off now."

"Did I say something—" she began, but I hung up.

Nineteen

January 2009

Kendra wasn't returning my calls. Poetic justice, I figured, since I didn't return Coco's next two calls.

I went through all my credit card bills and got the balances to zero with the money I'd been saving. There was plenty of money for that. There just wasn't enough to comfortably support me and a child. That was a different category altogether—always had been, I thought, as anger at my own stupidity flared up again.

I'd continued to spend a ton of time in the library by myself. But enough was enough. I unlocked the door. The library was officially open again. Of course, no one knew that except me. There was no chance Elmira would stop by; she was grounded for the foreseeable future. I would tell a few people at school, and word would get around.

Children would play hide-and-seek among the stacks again. In a quiet corner, three readers would be wedged against the cases, deeply engrossed in a novel, a historical narrative, and a biography. A couple of people would be piling book donations on the circulation desk, their covers gleaming like jewels. I could hardly wait to see that again (and to sniff the books).

Back in the living room, I hit the button on my answering machine.

"Hey, assbrain. Call Coco. What the eff is up with you? Stop acting like such a loser and call her back. You and I have already talked twice this week. Granted, you sounded like a coked-out zombie, but if my incredibly exciting life of takeout and hot games of grab-ass in the bathrooms of art galleries are enough to keep us entertained, I'm sure our bleeding-heart Samaritan sister would have enough of interest to say to you. So stop this bitchery and get your butt on the phone for real this time. Get on it like I'm about to get on this Viggo Mortensen–looking cowboy installation artist who walked in a sec ago." There was a pause. "It's Maddie, by the way."

Thanks for the clarification, I thought.

After another pause, the message continued. "Yes, right, Maddie, not Madeline. He keeps introducing me like that, but you can use my nickname as long as you don't mind if I call you Aragorn."

I heard a deep, sun-weathered laugh.

It was tempting to keep listening. Maddie's inability to hang up the phone was a gift equal to finding Hemingway's lost manuscript.

(Aragorn ended up asking for her digits.)

• • •

Mom caught me on the phone. She was on the case too. “Do, what’s going on with you and Coco?”

“Nothing. I spoke to her a few days ago,” I said a little too hastily.

“She told me you asked her about herself and hopped off as soon as you heard the answer. She’s hurt, Dodie. She doesn’t know what she did wrong. She feels like you resent her or something.”

“I’ve been really busy. I don’t resent . . .” My voice trailed off. “Mom, I’ve gotta go. I’ll call you later.”

I *did* resent her.

“Why are you being such a colossal bitch?” Coco demanded when she answered the phone. “It’s been over a week and a half since you jumped off the phone in the middle of our conversation.”

I was silent. Like me, Coco never swore. We left that to Maddie.

“Has it really been that long?” I asked. I knew it had.

“You know it has!”

“Well, I’ve been busy.”

“Doing what? What have you been doing that is *so* important?”

“Just because I’m not working with genocide orphans in Africa doesn’t mean I’m not doing something important," I snapped. Why was I being so mean? I couldn't postpone the inevitable any longer. *Let go.*

"I never said that! I'm not comparing us. Jesus, Do, I just want to know what's going on with you. Help me understand. What did I say that made you so angry? Where have you been disappearing to?"

I gritted my teeth. "I've been distancing my family, jeopardizing my relationship, neglecting the library, failing at painting, and trying to adopt Terabithia by myself."

Silence.

"Holy crap," she finally said. "I had no idea."

"Yeah, well, how could you? I've been like some deranged jam-making, oil-painting Macbethian witch guarding a deep, dark, rose-and-raspberry-flavored, mermaid-covered secret over here."

"That doesn't sound very threatening," Coco observed. We both laughed. I had missed that.

"So what are you going to do?" she asked. "How can I help?" Her voice was so full of hope that I swallowed hard against the pain in my throat and said, "Actually, the real reason I haven't been calling you is because . . . I think you should adopt Terabithia. If Mackie and Jeff are okay with it."

There was another long silence from the other end of the line. "What?" Coco said faintly.

"I think you should adopt Terabithia. You and Mark. Maybe you two are supposed to adopt Boo."

"That's crazy, Do. *You* want to adopt him."

I swallowed hard and let the thoughts I'd been pushing away too long surface. I had to face them, and I had to do it now, before it was too late. Before it became even more difficult—or suddenly impossible—for Mackie and Jeff to take care of Terabithia. Before another nice couple of strangers looking to adopt came along. "I do. I did. But it's not the right thing for him. Or me. You and Mark are ready. You can provide him with a wonderful home and love, and you have the resources to give him what he needs. I don't."

"But Dodie—"

"No. Listen, it's taken me a long time to admit it to myself. But I can't do it now. And it's not as though I can ask Mackie and Jeff to wait."

"Couldn't you, though?"

"They already have. It's been almost a year since Sullivan died, and three months since the previous adoption fell through. Jeff's not well. The stress is making it worse. And Terabithia is going to turn two soon."

"But I can't just . . . we can't just . . . adopt the child you've been breaking your back to try to adopt. I know from losing Sianeh. It's specific. It's personal. Even more so in your case because of your relationship with Terabithia. You know him. He knows you."

I understood why I had to keep talking about this with Coco. Why I had to insist that she consider it. But damn was it painful. Like I was operating on my own organs. "Yes, it is personal. And for a long time, I kept thinking I could rise to the occasion. But this isn't only about me and what I want. It's about Shep and what he wants. He's my fiancé—I have to take that into account. I may have already messed things up beyond repair. The fact is that he's not ready. And this is also about my friends in Chatsworth. I started this library for them, and I have been neglecting it and the people who need it. And it's about Terabithia and what's best for him. If you and Mark adopt him, I'll get to be a meaningful part of his life. And so will Mackie and Jeff. If someone else adopts him, there's no guarantee."

"I don't know, Do. I have to think about this. And talk to Mark about it. I'm so grateful to you for this incredible, generous thought. But it feels strange."

That night, lying in bed, Mark and Coco held hands and talked about what I'd told her. They discussed it for hours. Coco was worried. Mark told her that it would be hard for everyone involved but that everything would be all right.

"Okay. I believe you," Coco finally said. "Should we go meet him, Mark? Are you ready?"

Mark brushed hair away from her earlobe, gave it a kiss. "Of course I am," he replied. "And you are too."

I desperately needed blush. I rubbed some into my cheeks. Better. Now I was ready to don my imaginary tour director's cap for the day. I had made granola jam bars in case Terabithia needed distracting with sugar and filled a tote bag with construction paper, stampers shaped like frogs and beavers, and pop-up books. After giving it some thought and talking to Mark, Coco had decided to come meet Terabithia and Mackie and Jeff. And, I suspected, to see how I was holding up under the circumstances.

"Shep and I will be there at noon," I promised Mackie. She and Jeff were nervous. I'd told her all about my sister, of course, but the idea of Coco—or anyone—possibly becoming Terabithia's new mother . . .

Mark and Coco arrived at one. "Come in, come in," Jeff invited them, and I attacked them with a bear hug. Coco smelled like the crème brûlée shower gel she always used. She had blush on too. Her hands were freezing cold. I gave them a squeeze as our eyes met.

They both hugged Shep, who was with me purely for moral support. He planned to make himself as scarce as possible. I knew, though, that because he loved me and had grown fond of Terabithia, he would be observing the proceedings with eager interest too.

"Please, have a seat," Mackie said to us. Jeff patted her lovingly on the shoulder as he passed into the kitchen to get drinks. Terabithia was having his nap upstairs.

"How was the drive?" Mackie asked when they were settled in, Mark's arm comfortably resting behind Coco's shoulders. She leaned into him unconsciously. Mackie registered it too.

"I like a morning drive," Mark said. "It's a nice way to get going."

The corners of Mackie's mouth twitched upward.

"We saw a field of alpacas!" Coco said. "It's so cute how their twiggy little legs stick out under that saddle of fur." She smiled directly at Mackie, putting her at ease.

As I listened to them make small talk, I didn't know what I'd been worried about. It was impossible not to like Mark and Coco. That would be similar to not liking Canadians or something else that pretty much everyone in the world liked. Maybe a peanut butter and jelly sandwich. The sophisticated kind—with farmers market Concord grape jelly and organic peanut butter. Or even almond butter, which was better for you and actually even more delicious. Unless you had nut allergies, in which case Mark and Coco would be like some other delicious yet hypoallergenic sandwich.

"Here you go." In the center of the coffee table, Jeff set down a tray with a cluster of mugs and a pot of tea. Mark served us all some pumpkin rooibos. Wreathed in a cloud of spices from my cup, I felt a calm settle over me. A sense of relief I hadn't expected to feel. Mackie and Jeff would love Coco and Mark, and Coco and Mark would be generous to all of us with Terabithia's time. Everything was going to work out fine. Just fine. Probably fine. In time.

A little before three, as Coco and Mark were describing the day the school in northern Sudan was dedicated, Terabithia's babblings became audible on the monitor. "Gamma Gampa Gamma Gampa get me get me get me," he was saying.

"That's my cue." Mackie excused herself.

Coco's hands fidgeted with the hem of her dress, and Mark shifted in his seat. I smiled at both of them and, like a good tour director, said, "He's on his way! You're going to love him."

"I know we will, Do," Coco said. "Because we've heard how much you do." Her smile was tight.

Over the monitor, I heard Mackie murmur, "Dodie's here to see you. And she brought some very special friends. Including her sister."

"Dada? Yay! See Dada now!" I could hear the

bars squeaking as he pulled on them in his haste to get out of the crib.

"Yes, her sister's here," Mackie repeated. I wasn't sure if Terabithia knew what that meant yet.

Mackie was carrying Terabithia down the stairs. He liked to be held sometimes when he first woke up, as if leaving a nap was a little like leaving the womb. I couldn't blame him.

"Dada! Dada! Dada! Dada!" My heart twinged until she could pass him over. I noticed her grimace of relief. Terabithia was getting big. He couldn't have been easy for her to carry these days.

I gave him a huge smooch on the cheek, so long and so loud it turned into a raspberry, as he giggled hysterically. "Hi!" he said, waving up at me after I set him down.

"Hi!" I said back. "Can you say hi to these people, Terabithia?"

"Hi, Shef," he said.

"Hi, Boo." Shep kissed him on top of his hair.

"Hi!" he said to Coco and Mark.

"That's my sister Coco and my brother-in-law, Mark."

Terabithia toddled over to Coco. He grabbed a handful of her hair but didn't pull it. Our hair was similar except Coco's was nicer. "Caca," he attempted.

Mark and Shep stifled nervous giggles.

“Coco,” I repeated for him, slowly and encouragingly.

“Caca,” Terabithia repeated. Um, okay. Well, they could figure that out later.

Coco put her hand gently, tentatively, on his back. No doubt she’d held a lot of babies in Africa, but this would be a huge new learning curve for her. Maybe I could help.

Terabithia pivoted, releasing her hair and running over to where Mark was sitting on the couch. Terabithia gave him an intense stare. Mark laughed. He would have stood up, but his height might have intimidated the little guy. “I’m guessing he hasn’t seen a lot of other people around here with skin color like his?”

Mackie and Jeff exchanged a glance. “Around town, here and there, but we don’t have a lot of friends who are African American,” Mackie said apologetically.

Mark nodded. Terabithia bonked Mark on the knee, testing him. Mark reached out to tickle him, and he scooted away, shrieking, “No tickle!” We all laughed. A few seconds later, Terabithia was back for more.

Like the solar heat factory he was, Terabithia melted their hearts in ten seconds flat. Mark and Coco wore the same gorgeous, sunny smiles on their faces as they had on the night of their return party . . . as though this was another kind of homecoming.

While Terabithia played with his musical keyboard, we adults spoke quietly.

"I can't even imagine how hard this must be for you," Coco said to Mackie and Jeff. "You've lost so much in the past year. I don't want this to feel like another loss for you." Her face blanched as if she'd said the wrong thing.

"We'd be lying if we said it wasn't one. But we keep reminding ourselves that Terabithia stands to gain so much. We've asked ourselves over and over what Sullivan would have wanted. We'll never know what her preference would have been. But we're pretty sure that this is what's best for Terabithia—a forever home, with parents who can give him love and energy and help him grow. Without worrying about getting stuck on the floor due to arthritis," Mackie joked, but her smile was wan.

"Or having a massive heart attack," Jeff added, not smiling at all.

We sat there awkwardly for a moment, taking it in. There was no perfect situation. Everything felt strange and painful, and it had since Sullivan's death. And it would for a long time. But we would all get through it together. There was no other choice.

Terabithia was swaying back and forth to what sounded like a kazoo version of "The More We Get Together." He looked over his left shoulder at us and grinned, happy to see so many people he loved—and some nice new ones—in the same place. It was important to let him be a child, and Mark and Coco were the ones who had the best shot at doing that for him.

Back at our house, I thought about the light in my sister's and brother-in-law's faces, about how Terabithia had shone it right back. Coco and Mark had gone upstairs to the guest room, exhausted, after a wonderful Thai take-out dinner.

"We adore him, Do," Coco had said. "But how are you feeling about this? Are you sure you're okay with it?"

I wasn't, really. But I was convinced more than ever after today that it was the right thing. I had looked at Shep and saw his jaw clenched with tension. And hope. He really, really wanted things to work out with Coco and Mark. Which meant he wasn't going to have a change of heart or make some big gesture to me or with me. I tried to be honest without dissuading her. "It's going to be hard for me, but it's for the best." The words had gone sour in my mouth. I had said them and thought them so much.

"I know," Coco said. "Mark and I are going to make it as easy for everyone as possible. We'll come here, you all will come there . . . we'll figure it out. Nothing seems far after you've been on a seven-hour bus ride with no bathroom and live chickens at your feet on a flooded road in Africa."

Mark had been very quiet. He was trying to be respectful of this moment between us. I imagined he was also exhausted. When we finished the dishes, I gave them an out. "Shep and I are going to turn in pretty early, but you guys stay up as late as you want. Coco, you know where the movies are."

"Actually," Mark said eagerly, "we're pretty beat from that early drive. I think I'll turn in."

"Me too," Coco agreed.

Shep and I headed up soon after. I slipped under the covers and lay on my side, facing him, lost in thought.

"You'll always be Terabithia's favorite aunt," he said, rubbing my arm. My eyes welled up with tears. I didn't want to be his aunt. I wanted to be his mother. And Shep knew that. "You would have been his favorite aunt if Sullivan was still alive, and you will be now. And you and Coco are so similar. I'm sure he feels comfortable because he sees a lot of you in her."

"I'm unbelievably excited for them," I said, trying to convince myself. "I really am. So excited."

Shep kissed a salty tear off my lip. "Of course you are," he murmured. "I am too."

Twenty

February 2009

A few weeks later, once the paperwork had been expedited and the home study had been done, the unofficial adoption ceremony took place at Mackie and Jeff's. I tried not to think about how quick and easy it had been for Mark and Coco since they had money. Instead, I focused on how radiant they looked and how squee-worthy Terabithia was in his minijeans and blue dinosaur shirt that read I'M THE BOSS AROUND HERE.

Mackie and Jeff placed Terabithia in Coco's arms as part of the symbolic ceremony. I could tell that when they looked at Coco, they recognized a little of Sullivan's generous spirit in her, which must have helped as much as anything could at that moment. They would see Terabithia a lot less now, but my sister promised to visit us often, and she made sure Mackie and Jeff knew they were welcome whenever they wanted to make the trip.

With all the excitement, Coco and Mark felt that it would be best to take Terabithia straight home to start the acclimation process as soon as possible. We sent them off with a Lady Baltimore cake I'd baked to keep their strength up and a car full of toys and blankets that smelled like Terabithia's yummy baby scent.

After I clicked Terabithia's little seat belt and kissed him goodbye, I bit my lip so hard I could taste blood. The sides of his mouth curling up a teeny bit, he looked at me with those heavy, trusting eyelids that meant he was ready for his nap but knew you would be there when he woke up. *He'll be okay because Coco and Mark will be there,* I reassured myself.

"What will you all do now?" Shep asked Mackie and Jeff when we were no longer in waving distance of the car. "Could we take you out to lunch?"

Mackie shook her head. "We planned to meet friends for bridge at noon."

"Just, you know, to have something scheduled," Jeff added.

"Good idea," Shep and I said in unison.

"Okay, then, we'll see you soon." I kissed them both on the cheek. I wanted to get away from them, from everyone. I felt like I was suffocating.

Shep's phone jangled. He shoved his hand in his pocket and glanced at the screen. "Excuse me a second." His face was expressionless as he walked down the driveway.

"Want us to wait?" Mackie asked.

"No, no, I'm sure he'll only be a minute. Go ahead and break a leg at bridge."

Jeff gave me a little half smile. They looked

like they couldn't wait to escape the scene of the morning either. My heart ached for them. Hell, my heart just plain ached.

Shep was pacing. The call went on a while. I was tracing my finger through the dirt in the back window of my car, writing "D hearts S." It had been a while since I'd cleaned the car. Or the house.

When the call ended, Shep stared at the phone for a moment, shaking his head slowly. Then, equally slowly, he walked back to me. His face was white.

"You okay?" I asked.

He nodded, a quick jerk of the head.

"Who was that?"

Shep's jaw set as he gazed back at me. "Work," he said, blinking.

"Do you need to go in?"

"Not . . . right . . . now," he said. "Maybe later. Probably tomorrow for a bit."

We got in the car. I was having this strange, unfamiliar feeling. It was sort of like hearing a raccoon rooting around in the trash cans outside your window. When you went to chase the raccoon away, he was gone.

I looked at Shep's gorgeous face—the face I loved so much—and those beautiful eyes, usually so warm, were now as empty as the windows in a Hopper painting. I realized what was bugging me: Shep was definitely lying to me.

Through gritted teeth, Shep suggested that we should probably do something too. "How about a trip to Little Duck Park?"

I nodded. Some fresh air might help.

From the top of the hill, it was comforting to see how far the blanket of branches extended out into the distance. They were bare, but they were still beautiful. I wondered if Terabithia was sleeping peacefully on the car ride or if my sister was trying to distract him with the hanging elephant toy whose legs stretched when you pulled on it. Shep slipped his hand into mine. "C'mon," he said after a long time. "Let's go get some food."

Neither of us felt like eating until the evening, though. I paged through all the silly tabloids he had preemptively bought to take my mind off things, and by five o'clock, after he tried to make me dinner but burned the last of our tomato sauce, we decided to order takeout from Thai Village again so we could just call it a day afterward.

"Early-bird special," he joked, shoveling noodles onto my plate.

"Stop." I put up my hand. I probably wouldn't even eat half of the small portion. Shep picked at his own helping. He may have been remembering when he'd once helped me at Terabithia's bath time and how Boo's stomach pooched out when he was sitting in the tub, intently focused on pushing a floating airplane around in the inch or two of water. I smiled thinking about how Terabithia loved pulling out the plug and never seemed to figure out (or care) that all the water started to disappear when he did.

We stuck the rest of the food in the fridge and went up to bed. I was so exhausted that I expected to be out like a light. As soon as I lay down, I thought about how I'd cried myself to sleep the night Sullivan died. *Snap out of it,* I commanded. *These two nights are not at all alike.* Back then, Terabithia had tragically lost his mother. Tonight, he was with his new one, and a wonderful new father, beginning a whole new life filled with love.

Shep was gone the next morning when I woke up. He left a note saying, "Gotta go take care of something. Call you later. Marvel B's for lunch? Banana bread pudding!" he wrote, underlining it three times.

Maybe I'd imagined things yesterday. It had been tough for all of us.

I took a hot shower and wrapped myself in my robe. When he came home, I might greet him at the door with something he liked even better than banana bread pudding.

I plopped onto the couch, watching the end of a rom-com so delightfully bad and predictable that I enjoyed every last second of it. I luxuriated in the feeling of having nowhere to run to. No jam to make, no empty canvas to sit in front of, no Terabithia to rush to see . . . okay, maybe it would take me a little while to get back into the whole luxuriating thing, but I knew that if I put my mind to it, I could luxuriate again. I had very strong luxuriation genes.

By one o'clock, and still no word from Shep, I was starting to feel like my brain had a stomach-ache from all the candy I'd been feeding it. If I had to watch one more doe-eyed ingenue muster the moxie to fight for her beloved, I was going to need a drink. Times had really changed since the days when the highlight of my month was watching the twenty-four-hour Nora Ephron marathon on TV.

Where was Shep?

At two thirty, my phone bleeped. A text from him said, "Caught up. Go ahead to Marvel B's without me. Call you when I'm done." I sighed. I had eaten every snack left in the house, so there would be no Marvel B's. But it definitely was time to go out. I shlumped down into the sunroom, where Geraldine was womanning the library for me. "How's it going?"

"It's been dead. I'm plowing through *The Help*, though. It's really good."

I was grateful that she didn't say what she was probably thinking: a lot of people still didn't know whether they could trust me—or a faithful volunteer—to be there.

For the first time in weeks, I checked the Secret Santa box. A copy of *Merry Hall*. The note card tucked inside read MACKIE O'REILLY. Someone knew that Mackie wanted to take up gardening now that Terabithia was gone. And this book, with its hilarious, lovably cranky narrator and his quirky little British town and his grumpy, excellent gardener would be a perfect distraction for her and encouragement in her new hobby. Tears sprang to my eyes.

"What do you want to do?" Geraldine asked when I replaced the top of the box and laid the book aside to pass along for Mackie. I pulled a bookmark out of the desk drawer with a Mary Cassatt painting of fresh-picked flowers in a vase on the front and wrote "Tender new shoots will bloom" on the other side.

"Let's read," I said.

"Do you want to talk about what's going on with Shep?"

"Nothing's going on with Shep."

"If you say so. Have you heard from Kendra yet?"

"No, she still won't return my calls. I've stopped by her house, but she never seems to be home. I don't feel comfortable storming Benton's place to see if she's there. I sent her an engagement card and two long letters apologizing. I guess she's really pissed at me. I can't believe I don't even know the story yet."

"I'll tell you if you want," Geraldine offered.

My stomach fell. "No, thanks."

Kendra and Geraldine had become acquaintances because of me and closer friends because of trading hours at the library when I needed backup. Now Geraldine knew the story of Kendra's romance, and I didn't? Even though I worked with her and Benton? I buried myself in the pages of the new Sophie Kinsella. I didn't think I could handle any more sadness or soul-searching at that moment.

When Shep came back that night, he wouldn't look me in the eyes.

"What's going on with you?" I asked.

"Sorry about lunch."

"Did you have to take care of something at the site?" I helped.

"Yes, exactly."

"What?"

"Oh, there was this project that I thought I might be signing on for, but now I'm not."

"I feel like there's something you're not telling me."

"Why would you think that?"

"Because you're pacing like a caged animal, and you haven't looked me in the eye. We don't usually keep secrets from each other—"

"Oh, really?" he cut me off. Now he was meeting my gaze defiantly.

I backed down. He was right to be angry. I had

kept a big secret for a long time. Though it did seem like an unfair time to bring it up. "I just want to know if I can help," I whispered, reaching out for him. He sank down on the couch, raking his hands through his hair.

"When you first told me about Terabithia, I was hurting for you and with you. I know how much he means to you. I didn't realize it was so much that you were willing to risk everything for him. I remember how bad it was when Sullivan died—when I was starting to get to know you—and I can't even imagine what it must be like to have Terabithia move away after that.

"But for the past few months, I've been feeling like a second thought. I hate the way that sounds, and I hate complaining. But I honestly don't know if you want to marry me. If you see a future with me."

"Of course I do."

"Then why aren't we planning it? Why aren't we talking about it?"

"Let's talk about it. I'm here, Shep. I want to marry you. I'm sorry if I've been distracted."

Shep snorted.

My thoughts flashed to the abandoned calendar under my bed. I hadn't touched it in ages. In a few more months, it would be May, which might be the end of my reproductive system.

"And what if I don't want to have kids for several years?"

Several? "Is that what you're thinking right now?"

"I don't see it as such a rush."

"If you want a biological child, the chances are about to go way down with me . . . and adoption usually takes years."

"Enough already!" Shep snapped. "I'm so sick of hearing about this. You are obsessed."

I reared back like he'd doused me with cold water. "I'm not obsessed. I just know what I want."

"What do you want? Where do I fit in? Or do I?" Shep grabbed my arms. I gasped from surprise. It didn't hurt, though. It felt amazing, as if he had the strength I couldn't find in myself. Our faces were so close I could almost kiss him. I wanted everything to be all right again.

A surge of courage rose up in me. Or maybe it was fear. I hadn't wanted to tell him this way, but there was no other choice. Time had run out, both literally and figuratively. I could suddenly see that clearly. I touched his face. "I want you. And a baby. Not in five years. As soon as possible. I want to find a way to have that and still keep running the library and making the people of Chatsworth happy. I want us to be happy too."

Shep was standing as still as a statue. His face had gone white. I could hear him swallow as he stepped back and released me.

We stood there for a few minutes looking at

each other. His eyes were as dark as the trees in a Bierstadt painting. I felt the blood drain from my heart. He had no response. He didn't want a baby with me right now. From the horrified, trapped look on his face, I wasn't sure he wanted one with me at all anymore.

"Shep? What about you? What do you want?" I had waited too long to ask him this question, but it was my last hope.

His voice was quiet, eerily calm. "I want to go to South America."

Twenty-One

March 2009

Coco called twice each day with reports of Terabithia. It soothed me enormously. I could hear him chatting happily in the background. It didn't sleet anymore in the weeks after Shep left. Every day was sunny. It seemed cruel that the warm weather kept breaking through while I shivered in bed at night without him next to me.

I hadn't called Kendra to let her know. The day after Shep broke up with me, Geraldine had come to sit with me. She would tell Kendra, or Kendra would hear it through the grapevine. After dozens of unreturned calls to her, I couldn't bear another rejection. Maybe my friendship with her wasn't as strong as I had thought. Sullivan had been our connection, and while it seemed like our friendship had taken on a depth of its own, it had been less than two years that I'd known her well. Even if she cared but was still angry at me, we'd have to have a conversation to repair our relationship, and I didn't know if I had the strength to rehash the ways I'd failed her too.

Kendra didn't call when she found out about Shep; she came right over with a hot pizza and a bottle of wine and more cannoli than any two people could eat. Except us.

"Are you all right?"

"I'll be fine," I said as brightly as I could, still in shock about the breakup. It was too strange to be real, too impossible to sink in. I loved him too much to believe he had really left me, especially right after I had lost Terabithia. But I had already taken off the ring because it hurt to look at it.

"How are you now?" she insisted.

"Fine, really," I mumbled.

Kendra opened the box toward me. I took out a piece of pizza, dropping it onto one of my dark-blue plates with the white flowers etched into the rim. These plates always made me happy. They reminded me of dinners with my family. My mother gave them to me when I graduated from art school. Sullivan and I had eaten tons of takeout and a few home-cooked meals on them in New York, and a few—too few—here in Chatsworth.

Kendra put a slice on her plate. The pizza was steaming hot. I took a huge bite anyway, feeling the lavalike cheese slip over my tongue, all grassy, garlicky, buttery goodness.

We munched in silence for a few minutes. I still didn't want to talk about myself or about what had happened between us, but I wanted to hear about her, and I knew that I had to plow through the mess for that to happen.

“Kendra, I am so sorry for being MIA. For causing you pain, for not being around to hear about Benton, for being so selfish.”

“You really pissed me off, Do. I told you I would help you with the library. And you let me a little, but then it was like you forgot what a big commitment it was. People were counting on you.”

“I know. I let everyone down.”

“You have to be better, or you have to take more help, or you have to close it up for good.”

“I know. I will. Be better, I mean.”

“And will you keep it up even if you decide to adopt or have a baby?”

“I can’t say for sure.”

“Please think about it. Realize that the people in Chatsworth have come to count on it. At some point—who knows when—the town library is going to reopen. They’ve been making slow progress, but it’s moving along. If you don’t want to do this anymore, you could close when they open, and no one would blame you. They’d miss it, but they wouldn’t blame you.”

A terrible pain squeezed my heart. Close the library? I couldn’t do that.

“I’ll think about it,” I said anyway. “What about us? What can I do?”

Kendra sighed. “The thing is, after you dropped off the map, it got to the point where so much time had passed where I hadn't told you things because you weren't really there to hear them that it seemed too difficult to catch you up."

My heart sank. That sounded almost . . . irrecoverable.

"Will you catch me up now? I'm here, Kendra. I mean it. I won't disappear again like that."

"It's going to take time, Do. To catch you up. And to feel as though you're there for me. But I want to try."

She wanted to try. That was all I needed to know.

I sprang a huge hug on her. She hugged right back.

"I'm so happy for you." I changed the subject. "Let me see this ring." She shrugged, probably afraid of adding to my pain. I reached out and pulled her hand toward me. "How gorgeous." The square sparked in the light.

"Thanks," Kendra said, her cheeks tinged pink beneath the freckles.

"I don't expect you to repeat the full story for my benefit, but I want to hear as much of it as you're willing to tell."

She grinned and dove right in. "You know how we always used to think Benton could use a muzzle? Even though we appreciated how good natured he was? Well, in the past few months, he's been there every day. Almost every time

I was at the lending library as well as in the teachers' lounge. At first I think I mostly tolerated it. Maybe I was a little lonely." She looked up quickly. "I'm sorry. I didn't mean to make you feel guilty—"

I swallowed and shook my head, urging her on.

"Anyway, he was always talking, talking, talking. Sometimes I listened. Sometimes I tuned him out. It never diminished his enthusiasm for talking. One day, when he wasn't around, the silence felt strange. I missed the sound of his voice. I wanted to hear it *more* often. Can you believe that?" Kendra laughed.

I laughed too. Nope, I couldn't believe that.

"So I guess I realized it works for me. I went out on some other dates, but I found myself thinking I could never really imagine so-and-so confusing the daylights out of me—and intriguing me—by talking about the relationship between bird plumage and natural selection. Or even engaging in a really brainless conversation about whether it would be better to be the Wonder Twin who gets to be an ice cube or the one who gets to be an animal."

I grinned. This gave me an idea for a Celebrate Cartoons Day at the library. The kids in my class were always talking about the cartoons they watched, and the cartoons were beautiful and fantastic and transporting. But it was clear that my students didn't know the magic of classic cartoons—the ones with outlines and only two dimensions.

"When summer was coming, I realized that it wouldn't be as easy for him to appear in my day-to-day. I said, 'You know, Benton, maybe we should go out to dinner sometime.'

"He gave me a big smile. I had come to love that smile. It is always so earnest. Then he said, 'Thank God you finally asked me. I was afraid I was going to run out of things to say.'

"Obviously, that cracked us both up. We didn't plan a date for another night. Instead we went directly to this amazing restaurant at an inn he knew of about an hour from here. I kept thinking, *Dodie would love this place*.

"It was the best date I'd ever had. He asked me if I wanted to meet for breakfast the next morning, and we did. I love spending time with him. I miss him when he's gone. So yep, this fall I'll become Mrs. Benton. I can hardly wait."

I gave her another bear hug. "Kendra, that is wonderful. A story-circle-worthy tale! You deserve it. You both do. I can't wait to spend more time with him. Outside of the teachers' lounge and the library!"

"Speaking of which, how are things going with the library . . . um . . . situation?" Kendra asked gingerly.

"Much better." I sighed with relief. "It's up and running, and I have a plan to get the word out at school, with Elmira's help, of course."

Kendra squeezed my hand. "I'm so happy to hear it. It's your Tara."

My Tara?

"Listen, Do, Benton's parents are in town, and they want me to meet them for cocktails. I could stay here instead and hang with them some other time, though."

"No, you should spend time with your new in-laws-to-be," I urged her. "Thanks for coming over. For being patient with me while I figure it all out."

"I am sorry I shut you out. As mad as I was, I should have been there for you. I didn't realize what a rough time you were going through."

"I'll be okay."

"I know you will," she said, putting her hand over mine. "But just to be sure, have the last cannoli when I'm gone."

Maddie took off work to come and stay with me. She probably expected to find me completely depressed, but she was surprised.

"What do you want to watch?" I asked her, holding out a bouquet of DVD cases. We were both wearing pj's—my idea—and I had made a heap of popcorn sprinkled with cumin as well as a big batch of brownies (well, actually, not that big since we'd eaten most of the batter). It was exactly like when we were girls.

Maddie pulled a face.

"What's wrong, Mad?" I asked her. "These are our favorites! What do you think, *Pretty in Pink*? Or *Amélie*? *Bridget Jones's Diary*? *Sixteen Candles*? *Thirteen Going on Thirty*? Or . . . or . . . wait . . ." I dug through the pile in front of me. "What about *Some Like It Hot*? *Serendipity*?"

"Jesus," Maddie said, pawing through the cabinet under the TV. "It's like the Romantic Comedy Library of Congress in here."

"Of course!" My face hurt from smiling. "Just like always for the Fairisle girls!"

"Noooo . . . ," she countered, shaking her head. "*I* have horror films too. And action films. So does Coco . . . at least she will now that she has a DVD player and not a banana leaf filled with water for her entertainment. This is crazy . . ." Her tone was light, but I could feel her studying me.

That was nothing compared to when we finished watching *Sabrina* (the Audrey/Humphrey version, bien sûr) and headed up to bed. When I got back from brushing my teeth, she was standing in front of my bedside table, forehead deeply creased as she took in the tower of books that topped it. I tried not to look her in the eye as I slipped under the covers.

Maddie perched on the edge of the bed,

transferring the books, one by one, into a row in front of me.

Far from the Madding Crowd. That scene with impetuous Bathsheba and patient Gabriel, who had loved her steadfastly and silently for so many years after her first rejection and finally found the moment and the courage to try again:

> "If I only knew one thing—whether you would allow me to love you and win you and marry you after all—If I only knew that!"
>
> "But you never will know," she murmured.
>
> "Why?"
>
> "Because you never ask."

Emma. When Mr. Knightley finally declares himself to her: "If I loved you less, I might be able to talk about it more."

On it went. Maddie was watching my expression. My face didn't lie; I could feel the pain and then the pleasure wash over it as I relived each scene that I had reread so many times I had committed them to memory.

"Do, what are you doing with these?" Her voice was so kind, so gentle, and so unlike Maddie that it was a little troubling. She was obviously worried about me.

"I like to read."

"Duh," Maddie retorted. Then more softly, "You know what I mean."

"They make me feel better. It's like . . . like . . . romantic catharsis," I explained.

"But how much catharsis does one person need? It's as though you're drugging yourself with other people's happy endings."

I gasped. Maddie was absolutely right. As she flicked out the lights, I felt the dark sadness I'd sewn up inside me spill out.

I managed to put on a brave face for the rest of Maddie's visit, not letting on that our conversation had opened the huge wound I'd been denying.

Once I admitted to myself how terrible I felt, everything shifted downward. My art projects at school were lackluster at best. At night, after work, I would sit at the circulation desk and help all the happy visitors who had returned, but I couldn't concentrate on reading anything myself. When I wasn't in the library, I would avoid being in the rest of my home, where there were too many memories. Geraldine and Kendra kept me busy with dinners and drinks as much as they could, but there were still plenty of evenings where I would close the library at seven as usual, rush to the gym I had joined as a distraction, then wander aimlessly around the grocery store inventing recipes with complicated ingredient lists that would take time to hunt down among the aisles. The house I loved so much waited for me like an old friend I'd grown apart from. I couldn't find the appetite to eat the meals I made or take any pleasure in making them. My fridge was full of leftovers, and soon so was my freezer.

After "dinner," I would put on my pajamas and plunk down at my desk, as if it might inspire me to do something creative or just . . . something. Instead, the only remedy that remotely soothed the ache in my chest was stroking the back of the small horse statue that my student Barnaby had given me. It looked like . . . well, let's just say it wasn't perfect. First of all, there was the brown lumpiness. Second of all, one of its ears had broken off. *Well,* I thought defiantly, *none of us are perfect*. Even though I knew that wasn't why Shep had left, I couldn't help but feel slightly self-righteous, like he wanted me to be flawless and couldn't handle it when I wasn't. To the point where he hadn't even called to check on me. Or written. As time passed, I had to admit it: he hadn't loved me enough. When things had gotten difficult, he hadn't been there for me. He hadn't cared enough to stay.

• • •

On one of my grocery store trips, I ran into Mike in the cereal aisle. "Hey there! Haven't seen you in a while."

"Hey, Do."

My chest twisted. Mike only called me that because Shep used to.

"How're things?" I managed to say.

"Good, good. Sorry I haven't been at the library much lately. I didn't want you to feel awkward. If, like, my presence reminded you of . . ." He paused, debating inwardly. *Oh no.* "You know, Shep is in—"

I held up my palm, shaking my head. Mike's jaw snapped shut.

"Unless he needs a book recommendation . . . ," I whispered, not trusting my voice, worried I'd been rude.

Mike's eyes grew wide. "No . . . no, he's okay."

"Then I'm sure he'll tell me if he wants me to know."

"Gotcha. Okay, anyway, the kids and I will see you at story circle on Saturday."

"See you then."

Concerned about Maddie's report, Coco came to stay with me and brought Terabithia, knowing he would cheer me up. She looked more beautiful than ever. Helping other people and being a mother really became her. I thought about all the funny postcards she had sent me while in Africa. Especially the one where she was looking at her arm, waiting for a three-foot-long guinea worm to burrow excruciatingly through her skin. I felt like I had guinea worm of the heart.

"Have you tried to talk to him?" she asked after we put Boo to sleep.

"No. It seems pointless. He would come back if he wanted to."

"Maybe what he wanted was for you to *fight* for him."

That stopped me for a second. "Shep doesn't play games like that," I murmured. Out of habit, I brought Barnaby's horse out from my drawer and began to stroke his back.

"Doodoo Horse!" Coco cried, snatching him out of my hands. "I was wondering what happened to him."

A faint smile played over my lips. Coco and Maddie had burst into a fit of giggles when they first saw the little statue. I hadn't minded. Too much. After all, in French, *doudou* might be one of the nicest words you could think of. It means that deliciously soft stuffed animal that you carry around all the time, your very own Velveteen Rabbit. Still, I had made the executive decision not to share the statue's nickname with Barnaby since at six he probably hadn't learned French yet.

"Yep, Doodoo Horse," I repeated joylessly. Coco gave me a hug, and we headed to sleep.

It was time for Terabithia's snack. I found the rhythm of his and Coco's days—the specific routines, with space in between for play—comforting.

"Want to take him to Olive's for a bite?" I suggested after we had a rousing rendition of *The Piping-Hot Frog Book* in the library for old time's sake. "If we leave right now, we might be able to get there when the chocolate chip cookies are coming out of the oven."

"Well . . . ," Coco mused. "We're trying to watch his intake of sugar. When I gave him chocolate, he got a little deranged. He practically lobotomized Sheepy. Maybe there will be something healthier at Billybee's Bakery?"

"Right," I agreed. I wasn't exactly sure what that would be, but I wasn't about to argue. "Benton, would you take over for me?"

"Sure thing, boss," he said without even missing a beat scanning books in. Kendra continued to help out at the library, but now Benton came without her too. Apparently she wasn't the only thing about the library he liked. He liked the volunteerism. The can-do spirit. The people. Being surrounded by knowledge. A chance to meet his students' parents in a more informal setting. The funny things people asked for in the request envelope. Benton was one enthusiastic guy, luckily for Kendra. Luckily for me and the library too. I was now willing to admit I needed help even without a baby.

Coco pushed open the door of Billybee's, and Terabithia ran through it. "Yay! Yay! Yay! Candy!"

Well, yeah, okay. He wasn't wrong.

Against a bright white backdrop, Billybee's had added pale-blue and mint-green checkered gingham tablecloths, and all the cakes sat on vintage jadeite cake trays. Fruit-covered and pastel-colored cupcakes lined the shelves of the display case. Stacks of snickerdoodles, chocolate meringue clouds, and oatmeal raisin cookies beckoned from jars with pale-green lids.

Terabithia's face was pressed up against the glass. "Want dat, want dat." He kept looking over his shoulder to see if we were paying attention. "Nanas. Yehyo." He pointed.

There on the middle shelf was a huge crystal bowl brimming with banana pudding. The creamy top was unbroken, and layers of cut bananas and crumbled gingersnaps bisected the pillows of pudding underneath.

"Of course! That's my favorite too." I squatted down and hugged him.

Coco was standing beside us. What did she expect, bringing him to a bakery? *At least he picked something with fruit in it,* I thought.

"I have, I have," he pleaded with Coco, patting his belly.

She looked at me and shrugged. "At least he picked something with fruit in it."

Ha! "Yeah, and there's the . . . um . . . calcium," I improvised.

Terabithia sat in my lap while I spooned pudding into his mouth. He got bored of it pretty quickly and made me dig out the banana and cookie pieces. "Down," he commanded. "Dada put Bissia down."

"What do you say?" Coco prompted.

"Peez."

I set him on his feet. He had left plenty of pudding for us. As he began exploring, Coco took a spoonful, slurped it off the spoon, and said, "It's good to see you smiling."

I'd tried to put on a brave face.

"It's pretty obvious you've been feeling profoundly miserable," she continued.

"Really?"

"Yes. You haven't looked like your normal fashion-plate self, dressed up for our video chats, in ages."

I took the bait. "Sorry."

"C'mon, Do, I'm only teasing. You always look great. How are you doing, really?"

I was tired of pretending to be fine when I wasn't. What was the point of keeping it from my family and friends anyway? It wasn't like they expected me to be happy all the time. I was the only one who had put that kind of impossible burden on myself. "Terrible."

Admitting it made me feel lighter. Kind of.

She patted my knee. "I know. What can I do?"

"Move here with Mark and Terabithia?" I said, half joking—and obviously half not.

Coco gave Terabithia a long look. He was licking the side of a container of lilac-colored frosting, saying "Bissia purpuh."

"I wish we could, but we're getting him settled. I wouldn't want to uproot him again . . ."

"Oh, of course." I waved away the rest of her words. "I know. I was totally being selfish."

"Well, I wholeheartedly encourage that. You haven't done enough of that in the past thirty or so years. Remember when you used to give all your dessert to me and Maddie? And the front seat of the car? And your toys?" She shook her head fondly. "Why don't *you* consider moving in with *us* and letting us spoil you for a while?"

I hadn't even thought of that possibility.

No, I couldn't move away from Chatsworth. Elmira, who was still grounded, needed me. So did . . . *No, Dodie.* I stopped myself. *What do* you *want?*

After Coco and Boo were asleep, I crept downstairs and turned on the light in the sunroom. I sat behind the circulation desk and felt my heart swell with excitement thinking of all the new books that waited on the shelves for me—and the patrons—to discover. I plopped down in the wing chair and remembered all the times I had seen Elmira sitting here looking peaceful or stifling a laugh. I shook the folded pieces of paper out of the request envelope.

More razberry bars please!!!

Could you get another copy of Llama Misses Mama*? My son's favorite and it's always gone*

Elmo books!

I love library please stay open forever thank you!

I sighed with relief. What I really wanted was to stay in Chatsworth. To be around these people that I loved. To make them happy as well as myself. I knew now how blurry the line sometimes became between the two. I wouldn't figure it out right away. But I had learned that a lending library was something I needed as much as they did.

While Terabithia napped on his and Coco's last day in Chatsworth, I stood under the shower long after washing off the Moroccan rose oil gel, feeling the cleansing heat pelt down on my head, breathing the steam in deeply, and feeling the tingling in all my cells.

Coco picked up lobster rolls for lunch. We brought them onto the deck and ate them with our faces toward the sun, washing the buttered grilled buns and sweet briny meat down with black cherry soda. Coco fed Terabithia English muffin pizzas. He seemed to feel his lunch was as indulgent as ours. Afterward, we took him into the backyard to run around. He pulled on my leg, and I knelt down over my stretched and satisfied stomach.

When we were at eye level, he pat-pat-patted me on the shoulder. “Hide-and-seek?” I checked.

“Yeah,” Terabithia agreed, then waited expectantly.

“Okay, if I find you”—I pretended to think hard—“then I’ll buy you an ice cream.”

With a huge grin he was off like a shot, crooning “Chocolate ’nilla ’stachio,” his little legs remarkably fast even though he ran akimbo. I counted to twenty—long enough to build the suspense, an eternity for a little boy—then headed for the honeysuckle patch.

As I stood there inhaling, the scent of the flowers was as thick and spicy as gingerbread baking, then as sweet and light as a sip of liquid sunshine. Behind a slip of flowers, the top of Terabithia’s hair peeked out, his curls—and no doubt his whole body—shaking with excitement. The slow rising within me grew until I felt double oxygen, double blood, double happiness. So much happiness that I couldn’t measure it—and for the first time in so long.

Twenty-Two

April 2009

I was on speaker with Maddie when Kendra arrived to keep me company one night. Kendra overheard my sister saying, "The only way to get over someone is to get under someone else."

"She's so right!" Kendra cried. Ever since meeting Maddie, Kendra had become the other number one member of the Maddie Fairisle Fan Club. Female member, at least. She thought Maddie's idea was a fantastic one.

"A fling would be perfect for you right now!" She offered to set me up on dates or wing me at bars, but queasiness rolled over me whenever I thought of any lips touching mine besides . . . *those* lips . . . the ones I'd planned to be loyal to for the rest of my life. Maybe he had changed his mind about that promise . . . he obviously *had* changed his mind . . . and skipped town to no-one-knew-where . . . but when I tried to envision the spine-tingling pleasure of someone new, my body revolted. It was impossible.

More time, I reassured myself. *That's what you need.*

One afternoon, when I was walking on a woodsy path about a mile from my house, I discovered a little pond I'd never seen before. I started to walk a lazy circle around it. The chilly air was still as soft as the underside of a rose petal, and the sky was almost the same color. It was later than I had thought, but I didn't care. For the moment, I had nowhere to be. It was a delicious, forgotten feeling.

I had stopped looking for Shep around town. I'd never let myself count the weeks since he'd been gone; a haze of time was better than a certain amount of absence. Where was he? Still somewhere in South America? Back but keeping to himself in Chatsworth? Frequenting places where he knew I didn't go? Doubtful. It seemed as though he was farther away, as if Mike—and the town—missed him too. I wondered if he would ever come back. The fact that I could consider the possibility he wouldn't was a relief—it showed my denial was over even if my heartache wasn't.

Facing my denial was the only way to move forward. I went directly upstairs to my room, knelt down beside the bed, reached underneath, and pulled out the toile-covered box. A skin of dust sat on top. May 2009, the final month of my supposed fertility window, which I had circled in red and starred in gold and drawn fireworks around in orange when I first bought the calendar, was next month.

I hadn't looked at the calendar in many months. Thank heaven. This was one project I was proud to have given up on. I ripped each page into confetti so small it was like snowflakes. That seemed fitting. No day, no week, no month out of all that time had been exactly alike. Not one of them had brought me a baby, but each and every one of them had been singularly beautiful and important anyway.

I uncreased the piece of paper where I'd figured out the math of it after the dinner with Maddie. I laughed as I looked at my confused scrawls, calculations, and recalculations. It all seemed so arbitrary to me now. Would my ovaries really obey such a silly-seeming rule? It could have been a coincidence about my mom and grandma. I ripped that page to shreds too. Either the math was right, or it wasn't. Either I would be able to have a baby biologically, or I wouldn't. I could probably do it alone, but I could now admit to myself that I didn't really want to, and—what's more—I didn't really have to, at least not yet. I knew my mom was right: everything would work out the way it was supposed to. It didn't matter if my child was conceived or adopted. Whatever child came into my life, however that child came into my life, I would be an amazing and loving mother just like I'd always wanted.

For now, I would be a good mother to the library. I had a lot of catching up to do.

Twenty-Three

"This may be the most delicious thing you could ever make," Chloë pronounced. "My *grandmère* used to do a dacquoise for special occasions, but this one puts hers to shame." As soon as the words came out of her mouth, Chloë looked back and forth over both shoulders as if her offended grandmother might materialize.

"Aw, you don't have to say that," Sam replied with a delighted smile. At our first Foodie Book Club, she had made inedible hardtack. Now she was responsible for the almond-hazelnut meringue confection with mocha buttercream that all of us were snarfing down from a recipe in Ruth Reichl's *Comfort Me with Apples*.

Kendra licked her fingers. "I love her honesty in this book. The story of how she tried to adopt Gavi and then Gavi's parents took her back was one of the most heart-wrenching things I've read in a long time." She glanced over at me.

I swallowed. That part of the book had definitely struck a chord. There was Sianeh. And Terabithia.

Melissa looked at her watch. "I've gotta go pick Deandra up at ballet, and then we're going to the Cherry Blossom Festival in Eagle Ridge with Trey." A glow suffused her face as she said it. Apparently, she had read *Far from the Madding Crowd* and had gotten the message. Or maybe getting to know the boneheaded, arrogant Channing Robison had soon made her realize that Trey was a much bigger catch and a man who would actually respect and be kind to her and her daughter. "Trey calls this 'Food and Feelings Book Club.' " We all laughed.

Geraldine burst through the front door. "You're done, right?" she asked unceremoniously.

"Yep," I said. "We were finishing up."

"Good. Dodie, I need to talk to you *stat*."

"All right. Bye, everyone. Amazing dacquoise, Sam, really."

As soon as we were alone, Geraldine said, "Sit down."

"What's going on? You're freaking me out."

"Okay, so you know how I missed Foodie Book Club today because I got called in for an update on the progress at the Chatsworth Library?"

"Yeah."

"Well, guess what?"

"It's almost done?" I had driven by the library dozens of times, and while I didn't know how long the inside stuff would take, it had a welcoming air again instead of a deserted one. It seemed like it was almost . . . ready. Geraldine had told me that they were expecting to finish sometime this spring or summer. But after more than two years of waiting, I wasn't about to believe it until the news became official.

"Yes. And guess why?"

"I have no idea."

"Shep has been assigned as the foreman for the rest of the project."

So Shep was back. I felt like all the wind had been knocked out of me. "Oh?"

"Yes. And not only that, but he secured the funding from the investors of the mall he worked on and got an architect on board for the last details for some crazy-low price because she is a major bibliophile. He cut through the last of the red tape, and now it's really happening."

I was stunned silent. Shep was back. Part of me wanted to throw up. Shep was going to get the Chatsworth Library finished. The other part of me thought that might have been the most romantic thing I'd ever heard.

"He practically pounced on me to ask about you," Geraldine continued.

"You spoke with him?"

"Yeah. Sort of. I didn't say much because I wasn't sure what to say."

"So what did you say?"

"I told him you were doing great, that things are going really well for Terabithia with Coco and Mark."

"Okay."

"Dodie, how do we feel about him? Are we . . .

angry? Or are we . . . friendly? Because I wasn't sure how to act."

"Can I get back to you?" My voice was shaking.

"Sure, honey."

Kendra was next. Then Mackie and Jeff. Everyone I knew was running into Shep, and I hadn't seen him once. Heck, he was probably having tea with Elmira's mother by now. Then the first postcard came.

I was in the library after a rousing story circle that somehow devolved into a recounting of the craziest things that had happened at the bachelor and bachelorette parties we'd been to.

When everyone cleared out, I pulled *Remembrance of Things Past* off the shelf. *Swann's Way*, the first of the seven books in Proust's masterpiece, was as far as I'd gotten. I'd dipped into the other volumes but was always happiest to return to Marcel's childhood with him even though it was fraught with the loneliness of nighttime.

In my mind's eye, the gorgeously vibrating, unfurling sentences in the book had swept me outside, onto the Guermantes Way, under bowers and among bushes of hawthorn blossoms as pink and ruffled as little bloomers for a baby girl. Like Marcel in all his wide-eyed wonder, I imagined soaking up the smells of freshness from the grass and the wet soil and, most of all, those divine trees. They left us both—Marcel and me—literally gasping for breath.

As if the universe was determined to make me faint dead away, Anoop arrived at that moment with the mail, and he handed me a large envelope that smelled like the kind of earthy, irregular Irish soap that's handmade. It was filled with postcards from Shep. The dates written on them went as far back as September, but the postmark on the envelope was from the day before in Chatsworth. I read them in order.

> Dear Do,
> It's only been twenty-four hours since our breakup, but so much has changed already. I took the first flight I could get this morning, and now I am on a different continent. I am so tired that I feel like I could fall asleep for a hundred years, but I know that I'll be lucky even to get one hour of rest. I really do think this is best for us, though.
> All my love, Shep

Ouch. Way to send a message. It was amazing how much a wound that had healed could still hurt.

By the time I finished reading the postcards, I felt intruded upon.

Because of the sadness that filled them, proving

how hard it had been for Shep, I also felt more hopeful than I wanted to admit.

I made a decision.

"Hi," I said when he answered his cell.

"Hi."

"Shep, this has got to stop."

"I'm sorry?" His voice rang with curiosity.

"I don't think we have a choice but to talk about this situation," I announced. "I'm coming over to your place tonight at eight."

"Oh, um, okay. Do you want me to come to yours?"

"No. I'll see you at eight." I hung up quickly.

Going to Shep's apartment meant I had more control over when I left. I could escape as soon as I needed to, if I needed to. Since moving to Chatsworth, he had been living in a furnished long-term rental apartment that was perfectly fine but pretty impersonal. He'd been more than happy to spend all his time at my cozy house, so his apartment was a much less fraught place for us to meet now.

I stood outside his door for three full minutes. I breathed very slowly through my nose. It would suck if I hyperventilated and passed out on his doorstep. Finally, I summoned the courage to knock.

The door opened so fast it was as if he'd been standing behind it waiting for me.

With effort I lifted my eyes from the doorknob.

Shep was the tannest I'd ever seen him.

He looked taller than I remembered.

His sleeves were rolled up to the elbows.

And his hair was wet.

I took little sips of air through my mouth. That didn't do much good. I felt like I might black out, and his scent was as strong as if my face had been pressed against his neck, his chin tucked over the crown of my head.

"Are you moving out?" I asked, embarrassed at the obvious alarm in my voice as I spotted the boxes all over the apartment.

"No," Shep laughed. "It does look like that, though, doesn't it? I guess I got carried away buying souvenirs for the Chatsworth crew."

"How nice," I said.

"There's one for . . . well, let's have a drink first, okay? I mean, I could certainly use one. Only if you want a drink. Otherwise—"

"Sure, Shep," I said as brightly as I could. "A drink"—(or five)—"would be perfect."

The white wine was cooling on the back of my throat. A few sips later, I began to relax. It had been eight minutes, and I hadn't burst into tears or yelled at him. Shep was drinking his beer more quickly. I forced myself not to follow him with my eyes as he got up from the couch to grab another from the fridge and then sat back down.

"Where have you been?" I asked as lightly as I could, running my finger over the nubby fabric of the cushion.

"All over South America." His eyes sparkled. "Buenos Aires, Cuzco, the Pacaya-Samiria National Reserve, Iguazu Falls . . . little beach towns totally off the beaten path . . . on a traveling houseboat, for some of the time, with a guy who builds boats based on ancient Amazonian techniques. It was amazing."

Wow, I thought. It was what Shep had been dreaming of doing for so long.

"That's amazing, Shep," I said. He winced a little. "I'm really happy for you." In spite of myself, I added, "I can't wait to hear all about it."

"Really?" he said, and his voice was so full of boyish excitement that I swallowed the lump and nodded.

"Dodie, please . . . ," he began, and I already knew what he was going to say.

The words rushed out of my mouth before he could speak. "No, Shep. How can I trust you again?"

Shep hung his head. "I—"

I wasn't done yet.

"You left me like *that,*" I accused him, cutting the air with my hand. "Like it was nothing. Like you were gone and never coming back. When you *know* that is probably the *one* thing I can't handle. Because you did exactly what my birth father did. That is *exactly* what my birth father did."

I didn't care that I was repeating myself. This had been pent up in me for months.

Shep reached out as if to comfort me. Realizing he didn't have the right, he raked his hand through his hair instead. "Of course you would see it that way," he said, anguished.

"Anyone would," I shot back.

"That's not what I meant—I mean, of course they would—but . . . but Do, I didn't leave without thinking of you. I thought about it all the time—what it might do to you—"

"Could have fooled me," I interrupted. I couldn't seem to stop myself. "You were willing to risk causing me that kind of pain?"

Shep looked at me imploringly. "Please," he said. "Give me a second to tell you, okay? I thought of you constantly, Do."

How could I believe him when I'd heard nothing for months?

He handed me another fat envelope that had been sitting on the side table. "You're probably wondering how you were supposed to know I was thinking about you when you didn't hear from me? Well, I was telling you every day . . ."

The flap of the envelope was torn in a few places. The edges of dozens of postcards peeked out of the top. Like the ones he'd sent me . . .

but more. So many more. Dozens and dozens of them . . .

He held the whole thing out to me and scootched closer. Too close. His scent was distracting, and now there was absolutely no hiding the fact that my hands were gently shaking.

He was still getting closer, and I suddenly found my head against his chest, his chin tucked over it. Lightly touching some of the postcards I'd turned out onto my lap—postcards that I could see, even as tears of relief filled my eyes, contained more stories from his months of travel, each and every one of them signed "All my love, Shep"—he said softly, "I'll tell you everything now, but since I couldn't wait until I saw you again to share it with you, I wrote you these . . ."

It took a long time before I could speak. Shep waited. Finally, I said, "For now, tell me the best part."

"I hardly remember the first few weeks," he admitted, his voice contorting with pain.

Our faces were so close. He wasn't going to finish the thought; he was lifting my chin. I knew what was about to happen, but I was almost too dazzled by the smell of him, by the ache of remembering how his lips felt. Almost.

I stood up quickly, knocking the pile of postcards onto the floor. "Sorry," I mumbled, grateful to avoid his eyes as I bent down to pick them up.

"No, I'm sorry." He knelt down to help me. I handed the ones I'd collected to him, and he stuffed them back into the envelope.

"I—I have to go, Shep."

He sighed. "I understand. Let me walk you out."

"Thank you for the wine. I'm glad you're back." The warmth in my own words surprised me, and it was all the encouragement Shep needed.

"Do—" he began again.

"No, Shep," I objected, pressing the elevator button but half hoping it would take forever to come.

"Please, Do. I don't know if I'll see you again after this—if you'll want to—so I *need* to say this. Being away made me understand everything. How I must have hurt you.

"Then I realized two things:

"First of all, no man will ever deserve you, so if I'm the lucky bastard you love back, that's a gift I'm too selfish to give someone else. I can't live without you—it feels wrong.

"Second, I have to compromise more. What you want is important. If you need me to be ready for something, and I'm not—if it's really important to you, whatever it is—then I will try to be ready too. I know we won't always be on the same timeline about things, but if you let me have another chance, I promise I will spend the rest of my life trying to make you happy and to grow with you."

It was hard for Shep to say things like this. I could see that he'd probably thought about them everywhere from the Pampas to a puddle jumper.

Wiping the tears off my cheeks as I turned to go, all I could say was, "How do I know you won't leave again?"

His fingers alighted on my wrist, staying me.

"Do, please. There's more; there's a story that these postcards don't tell. Will you let me explain?"

"No, Shep," I murmured. "It's too much." *Don't look at him.*

Just as the elevator doors slid shut, he pushed one last postcard through. At the top he had written today's date. There was a picture of an heirloom tomato on the front. It said only,

> I didn't expect you to wait for me, but I've come back to you anyway. Now I will wait—for as long as it takes—for you to come back to me.

I lay in bed that night remembering the look of shocked disappointment on his face as he disappeared between the elevator doors. He had really believed it would work. The last postcard, well, that was just . . . romantic and maddening.

More importantly, how did he know I would

come back to him? Was he prepared to wait 62 years if it took me that long to forgive him? Or 117, if Jonah Brownlee's first attempts at a Divine Life Potion proved fruitful? It made me angry that Shep still assumed he knew the person I was after months of absence and that we could go back to how we were the second he decided that was what he wanted.

Except, a part of me argued back, *he* does *know you. And he still left.* I wasn't ready to accept any kind of love that seemed conditional. I still wanted it all, and I still believed that wasn't an impossible thing to ask for.

At 3:00 a.m., mind fuzzy, I tried to snuggle back into sleep as if it were a warm robe. The smile I wore when I woke again at 4:00 a.m. quickly faded. I lay very still, focusing on the tendrils of the dream that were slipping away.

Scattered snippets caught and held; the tan oval of Shep's face above me, laughing; wondering why I was flat on my back on the ground; his arms lifting me up, brushing me off, a kiss on my cheek that was publicly chaste but secretly contained a gentle lick, a promise for what was to come later; my face flaming in the midnight darkness as he shucked off his shorts and ran into the water; the ache of longing as he stroked up and down my arm distractedly while talking to my parents.

I rocked around in my sheets like a malcontent caterpillar. Shep was in town now. Minutes away. My bed was still so empty that I might as well have been the one mosquito netted into a bed, in a clutch of trees, somewhere on the South American plains.

It was no use. I couldn't sleep. Maybe a good book would help.

Outside the windows of the lending library, the trees were starting to puff green. Some perennials from the previous owners popped up every year, making me look like a chrysanthemum-yellow-and-azalea-amethyst-colored thumb instead of the brown thumb I probably was. I could make out the heads of some of the newly bloomed flowers bowing in the morning air. I settled into the squishy chair and picked up *Trading Dreams at Midnight*. The hours sped up as I disappeared into the story of Neena and Tish and the ways they dealt with the pain of their absent mother. At six, I texted Shep: Come by after you've had coffee. Let's go for a walk.

Shep was there by seven thirty. His hands were in his pockets as he leaned against his truck, his eyes riveted on my face. He swallowed hard. We drove in silence to Little Duck Park.

We headed up the side of the hill we'd climbed the day Terabithia had gone home with Coco and Mark. I could say that now: home. I knew it was true. I hadn't lost Terabithia; he was still in my life.

Losing Shep had been the most painful thing I'd ever experienced because I wasn't sure I had sacrificed him to something that would make him happier. I didn't know what I'd sacrificed him to at all anymore or whether we could ever go back to the way we had been.

The spring sun was strong, but as we climbed higher, the weight of the air compressed into coldness. From the top of the hill, the roads led out of Chatsworth toward the highway in a haze of bright leaves.

Shep reached for my hand. He had been pacing ever since we reached the summit. Now he led me over to a rock to sit.

"Do you remember soon after we started dating, I was acting sort of oddly, and I never really told you why?" he began. I nodded. "And how a number of other times, I got up from bed when I heard something at your window?"

A number of times? There had been that once. I half nodded, half shook my head.

"Well, it was my ex, Quinn. They were all Quinn."

Quinn? What was she doing?

"You know how I told you she and I broke up partly because she wanted a baby?"

I nodded.

"Really, really badly. She wanted one so badly that she . . . that she . . . ," he faltered.

I started breathing slowly through my nose. "Go on."

"She threatened to get pregnant whether I wanted it or not." He raked his hand through his hair. "By that point, I had already fallen out of love with her. It wasn't the idea of a baby. It was the way she always tried to make me feel small. She talked all the time about her ex-boyfriend whenever I told her no about a baby, and she said I treated her badly. It was all manipulation to try to get me to do what she wanted.

"Then I met you. Suddenly, this whole world opened up to me. I didn't feel small around you. I felt like you were part of my team. Part of everyone's team. I fell in love with you, and that filled me with guilt for having stayed with Quinn at all after I realized I didn't love her—even before I met you."

"So I broke it off with her—the weekend you and Maddie went away together. She couldn't believe it. She went nuts. She trashed my apartment. She followed me everywhere for the next few weeks. Followed us. I protected you from it. I knew she wouldn't do anything serious, and I wanted you so badly I was afraid she would scare you away. I worried that she would contact you. Instead, I kept intercepting her before she could.

“One night, when she started getting bolder, she came to my apartment. You weren’t there, but you could have been. Instead of telling her to go away, like I had the other times, I decided I needed to try to make her understand, so I told her she could come meet me at the site the next day. Neutral ground.

“She looked different. Scared, somehow. As if she’d been caught committing some kind of crime, and now she was frightened by the consequences. I thought it was just because she understood it was over and had to figure out what to do now.

“I told her it had to stop. She said she knew, and that was why she was leaving town. ‘Unless you want me to stay?’ she asked.

“I said no, it was definitely over between us, and not to stay for me.

“Quinn started crying. I let her cry on my shoulder for a second, and then I told her goodbye and wished her luck. She cried all the way back to the car. She seemed so broken. I couldn’t believe she loved me that much and had treated me so badly. But I didn’t dig deeper, didn’t ask any questions; I was off the hook with her, and I was crazy about you, and all I cared about was that she was going away.”

He paused. “You okay?”

“Yes, go on.” Something worse was coming—I could feel it.

"For the next few weeks, she called me dozens of times. I never picked up. I put my phone on vibrate so that I didn't have to hear it ringing. I screened my calls. I wanted a clean break. I wanted you. Being with you made me so happy that I forgot all about her, as awful as that may sound. The phone calls, any shred of guilt I might have felt, became like a gnat I could swat away.

"I didn't hear from her for more than nine months after she finally cut it out. One of the guys at the site told me she'd moved to New York. I figured she'd gotten on with her life. Then, the day Mark and Coco took Terabithia home, she called me. Remember when I got the call at Mackie and Jeff's?"

Of course I remembered.

"She said she had to see me and was heading back to Chatsworth to meet up. Turns out she'd been living at home with her parents in Greenwich, not in New York. I tried to dissuade her, but she insisted on coming. The next day, she showed up at the site. With . . . a . . ."

I steeled myself for what was coming.

"A two-month-old baby boy. Who looked a little . . ."

"Little what?" I whispered.

"Like me. As much as a two-month-old baby can." He pushed himself off the rock and knelt down. "It's not what you think," he rushed to say, taking my icy hands in his.

"Quinn said, 'Meet Max. Your little boy.' I nearly fainted on the spot.

" 'Max is your son.' She was smiling and told me to do the math.

"I did the math. It would have been a little less than a year earlier, before I admitted my feelings for you. It was before Quinn and I had stopped . . . well, it was when I was still in denial about how wrong she was for me.

"I asked her how it could have happened when we always used protection. I had made sure of that; I didn't trust her. Dodie, are you sure you're okay? You look green."

I waved my hand to signal I'd be fine. Hearing about Shep's sex with his ex-girlfriend was the least of my worries now. I wanted him to get to the part where it wasn't what I was thinking it was. *Stat*.

"Quinn admitted to poking holes in the condom beforehand. I will not repeat what I said to her in response to that. She told me I shouldn't speak to her that way since she was the mother of my child.

"I said I didn't believe her and asked why she hadn't told me before, why now?

"She said she had tried, right when she found out, and reminded me that I wouldn't take her calls. She said she had to try again now because 'Maxie' would soon be aware of what was going on around him, that eventually he would go to school and see the other kids with moms and dads. She wanted to give me a chance to be part of his life and even hinted that maybe we could try again.

"I told her no way and demanded a paternity test.

"She tried to talk me out of it, but I wasn't having it. We did the test. It came back negative when I was in Peru. She admitted to me that she'd cheated on me with her ex when we were having problems and that he wanted nothing to do with her. It made me sick to my stomach to think how she'd lied to me. To think that down the road she would have told that little boy I was his daddy. To put me in that position!"

Shep was silent, as if waiting for me to sympathize or at least say something.

"Why didn't you tell me?" I finally asked, my voice breaking . . . my heart breaking for that little boy. None of this was his fault, and yet he was the one who was going to suffer the most.

"I felt like I couldn't. You had just lost Terabithia. How could I tell you that I might be the father of another child out in the world?

"Then the night we fought, when you said you wanted to have a baby right away . . . after you'd admitted that you were trying to adopt Terabithia a few months earlier without telling me . . . it was clear how determined you were. I know it wasn't fair to see any similarities in my situation with

Quinn and with you, but it was too much of a coincidence. I couldn't process it all. I panicked, and I ran."

"I was your fiancée," I said softly. "You didn't even give me a chance. You didn't even stay to talk about it. You left me . . . you made me think you'd abandoned me, just like . . . just like h-he did . . ."

"I know." His eyes filled with tears. "I know, and I'm so, so sorry."

I felt sick to my stomach. All my anger at Shep, which had been bubbling up under the hurt, came to the surface, and if I didn't get out of there, I was going to explode. "I need to be alone," I said through gritted teeth. He caught up with me where the hill started to slope downward and grabbed my arm.

"No!" I yelled, pushing him away. "You hypocrite! Don't follow me! I can't even look at you!" I choked out.

"Dodie, wait."

I turned around to face him. "No! You . . . you *asshole,*" I sobbed. "You have the nerve to lecture me about taking away your choice, when all this time . . . when you allowed me to think it was because of something *I'd* done. That *I* failed in some way. That you didn't love me enough. You can go to hell!"

Shep's mouth hung open. He was looking at me like I was a different person. That's exactly what

I was. Not the same helpless four-year-old. Not even the person I'd been three months earlier, who was only ever hard on herself when she hadn't deserved it.

I picked my way down through the heavy carpet of dead leaves and branches, stumbling occasionally on pockets of uneven ground, blinded by my tears. At the bottom of the hill, I stopped and retched until there was nothing left. And then I went home.

Twenty-Four

May 2009

School was almost over for the year. I would miss it, and the relief of losing myself in the smell of glue and the sound of construction paper tearing. And the kids, of course.

"Who's that in your picture?" I asked my second-grader Joon. She was drawing a man so tall he looked like his legs had been stretched. He was wearing a top hat. Come to think of it, he looked a little bit like Abraham Lincoln without the beard. A bright burst of bouquet covered his hand, which was extended toward us.

"It's my husband," Joon replied matter-of-factly.

Opening my eyes wide, I pretended to be shocked. "You already have a husband? Aren't you a little young for that?"

Joon giggled and pushed her hair out of her eyes. "No, silly, he's my husband in the future."

"Ah, I see. Why did you decide to make him your husband?"

"Well, because I like the look of him. Also because he listens to all my stories. And also because he brings me flowers every day. That's how I know he loves me so much . . . Miss

Fairisle, why is your face turning purple?"

I exhaled; Joon had made me see how simple it was.

If I wanted to trust Shep again and to believe he could love me unconditionally, I needed to see Not Dad. I needed to understand what had happened so that I could put him behind me once and for all.

Deep down, I'd been trying to fill a hole he had left. There was some part of me that was still afraid of not being deserving of love or unable to keep it once I had it. Was that why I also wanted a baby so badly? Because a baby would love me unconditionally, would be truly mine? Was that why I had been so unwilling to fail or ask anyone for help to the point where I had ended up risking what I loved, including the library? Maybe seeing Not Dad would give me some kind of clue.

In those first years after he left, when he was apparently living around the corner, Mom had evaded our questions. When we became teenagers, she would answer them, then add, "You can see him, if you want to." But I never had. Neither had Maddie. Or Coco.

At least, as far as I knew.

I texted Maddie and Coco and asked if they could video chat at six.

Maddie asked what was so urgent and if I was pregnant. I texted back, Not unless by immac concep, all fine, see you 2nite.

"Hey, Do," Coco said, blowing me a kiss when we signed on later.

"Hi, sis." I blew one back.

"Where are Mark and Boo?" I asked.

Coco smiled. "Boys' night out so we can have girls' night in." We each poured ourselves a glass of wine.

"They're going out for sushi with Mark's parents." Coco looked at me pointedly. I laughed sheepishly. They had introduced a lot of foods to Terabithia but hadn't been able to change his far and away inexplicable preference for sashimi.

"How are you?" Coco asked, her brow knitted with concern.

"Overall, better. I'm not as angry anymore. More disappointed."

"That's kind of worse, right?"

"Yeah. But I really miss him," I admitted.

At that moment, Maddie popped up. "If I had known you were both going to be drinking fancy wine, I wouldn't have bothered mixing up some of my Ice-Cold Hot-Pink Lemonade in your honor."

"Oh, Jesus," Coco and I said in unison. The last time Maddie had made her Ice-Cold Hot-Pink Lemonade, the three of us had ended up with absolutely no memory of where we'd been—or how we'd gotten the temporary (thank God) tattoos of the Chippettes on our right buttocks.

Never one to miss a trick, Maddie sweetly inquired, "Did I interrupt something?"

"No way!" I rushed to say. "We would never start the serious talk without you here."

"Good. Now we can focus on your pregnancy."

I considered it progress that I was able to laugh at that.

"Did either of you ever see . . . Not Dad?" I asked.

Maddie looked down. Coco's eyes widened. She frowned.

"NFW," Maddie said. "Coco, however . . ."

Coco sighed. "I almost did."

"How could you guys not have told me?"

"That's your first question?" Maddie retorted.

"Yes, it is. No, it's not." I pouted. "So what happened?"

"It was actually right before Mark and I got engaged. I was worried about saying yes to Mark. What if I had more of Not Dad's genes than Mom's? I was so scared that I might hurt Mark that way."

My mouth dropped open. "Really? I had no idea you ever had any doubt about marrying Mark."

"It wasn't a doubt about marrying Mark," Coco corrected. "It was a doubt about myself. And my genetics. So yeah, I was a little concerned that I might have a weird personality break after marriage and turn into a deadbeat."

"But wasn't Dad already kind of a deadbeat before he and Mom got married?" Maddie pointed out. "Like, when they were dating and she got the flu and he avoided her for three weeks to make sure she was rid of all the germs before he would see her again?"

"I know, I know. But I loved Mark so much I thought it would be good at least to . . . meet Not Dad. You know I was so young when he left that I don't have any memories of him."

"I get that," I said. "So what happened?"

"I called him up and asked him to meet me for coffee. It took him two weeks to return my phone call. And I decided, you know what? It's not worth it. This has already told me everything I needed to know. I never called him back."

"Do you ever wish you'd gone?"

"Not really."

"What about you?" Maddie said. "Did you ever think about going to see him? Or go but not tell us?"

"Sure, I thought about seeing him over the years. But I figured it doesn't really matter. We had the best dad ever in Walter." I raised my chin.

"I don't believe you," Maddie said. "And there are about six books in your towering collection having to do with little girls finding their birth fathers to prove you otherwise."

"She's right, you know," Coco said.

"Okay, fine." I sighed. "It does matter, but

I didn't see him because I figured it wouldn't change anything. I mean, he rejected us all those years ago. He's never done anything to rectify that or to try to have relationships with us. So I knew what the result would be. And it was painful to think of that rejection happening all over again. I'd rather not go there."

Coco and Maddie were silent for a minute, reflecting. Then Coco murmured, "But you *are* going there. That's why you called us here. And that's probably why you still aren't sure what to do about Shep. Regardless, if you went, maybe you wouldn't have to keep reliving that rejection over and over again every day. Maybe you could finally get some closure and see him for what he is. Maybe you would stop hoping it's going to change and really know, once and for all, that it never will."

Maddie was nodding, but her brow was furrowed.

I let Coco's words sink in. I knew she was right because a huge wave of homesickness for Shep washed over me, and I couldn't will away any of its dizzying impact. I put my head in my hands. Coco and Maddie waited.

"Would you think about going now? With me?" I asked.

"Yes, I will," Coco promised.

Maddie was conspicuously silent.

"So will Maddie," Coco said pointedly.

Maddie grabbed the toxic lemonade and poured herself a tall glass, then slammed it back on the table. "Nope. No desire to talk to that asshat."

"You might find out a thing or two about yourself, Maddie."

"Okay, Mother Teresa. Can we stop talking about ourselves now and start doing something useful like watching *Shag* on TBS in six minutes?" Maddie begged.

Coco and I both laughed. Conversation over . . . for now. "Oh, bluuuuue," Coco crooned.

"I can't feel my teeth!" I said in my most exaggerated southern slur.

There was a nervous feeling in the pit of my stomach. A bit like stage fright. The anticipation was the worst. We were going to see Not Dad.

The reception area at Not Dad's office was frigid. My hands were trembling, so I sat on them. The least I could do was leave my sweaty palm marks on his chair. *That would show him!* I thought wryly . . . then had to bite my lip to avoid breaking into nervous giggles. Even though it wasn't neutral territory, the three of us had agreed to meet him there. We could leave whenever we wanted. And at least it was somewhat private.

"Can I get anyone a glass of water?" Not Dad offered when his assistant ushered us into his office.

I shook my head, took a breath, and got right to the point: "Why did you leave?"

Not Dad sighed. "I knew you would ask me that."

Maddie tensed on the chair beside me but said nothing. I could tell she was trying hard not to interfere.

"Well, it's been about twenty-nine years, so I think the least you owe us is a few minutes of your time today," I retorted. How *dare* he be annoyed at me for asking what was my right to know?

"Of course," he said, as if he was trying to placate me, which only made me angrier.

"How could you do that to us? We were only kids."

Looking me straight in the eye, he said, "It wasn't you I was leaving. It was your mother.

"I loved her. Just not enough. I knew that even before we got married, but I thought it would get better when we had kids. Instead, it made me realize I couldn't yoke myself to a life with her. I intended to try to reestablish a relationship with you three after the dust had settled a little bit with your mother. Then Susan got pregnant. It didn't seem as important anymore."

Maddie got out of her chair and started whispering swear words under her breath. I thought I heard "I will strangle him with his tie" and "I will fill his balls with paper clips."

My nails were digging into my palms so hard I felt blood on my fingertips. Coco covered my hand with hers. My voice quavering, I managed to whisper, "Even us?"

He shrugged his shoulders. A shrug. That's what I got in response to putting my heart in my hands, asking these questions. A shrug, a hammer—they pretty much amounted to the same thing. "Why was it different with them?"

"Because of the way I love Susan," he said simply.

I remembered how I had wandered around the house opening doors looking for him for weeks after he left until Maddie told me to cut it out because it made Mom cry. Coco didn't talk about Not Dad for a year after that, but her little brow had been permanently knit. Maddie used to go in her room, even in high school, and turn up her rock music loud. But not loud enough to cover her sobs. "You are a bad person."

"You would see it that way."

I flinched as if he'd hit me. That was the most hurtful thing he could have said. Because underneath it were the words he wasn't speaking: *I love my real family. I am a good dad to them. That's how* they *see it.*

There were more questions. There was so much anger. I could feel it warring with the grief, the disappointment, the fact that there had been no surprises—he was exactly how I had thought he would be. Except a little worse, colder. He was so arctic, and I was burning up with anger like it was a fever. I wanted to throw a paperweight at his head. A computer. A chair. I wanted to wring his neck. For my mom. For Maddie. For Coco. And for me.

Coco stood up. “I think we’re done here. Right, Do?”

“Right.” I grabbed my purse.

“Oh, I disagree!” Maddie announced. She turned to Not Dad, seething. “You stink more than sporty testicles!” she began. Then the expletive floodgates opened. She used every swear word I had ever heard. She even made a few up. “Let’s go,” she said, slamming the door behind us.

But not before we heard Not Dad say, “Nice language, Coco!”

He couldn’t even tell us apart. It was clear now in a way it hadn’t been before: we shared absolutely nothing with that man but biology.

I didn’t dissolve into angry tears the moment we got to the parking lot. Instead, I thought about the shocked expression on Not Dad’s face during Maddie’s colorful and inventive tirade. A laugh bubbled up in the back of my throat. I let it come, giving into it until I was howling. And the best part of all wasn’t the brand-new swear words I’d learned or even the fact that my sisters were cry-laughing with me. The best part of all was that I finally felt free.

• • •

I dug around in the back of my closet, behind my shoeboxes, until my hands closed around a small white paper bag. There was a book inside. A receipt fell out of it. February 17, 2008. It was for the copy of *The Lady of the Camellias* that Maddie had bought me on my birthday day trip not long before Shep and I got together. On the day we got engaged, I gave him a copy. When he left, I hid my own copy away with the receipt in it. It had been a long time since I'd read the book.

I was emotionally exhausted from the day. I couldn't even think straight, let alone imagine indulging in some tragic romance. I would only read a few pages, refresh my memory. When I had gotten more sleep, I would finish the rest.

Four hours later, tears were streaming down my face, and my bed looked like a tissue bomb had detonated all over it. The real tragedy in the book was that Marguerite and Armand had never told each other how they felt until (spoiler alert!) it was too late and she was dead. I had always understood that. Now, I also saw what it meant for me. *Life's too short,* I thought. *You have to tell people you love them when you love them. You have to trust that they love you back just as much even when they make mistakes.*

Most of all, I told myself, *you* have *to stop blaming yourself. Sometimes terrible things happen. Sometimes it's your fault, and sometimes it's not. Sometimes it's no one's fault.*

Nothing I could have done would have changed Not Dad's decision to leave us. I finally stopped thinking that if I had been smarter, sweeter, less whiny, the outcome would have been different. I knew now that for me, the outcome of my love story, of my future children's lives, would be different from my mom's and Not Dad's.

I suddenly understood the biggest gift of all. The one that Shep had contributed to by leaving. The one that over the past painful months, my friends and my family and my loneliness and the townspeople and my books had conspired to give me: I could believe that everything would turn out okay even if I wasn't always perfect. Even if I stopped trying so hard to make everyone else happy that I forgot what I wanted, what I deserved for being the person I was, flaws and all. The person that Shep loved, and the person that Shep had come back to. But most importantly, the person that I had become on my own and for myself.

Twenty minutes later, Shep opened the door to my frantic knock. I threw my arms around his neck and felt his own wrap me in return, strong with love but weak with relief.

"You're back," he whispered happily into my hair.

"Yeah," I murmured, thinking, *So are you.*

Leading me to the couch, he watched me carefully, as if he was afraid I would bolt. He blurted, "If you want a baby, Do, we can start trying. Or fill out the adoption paperwork."

"I don't think so, Shep."

"I know it will take time to win back your trust. But an international adoption will probably take a couple years anyway. I'm ready when you are."

I had imagined someone saying those words—*let's go for it*—for such a long time. But things had changed. I had changed. I now knew that playing with Terabithia for a few hours, even every day, wasn't the same as being up all night with him when he had night terrors or when he couldn't sleep for missing Sullivan. I hadn't had to rearrange my schedule at the last minute and scramble for a school sub when he got sick. I could have and would have done all that and anything else to keep him safe and happy and well. I had already figured out that I wasn't ready to do it alone, though.

It seemed like Shep was back for good, but you never knew what the next day would bring. I owed it to my child-to-be to feel certain that I wouldn't need to move back home with my parents or to move in with Maddie or Coco and Mark. I didn't want to leave Chatsworth. I didn't want to leave the lending library. Those were important parts of me too.

"No, Shep. You were right. I'm not ready."

Shep's eyes widened. "Okay," he said finally. "Then we'll wait. I'll wait," he promised.

We were both different. He was steady and sure. He was there, and he was listening. I was there, too, in a way I had never been before. And I still loved him so much it was like liquid excitement coursing through my veins. If he kept gazing at me with that utterly-devoted-to-Do look, and if we kept slowly finding our new normal—eating long meals, reading together with our legs entwined, sharing my joy in the library, and talking about everything this time around—we could get back to where we had been and even move ahead.

With no comment, Shep placed the ring box on my bureau. I wasn't even sure when the box had appeared there—by then, he was already woven into the fabric of my life again, the gorgeously disorienting blur of day after day spent together. I began putting the ring back on for little bits of time. I found myself wearing it more and more.

Twenty-Five

June 2009

Elmira had finally been released from grounding in time for the summer. She was squirming on the car ride to our very special destination. I knew exactly how she felt.

After waiting in a line of cars to get into the parking lot, we found a spot toward the way back. That was fine with me, though; it gave me more time to drink in the sights as we approached.

WELCOME TO CHATSWORTH LIBRARY—RENEWED AND IMPROVED! the banner on the front of the building trumpeted. I was so grateful.

Elmira and I grinned at each other.

I couldn't believe it had been almost two years. First, the asbestos. Then the other systems. Then money problems with the recession. Still, while I'd been wrapped up in my own library dramas, the Chatsworth Library was slowly and surely being renovated. It was finally ready to reopen, thanks to Shep, with a big bash.

"Thank you so much for taking me, Miss Fairisle. I asked my mom and dad, but they said—"

"My pleasure." I slung my arm around her and squeezed so she didn't have to tell me why or justify anything. I felt a painful twinge but pushed it away.

"Hey, I forgot to tell you," she said. Her shining eyes revealed that it was something big. "My mom baked me a cake the other night to celebrate my good grades. And bought me five new books."

I was speechless.

Was it possible that Leila Pelle had changed?

"That's amazing," I said.

"I'll bring you a piece tomorrow."

A clutch of visitors stood inside the entry in their finery. Geraldine was back in action greeting people at the door. She had earned her library science degree while the library was closed and had recently been named the new head librarian here. Roberta and some of the ladies from the story circle were in the vestibule too. And Mike and Lula and Ramon, Chloë, Melissa, Deandra and Trey, Indira and Amisha, and so many other Chatsworthians.

The mood was festive as Geraldine cut the ribbon and everyone rushed inside. There were long rows of desks with computers down the west side, an audiovisual station and circulation desk on the east side toward the front door, and neat and tidy shelves parading in between a perimeter of tables and chairs. It looked modern, spiffy. I wrinkled my nose at the smell of newness, but I had to give it time.

"Do you want to walk around a bit? Go ahead," I encouraged Elmira. She rushed off to explore.

I wanted a moment to myself. Excitement welled up inside me when I saw all the people filling the spaces between stacks, sitting at the tables, asking the volunteers at the information desk questions, drinking punch, and eating sprinkle cookies.

There was an official public library for the people of Chatsworth to go to and check out books again. My heart burned enviously in my chest as I looked at Geraldine. Maybe now the people of Chatsworth wouldn't really need my little and much-less-organized library anymore.

Geraldine saw my expression and came over. "I know exactly what you're thinking. And yes, the townspeople will still need the lending library."

"I hope so. I'm thrilled for you and appreciate all the help you've given me. And, Geraldine, this place looks great."

She nodded. "It does, but it smells new, and it'll take a while for that to change in such a big space. Plus, there are no stacks of random books or nearby ovens for a Foodie Book Club. Although there is a comment board for the kids, and I'm thinking of starting a story circle for adults," she informed me. I grinned.

"Now let me show you something." She waved me toward the northeast corner.

It was the same key shape as the nook that had always been my favorite spot in the library. Instead of floor-to-ceiling windows, though, the walls were bookcases made of wood intricately carved with little scenes. I looked closely. One of the scenes was from *Peter Rabbit.* One of them was from *The Little Engine That Could.* One of them was from *The Snowy Day*. And one of them, I saw through tears, was from *The Piping-Hot Frog Book.* Terabithia's favorite. There was a squishy chair in the center of this nook, too, but it wasn't cozy and alone. It was cozy and surrounded by a dozen little chairs.

I took a few moments to drink it in. Geraldine had disappeared. I felt Shep's arms around me, his chin coming to rest on top of my head. "Do you like it?"

"It's beautiful. Thank you."

"There's one more thing," he said, leading me to the nook's entrance.

My friends were gathered there watching me expectantly. Mackie and Jeff had joined them. Everyone made a little space for me as I came up so I could see what was on the wall.

It was a plaque engraved with a list of names. "This is permanent," Geraldine told me. At the top read the words THE PEOPLE OF CHATSWORTH GRATEFULLY RECOGNIZE THE PASSIONATE AND KNOWLEDGEABLE LIBRARIANS OF THIS TOWN. My eyes raced down to the bottom. Geraldine's name was there. And right above it was mine. *Dodie Fairisle.*

The people around me clapped as I wiped my eyes.

"And we'll be carrying on your tradition of inserting little bits of sage wisdom in the books we recommend," Geraldine said through her own happy tears.

"Thank you," I whispered.

Twenty-Six

"I can't believe we're doing this," Shep said, clicking his seat belt and shoving a magazine into the seat back in front of him. He kept looking out the window as if already expecting to see the Mediterranean Sea when our plane hadn't even taken off from Logan yet.

I grabbed his hand and squeezed, feeling my own excitement bubble up. I hadn't had a real vacation in years. Now we would have a week together on the French Riviera, where my hardest decision would be between fish soup with garlicky croutons and Gruyère or a hot-off-the-griddle chickpea pancake with a dash of pepper and rosemary. We would visit Nice and stay for several nights in Saint-Paul de Vence following in the footsteps of some of my favorite artists and musicians and writers. James Baldwin and Pierre Bonnard. Miró and Chagall and Matisse. Nina Simone and Miles Davis and Ella Fitzgerald.

"I figured we both deserved a vacation," I said.

"Definitely. I'm just amazed that we're doing this knowing that we'll have a honeymoon to plan in the near future."

We grinned at each other.

"Besides," Shep teased, "I wonder if you can really take a vacation."

"Hey, what's that supposed to mean?"

"You know the biggest decision we're supposed to have to make is whether we want to stay in bed till lunchtime or get up and go for a swim."

Even better choices!

"So you're not supposed to be on your phone all the time checking in on the library or Elmira or Terabithia or that woman who was telling you the other day that your book recommendations were helping her survive her divorce. That could be hard for you."

He was looking at me with his eyebrows raised. There was no judgment in his voice, no concern. His lips curled up at the edges.

At that moment, the only thing I could think about was Shep and the beginnings of that smile. I was determined to make it bigger. In fact, I could hardly wait for the next seven days in France to begin.

So while I was saying to him, "You're probably right," I was thinking, *We'll just see about that . . .*

ACKNOWLEDGMENTS

So many people have fostered my love of books and made it a possibility and a pleasure for me to write this one. From the very beginning, my parents, Fred and Sandi Fogelson, instilled in me a deep passion for reading. My mother showed me that everyone is creative and can make beautiful things; she taught me to believe in my imagination. My father's constant support and interest mean so much, every day.

My sisters, Jen and Marni, inspire me with their generous, kind hearts. I've been incredibly lucky to have Marni as the first sounding board for my writing and always at the ready during the evolution of this novel. Jen's sense of humor and fun have been a lifeline too many times to count.

My agent, Meg Ruley, believed in this book from the start and buoyed me through its journey. Conversations with her are like a cross between a cozy cup of tea and a glass of sparkling wine. I thank her for finding this book a home.

Thanks to my editor, Danielle Marshall, for making that home such an enthusiastic one. Her patience and guidance along the way are much appreciated. I'm also grateful to Heather Lazare for the insightful edits; Erin Calligan Mooney for all her help in the home stretch; Kimberly Glyder for capturing the charm of Dodie and her world in the cover; Michael J. Totten, Stephanie Chou, and Emma Reh for their attention to detail; and Gabriella Dumpit and the rest of the team at Lake Union / Amazon for the warm welcome and for all their efforts to share this book with readers.

Many friends have offered encouragement and the best kind of distractions along the way; I thank them all. I am especially indebted to Jennifer Pooley for being an abiding cheerleader and fairy bookmother through the years and to Ashley Martabano for the moral support and huge laughs.

My deep gratitude goes to my husband, Richard Cannarelli, who may even love books as much as I do. Hearing our son giggling with him in the other room helped me through some of the toughest stretches of revision. The wait for my happy beginning with him was more than worth it.

Thanks to Benjamin for granting my own wish to be a mother. I hope that one day this book reminds him of how deeply he was wanted. Most of all, I hope he will already—and always—know how beloved he is.

HUMMINGBIRD CAKE

Banana. Pineapple. Cinnamon. Cream cheese. Heaps of powdered sugar and butter. As Sullivan said, "A strange combination of flavors." But what a delicious one! This cake seems to win over almost anyone who tries it. And it's an actual prizewinner. Sincere thanks are due (from about a squillion fans, including me) to Mrs. L. H. Wiggins of Greensboro, North Carolina. Her recipe for hummingbird cake, adapted below, first appeared in *Southern Living* in 1978, and it won a reader favorite award in 1990. The pecans are traditional, but I've made this many times without them, and no one knew they were missing. You can also swap in your favorite 1:1 gluten-free flour.

While the original recipe makes a three-layer cake, I find that a two-layer hummingbird cake is more than decadent enough (and I don't mind having some cupcakes around to give away or freeze for another day when the craving for this treat strikes). This cake keeps well in an airtight container in the refrigerator for a week. It tastes best at room temperature, so if you can, take it out of the fridge at least an hour before serving.

Makes one three-layer 9-inch round cake or one two-layer 8-inch round cake plus six cupcakes

- 3 cups all-purpose flour, plus more for flouring the pans
- 1 teaspoon baking soda
- ½ teaspoon salt
- 2 cups sugar
- 1 teaspoon ground cinnamon
- 3 eggs, beaten
- ¾ cup vegetable oil (I usually use canola), plus more for greasing the pans
- 1 ½ teaspoons vanilla extract
- 1 (8-ounce) can crushed pineapple, undrained
- 1 cup chopped pecans (optional)
- 1 ¾ cups mashed bananas (3 to 4 bananas)
- Cream cheese frosting (recipe follows)
- Pecan halves for decoration (optional)

Preheat the oven to 350°F. Grease and flour three 9-inch round cake pans or two 8-inch round cake pans and six muffin cups (or use cupcake liners in the muffin pan).

Combine the flour, baking soda, salt, sugar, and cinnamon in a large bowl. Add the eggs and ¾ cup oil, stirring until the dry ingredients are moistened. Do not beat the mixture. Stir in the vanilla, pineapple with its juices, and 1 cup chopped pecans (if using) just until the batter is well combined.

Pour the batter into the greased and floured cake pans and muffin cups (if using). Bake for 23 to 28 minutes or until a wooden toothpick inserted into the center comes out clean. Cool for 10 minutes in the pans. Gently slide a knife around the edges of the pan to help free the cake. Invert the cakes onto a wire rack, and let them cool completely.

Spread the cream cheese frosting between the layers and on the top and sides of the cake. Decorate with pecan halves if desired. (They look lovely in a circle around the top edge and with a couple more pecans placed right in the center.)

Cream Cheese Frosting

I love frosting, and I think cake is best when it has a nice, big layer of frosting on top. This recipe for cream cheese frosting makes more than enough to cover the hummingbird cake. Even with a generous helping between the layers and all over the outside, you'll probably still have some of this sweet, creamy goodness left over. I highly recommend dipping strawberries in it. Or just a spoon. Maybe with a few chocolate chips thrown on top for good measure.

1 cup unsalted butter, softened
2 (8-ounce) packages cream cheese

2 (16-ounce) packages powdered sugar, sifted
2 teaspoons vanilla extract

Cream the butter and cream cheese with a mixer at medium-low speed. Gradually add the sugar, beating at low speed until well blended. Increase the speed to medium, and beat until the frosting is light and fluffy. Stir in the vanilla.

ABOUT THE AUTHOR

Aliza Fogelson is a writer and editor living in New York. She specializes in lifestyle books, including those about decorating, cooking, and style. She graduated from Princeton University, where she studied literature and creative writing. Her first published work was her third-grade short story "Baby Cow's Adventure." This is her first novel.

Books are produced in the United States using U.S.-based materials

Books are printed using a revolutionary new process called THINKtech™ that lowers energy usage by 70% and increases overall quality

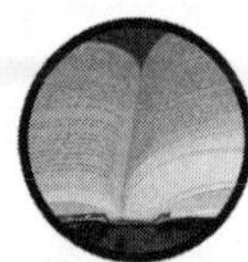

Books are durable and flexible because of Smyth-sewing

Paper is sourced using environmentally responsible foresting methods and the paper is acid-free

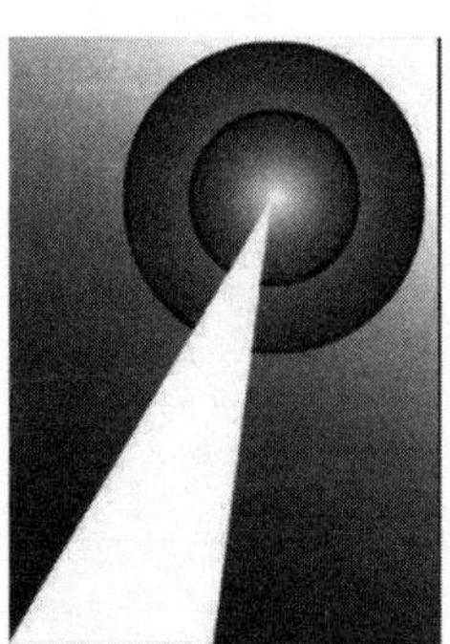

Center Point Large Print
600 Brooks Road / PO Box 1
Thorndike, ME 04986-0001 USA

(207) 568-3717

US & Canada:
1 800 929-9108
www.centerpointlargeprint.com